Mind
Games

A Demon Trappers® Novel

Other Books
by Jana Oliver

Briar Rose
Young Adult
Macmillan Children's Books (U.K.)

Tangled Souls
Paranormal Romance

Time Rovers Series
Time Travel/Alternate History Romance
Sojourn
Virtual Evil
Madman's Dance

The Demon Trappers Series
Young Adult
U.S. (U.K.)
The Demon Trapper's Daughter (Forsaken)
Soul Thief (Forbidden)
Forgiven (same title)
Foretold (same title)
Grave Matters (same title)
Mind Games (same title)

Mind Games

A Demon Trappers Novel

Jana Oliver

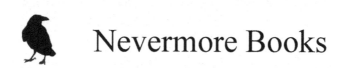 Nevermore Books

Published by
MageSpell LLC
P.O. Box 1126
Norcross, GA 30091

Mind Games
A Demon Trappers® Novel
ISBN: 978-1-941527-02-3
Copyright © 2015 Jana Oliver

Cover Image/Art: Yocla Designs
Angel Wing Graphic: Used with permission of
Macmillan Children's Books

For all those who nurture the light
in this often dark world . . .

Acknowledgements

Riley and Beck's stories don't come to fruition without assistance from other people. So here's where I mention those folks who've helped me make this book a reality.

First, a shout-out to Kathryn Fernquist Hinds, who served as developmental editor for this manuscript. Kathryn is like having a super hero(ine) in your corner who always pulls you out of trouble right before the big explosion. Thank you for helping me make this story the best it can be.

My copyeditor for the final manuscript was Mollie Traver (www.mollietraver.com), who was tasked with finding all those evil typos (no doubt put there by some sort of fiend). Mollie has a long history with the Demon Trappers: She served as my assistant editor at St. Martin's Griffin.

Where editors are the soul of a novel, a talented cover artist is the heart. Clarissa from Yocla Designs (www.yocladesigns.com) took my vision and turned it into reality. A special thanks to Macmillan Children's Books (London) for allowing me to use the gorgeous angel/demon graphic. The final result is a cover that is not only beautiful, but evocative.

My gratitude to my spouse, who typeset the print edition and did all the arcane formatting needed for the electronic versions. It's never a matter of just "pushing a button."

And finally, thank you to all my readers across the globe. Your e-mails asking "What happens next?" is what led to this book. It's always astounding when my characters take on a life of their own, but that's the case with these two. Hopefully Riley & Beck have even more stories to whisper in my ear down the line.

"The marks humans leave are too often scars."
— John Green, *The Fault in Our Stars*

"All men make mistakes, but a good man yields
when he knows his course is wrong,
and repairs the evil. The only crime is pride."
— Sophocles, *Antigone*

Chapter One

December 2018
Atlanta, Georgia

Riley Blackthorne's two apprentices were having too much fun, laughing and playing in the unusual Atlanta snowfall. It'd grown increasingly cold throughout the day, and at dusk the white stuff began to accumulate. This being the South, traffic had immediately snarled in the grip of a "snowstorm" that promised three inches tops.

Riley chose to ignore it. Though it was pretty in a fairytale sort of way, it was a distraction. When you trapped demons for a living, distractions could be fatal. Or at least earn you a lot of time clawed up and healing.

"Guys, let's focus here," she said, sounding at least two decades older than her eighteen years. It all came down to what life had thrown at her, most of it bad, and almost all of it during this last year.

"But the snow's so cool," Richard said, proving he was a true Southerner. Someone from up north would have shrugged and moved on.

Richard Bonafont was thirty-something, a former radio DJ, now on his second marriage. He wore wire-rim glasses and had a ready smile. He and Kurt Pelligrino had been with her since the summer, and were partway through their training. The third apprentice, Jaye Lynn, was out on family leave at the moment, but Riley expected her back in the trenches soon.

"Yeah, but how often does it snow down here?" Kurt asked.

Just into his twenties, he was single, tall, and sporting some serious muscles.

As apprentices went, these guys were sharp, not like some who were hotheaded or downright stupid—traits that did not promise a lengthy career in the Atlanta Demon Trappers Guild.

At least a hothead could change. Denver Beck, Riley's fiancé, had. Being stupid, on the other hand, was a lifespan-limiting issue, especially when you were dealing with Hellspawn.

"Here's a hint: We *are* in Demon Central," Riley said in what she called her "teacher's voice." She came by it honestly; both her parents had been educators and her father, one of the best demon trappers in the country.

"Demons should like snow too," Richard said. "They never get to see it in Hell. I wonder if they'd build a snowman if they had a chance."

"Probably make it look like Lucifer or something," Kurt chimed in. "Though I bet they wouldn't have the balls to give him a carrot for a nose."

"No snow in Hell." Riley knew that for sure, and exactly what the Prince of Darkness looked like. There were no carrots involved. "If you don't pay attention, this pretty, white, fluffy stuff could be the last thing you see."

"You know, you can be a real bummer," Richard said, shaking his head.

"Better a bummer than a corpse," she shot back. Then immediately felt bad.

In their own way, these guys were telling her to chill out. She'd been too serious since her trip to Scotland in late October. Nearly being killed by an Archfiend and a rogue necromancer would do that to you.

"Okay, message received," she said. "I'm far too grim tonight. Sorry."

Riley looked up, caught a snowflake on her tongue, and tried to lighten up. It wasn't like they were going to do anything before another demon trapper arrived. It was standard procedure now: The first time an apprentice trapped a Grade Three fiend, a pair of experienced backups were required. Tonight, those parts would be played by herself and Journeyman Trapper Lex Reynolds.

As they continued to wait for Reynolds, her apprentices horsed around in the snow while Riley executed a slow three-sixty to scope out their surroundings. Demon Central, as the trappers called it, was located just south of downtown Atlanta. With the depressed economy, it'd been a dumping ground for garbage by those trying to avoid paying the high trash-collection fees. Now, with the economy finally improving, it looked cleaner. The occasional deep holes in the pavement, a remnant of Civil War Atlanta, remained.

"'In a hole in the ground there lived a hobbit,'" she murmured. Maybe in Tolkien's Shire, but in this part of the city, holes meant Hellspawn. Grade Three demons loved them. Since their usual home was Hell, a hole in the middle of a major city had to be an improvement.

The guys behind her were too quiet. Riley turned to find that they had fashioned snowballs and were eyeing her as a potential target.

She grinned. "Remind yourselves that I assign who cleans the demon crap from under the holding cages at Master Harper's place. And I'll be doing that for the rest of your apprenticeships."

The snowballs hit the ground simultaneously. No one liked that task. At least she let them wear gloves and use a shovel, unlike when she'd had the job.

"So who can give me a rundown on the type of Hellspawn you're trapping tonight?"

The two looked at each other, and it was Kurt who answered.

"A Grade Three demon, also known as a Gastro-Fiend, is an all-purpose omnivore. It'll eat anything. They usually stand about four feet tall, have six claws on each paw, and one or two sets of razor-sharp teeth, depending on the fiend's age."

She nodded. "Why do they live here?"

"The holes," Richard replied. "They seem to like them. And all the garbage down here."

"At least until recently," Riley said. "The city is cleaning up this area of town. Why is that a problem for us trappers?"

That stumped the two apprentices.

"What happens when you alter a predator's natural habitat?" she nudged.

Richard nodded his understanding. "It finds another place to hunt."

"Exactly. The Threes have been branching out. They've always been pretty mobile, but clustered down here for the most part. Now they're regularly seen as far north as Midtown and Buckhead, and as far south as the airport. Though why they'd go down there is anyone's guess."

"This change of territory doesn't sound good," Kurt said.

"No, it's not. The Guild warned the city about what might happen if they messed with this area, but they're eager to develop the land after the casino went bust. The demons expanding their hunting range is a prime example of what my dad used to call 'unintended consequences.'"

Before either of them could respond, something crawled across Riley's skin, like the sharp skitter of thousands of clawed feet. A quick glance at the other two proved they'd felt it as well.

"What was that?" Kurt asked, his eyes widening.

"That would be magic."

"Really? How cool is that?" Richard said.

"Not at all cool. Not down here."

Another crackle of magical energy lit up the night, appearing farther south, near Alabama Street.

"Not our problem, right?" Kurt asked, his voice thinner now. "I mean, Grade Three demons aren't going to care if someone can sling spells around."

He was correct. A Gastro-Fiend wouldn't care—a necromancer would make just as tasty a meal as a demon trapper if he or she wasn't careful. Most of the magic users were brighter than that.

"It's not just Threes down here," she said. "That's the danger."

With each increase in grade on the demonic rating scale came a corresponding increase in lethality and smarts. Playing with magic in Demon Central was like laying a juicy steak in front of a hungry mongrel. Some of the demons would ignore it, but not all. Not the really badass ones. They'd love nothing more than to grab onto the soul of some clueless necromancer. If you delivered a summoner's soul to the Prince? That'd earn you special brownie points.

Hell was all about one-upping your fellow fiends, the ultimate corporate hierarchy. Mortal institutions were only pale imitations.

When the ground rumbled beneath her feet, Riley knew the magical bait had been taken. "Damn!" she said, pulling out her cell phone.

"What was that?" Richard asked.

"Big trouble." Riley sent a text, one that automatically went to all the demon trappers on duty tonight. One that meant they should drop whatever they were doing and get here as fast as possible.

FIVE IN DEMON CTRL

No other directions would be needed—a Geo-Fiend, or Grade Five demon, stood at least seven feet tall. No way you could miss it. All the trappers had to do was follow the lightning and the raging windstorm.

Once she finished the text, Riley looked over at her apprentices. Richard's and Kurt's faces had paled now. They knew what a Five was, and they knew they were nowhere near ready to confront this level of demon. It would be suicide.

She needed to reinforce that thinking, so they didn't try some of the crazy stuff that she had when she was an apprentice.

"Guys, this thing is above your pay grade. You stay here. Do *not* get in the middle of this."

"But—" Kurt began.

"No! This fiend will tear you apart." Riley paused. "This is the kind of demon that killed my dad. You know, Paul Black-thorne, *Master* Demon Trapper?"

"But you need backup," Richard insisted.

Her newbies had guts, that was for sure. But guts with no training would get them just as dead.

"Backup will be here shortly. What you can do is keep the civilians away. There are bound to be some nosy ones around," she said, pulling a blue grounding sphere out of her backpack. "Stay safe, okay?"

They both nodded, still in shock. There was a point in every trapper's career when the job bitch-slapped them, and she suspected that moment had just arrived. This was usually when the decision was made: Continue with the training or walk away? Riley would tackle that issue later.

Right now, she had a demon to trap.

Chapter Two

Riley took off at a trot. One street away, she found herself facing increasing gusts of wind and lightning bolts that slammed into the buildings nearby, causing debris to break loose.

As she drew closer, she found the source of the trouble: A man in a dark-blue robe stood in the middle of the street, magic arcing around him. Didn't he realize that he had attracted one of Hell's most lethal killers?

"What a total idiot," Riley said, picking up speed. If she could hold the Geo-Fiend in place until the other trappers arrived, they could ground the monster and send it back to Hell. If not, there would be more earthquakes, high winds, and casualties.

One of which might be her.

Riley had nearly reached the necromancer when he turned in her direction. He didn't look familiar, but then, she knew only a few of the corpse summoners. On the whole, she tried to avoid them. The necro smiled at her, pulled up the hood of his cloak, then vanished in a ball of bright-blue light.

"What the . . . oh no."

Had she just been set up?

The Geo-Fiend rose out of the boiling asphalt, its bull-shaped head resting on a pair of massive shoulders that would make any steroid-stoked bodybuilder proud. Horns curved out of its skull, and it had two massive canines. Coal-black skin contrasted with the blazing-red eyes, which homed in on her immediately. That wasn't surprising. If this behemoth could kill her, or obtain her soul, it would be given the biggest celebratory party Hell had ever seen.

"Blackthorne's daughter!" the fiend bellowed.

It hovered above the ground now, wind swirling around it, picking up snow and debris. The mini earthquakes were bad enough, but the debris could be lethal. She'd lost her father that way.

Riley ground to a halt about forty feet from the monster, needing to buy time for the others to arrive. Her heart hammered and her palms sweat, making it hard to keep hold of the grounding sphere.

She thought of the man she loved, how Beck would handle this. And then she knew the best way to play it.

"Hey, dumbass!" she called out, channeling her fiancé's mouthy attitude. "Yeah, you! What are you doing here? Don't you know Atlanta is a no-go zone for you losers?"

"Your soul will be mine!" it called back.

One-track mind. "Not happening," she replied, sweat now rolling down her back despite the chilly night. "How's old Lucifer nowadays? Still cracking heads like a good tyrant?"

The demon snarled at the mention of his lord. The fiends might serve the Fallen angel, but that didn't mean they liked to be reminded. The lesser demons would cringe at his name. This one just winced.

Without any warning, the ground in front of Riley cracked, heaving open. Heat and the stench of rot rose in a steady cloud.

"That again? Really? Don't you guys learn any new tricks?"

Where is my backup?

If a Five came to the city, every demon trapper on duty had only one response: They came to the battle.

Yet here she was, alone.

They wouldn't let me die like this.

Or maybe they would. At least some of them.

The demon laughed in amusement, knowing she was in trouble. "Pledge your soul to me and I will let you live," it offered.

"Yeah right." Riley smirked, trying to cover the fear that had wound itself around her middle and squeezed like an anaconda.

"Let me guess, that deluxe *"Sell Your Soul to Me"* package comes with a one-way trip to Hell, a personal welcome by the Prince himself, and an eternity of torment. Am I right?"

The fire in the demon's eyes grew brighter now. "Of course not."

"Liar. You forget, I've been down there. I know what it's like."

And no matter what it took, she would never go there again.

The demon flicked its hand, and a mini tornado formed on its palm. That was this kind's strength—the ability to command the weather and generate earthquakes. It dropped the funnel to the ground, and it immediately grew in size, spinning the snow as though she and the fiend were inside a hellish snow globe.

Usually Demon Central was littered with scraggly metal fencing, left in place because most people weren't brave enough to try to salvage it in an area full of monsters. The grounding spheres worked best by connecting with the metal and—if you were lucky—enclosing the Five in a circle of magic. Once the fiend touched ground, it would return to Hell. A quick check proved that the city's ambitious cleanup plan had robbed her of that option, at least when it came to the fencing.

"Thanks a bunch, guys," Riley muttered. Now she would have to lob the magically charged sphere underneath the fiend. If the sphere hit in just the right place, it'd work. Most times, it didn't.

Just as she was about to throw the sphere, a voice called out. A quick glance over her shoulder revealed Lex Reynolds running toward her at top speed. The bad news was that he was the only one.

He skidded to a halt by her side and, breath heaving, asked the same question she'd been thinking. "Where is everyone?"

"Polishing their nails, apparently."

He met her eyes and the message was passed: They were on their own. At least until someone grew a conscience. Or a pair.

The earth rumbled again and they dodged right to avoid another sinkhole, debris swirling around them. When Riley looked back, the demon had shifted closer. Too close.

"Stay or take off?" she called to Reynolds. Not that she wanted to run, but they were in deep trouble.

"Stay," he said. "Let's send this thing home."

"Then we'll kick some people's asses."

"You got a deal."

They flanked the Five, carefully avoiding the steaming pits that continued to open around them. It was harder to avoid the crap whirling in the air.

A low groan from Riley's left indicated that one of the derelict buildings wasn't tolerating the wind. "Reynolds!" she called out in warning.

He sprinted out of the way as a jumble of bricks cascaded to the ground, adding even more fuel to the demon's windstorm. A crackle of lightning made Riley look up just in time to avoid being speared by a sizzling white bolt before it slammed into the ground, scorching the pavement in a five-foot circle. Car alarms blared in the distance.

Reynolds's blistering expletive and "Hell no, you bastard!" told her that the Five had just made the same "Sell Your Soul" offer to him. So much for being special.

Her fellow trapper's grounding sphere fell short. As the demon roared in anger at the futile attempt, Riley took her best shot. Her sphere landed closer to its mark, which only infuriated the Five more. As the magic took hold, grabbing onto the fiend, her companion sent another grounding sphere under its clawed feet.

When the Five went ballistic, fighting against the magic, they broke open their shield spheres, forming a protective envelope of magic around each of them.

Riley's heart raced and her breath grew short as the storm roared around them. Another sphere arced near the demon, a long lob from somewhere behind them. That sphere caught as well, and with a final deafening roar, the Five sank into the ground, leaving behind one last, sharp shake that sent Riley tumbling to her knees.

As the debris pattered around them like rain, she covered her head, praying the shield spheres held a bit longer. Finally the fallout ended, and she regained her feet.

Reynolds raised his head. "You okay?" he called out.

"Yeah. You?"

"In one piece." A trickle of blood ran down the side of his face. "Jackson, you good?"

Master Trapper Chris Jackson joined them now, his face and ponytail covered in brick dust. "Sure am. Damned that was a big mother."

"Where the hell are the others?" Reynolds demanded.

"I have no idea," Jackson said. "I was at Georgia Tech. I figured I'd be the last to get here."

If he could make it all the way down to Demon Central, there was no good reason the rest of the trappers weren't here.

"We just got hung out to dry," Riley said. "And I'm willing to bet it's because I was the one who sent out the call."

The two men traded looks, but didn't argue. That only made her angrier.

"I owe you guys," she said. "Really."

"No, you don't. But you do owe the others some serious pain," Reynolds said.

She nodded grimly. *And I'm the girl to deliver it.*

Chapter Three

Riley's two apprentices had waited for her, doing just as she'd asked: keeping the curious out of harm's way. Tonight it was only a small knot of bystanders. One of them was filming her on his cell phone.

Every. Blasted. Time.

By tomorrow she'd be on YouTube. Again. It was a sure bet that Beck would see the video, and then she'd get a worried phone call from Scotland.

When she reached her apprentices, she gave them a pleased smile. "Thanks, guys, you did good."

Kurt shook his head, his eyes still wide. "My God, that thing was huge!"

"Yeah, they are just that," she said, trying not to show how much she was shaking inside. "But we took it down."

"I thought there'd be more trappers here to help you," Richard said.

Now was not the time to tell them why she thought that hadn't happened.

"You guys go on home. We'll trap a Three another night."

They looked relieved and she knew why: The sight of the Five had filled them with terror. She wasn't much different. Only two other of Hell's killers scared her more: Fallen angels and Archfiends.

"See you tomorrow at nine at Harper's," she added.

If her gut was right, they'd be there. If not, one or both of them would have phoned in their resignations. And she wouldn't blame them. Sensible people did not trap Hellspawn for a living.

"Good night, Riley," Kurt called out.

Richard seconded it and they headed out of Demon Central, talking back and forth animatedly.

She looked over at Jackson, who was just getting off his phone. "You called Harper?"

He nodded. "He wants you to head up to Stewart's house. He'll meet you there. They want a report. I already gave them mine."

Oh boy. "Who was on duty tonight, besides you and Reynolds?"

"McGuire, Stanfield, and Machen."

Riley snorted. "Why am I surprised? Those guys have never wanted me in the Guild."

"There are only a few," Reynolds said. "Most are fine with you being a trapper. After what you did for us last spring, everybody oughta be worshipping at your feet."

"Not likely," she said. Lowering her voice so none of the bystanders could hear her, she added, "Some think the only reason Heaven and Hell almost went to war was because of me."

"Then they're stupid," Jackson said. He walked to where the small knot of locals was clustered. "Time to go home, folks. The demon is gone."

To Riley's amusement, a young lady offered him a scrap of paper and asked for his autograph.

"Groupies," Reynolds murmured. "Gotta love 'em."

A few more cell phones flashed, capturing Riley in her post-Five-whirlwind glory. Just once, she wished they'd see her looking good. Unfortunately, for a trapper, this was the norm.

She hadn't mentioned the necromancer to either Jackson or Reynolds, saving that newsflash for the two senior masters. Because if anyone knew how to handle that problem, it would be them.

~~*

Grand Master Angus Stewart lived in Riley's dream home, a multi-story, blue Victorian, complete with a turret and a ballroom. Because it had once been the Vatican's requirement that Stewart keep an eye on her, she'd lived with the grand master since earlier in the year. Now that Beck was away in Scotland, she split her time between here and his place across town. Once Beck was back home for good, there'd be a wedding to plan and . . .

Not yet. There was just too much going on to think about all that.

Her own master's truck was already in the driveway, which meant Harper had headed over here the moment he'd gotten off the phone with Jackson.

He and Stewart are going to be furious.

The scent of aromatic pipe tobacco greeted her as she entered Stewart's favorite room in the huge house. The stone fireplace currently hosted a warming blaze. Her eyes automatically tracked to the Scottish flag above the mantel, the white St. Andrew's cross on a blue background. Family pictures adorned the walls, and a couple new photographs of grandchildren had been added.

Stewart sat in his usual chair, one of his legs propped up on an ottoman. Unlike usual, he didn't have a glass of whisky at his elbow, no doubt in deference to Harper's battle with alcoholism.

Harper gave her a quick look, then shook his head at her appearance. "Yeah, it was a Five alright," he said.

"That's for damn sure," Stewart said.

"I look that bad?"

"A lot like Dorothy after the tornado blew her ta Oz," Stewart said, his light accent a reminder of his homeland.

He was in his sixties, had spent the last decade in Atlanta, and was a member of the International Demon Trappers Guild. Though as a grand master he technically outranked Harper, it was Harper who ran the local Guild. When she'd asked why, Stewart had explained that Harper deserved to be the head of Atlanta's trappers, that he'd paid a very high personal price for that job.

Her master, on the other hand, was in his fifties, but looked older. Part of the reason was the wicked scar on Harper's face. His years of living in a bottle hadn't helped, but now that he'd joined Alcoholics Anonymous, Riley'd had the opportunity to see the real Harper. Still a tough old bastard, he had a heart buried down under all the attitude, something she hadn't always thought possible.

Riley chose her favorite chair in the room. Fortunately, it was leather, so she wouldn't leave too much of a mess behind. It was also close to the fire.

"Sorry. I was going to clean up, but I wanted to talk to you guys right away."

"Not a problem. If ya need somethin' ta drink, help yerself," their host said.

"No, I'm good." She pulled out a water bottle from her backpack and took a sip. The silence filled in around them.

This was familiar territory. More than once, she'd been here with these two men after one momentous event or another. Back then, Harper had been the enemy, but now they had a truce in place. From the fire in his eyes, she could tell he was mad. At least it wasn't at her.

"Give us your report," her master ordered.

Riley did as he asked, laying it all out, including the necromancer who had summoned the Five and how it seemed as if he'd been waiting just for her.

"Shite," Stewart muttered. "Lord Ozymandias has killed enough of the fools, ya'd think they'd learned their lesson."

"Apparently not."

Harper fumed. "So we've got two separate problems here: the necro calling up a demon, and the fact that three of our trappers didn't back you up tonight. Is that right?"

She nodded. "If Jackson hadn't shown up, Reynolds and I would have been in big trouble."

"Dead, you mean. And I *do not* want to be the one who has to call Beck to tell him his squeeze is history because no one was there for her," Harper said.

Squeeze?

"Trappers' meetin' tomorrow night?" Stewart asked.

Harper nodded in response. "The sooner the better."

"Telling them they have to treat me like any other trapper isn't going to work," Riley said. "Some of them are always going to hate me."

"It depends on how they get told, lass," Stewart said. He looked over at Harper, and her master gave a nod. "Get some rest. Ya did a fine job tonight."

She knew that, but it felt good to hear it.

Harper cleared his throat. "I agree."

A compliment from her master? That was rare too. "Thank you. I'll be staying at Beck's tonight," she said.

"Keep yerself safe, lass."

"I will. Thanks."

As Riley reached the front door, they began to talk back and forth. She couldn't hear the exact words, but she caught the undercurrent of righteous anger. Once again, she was unwillingly causing hassles within the demon trappers' ranks.

This crap has to stop.

Chapter Four

Rolling out of bed the next morning, Riley felt like she hadn't slept at all. Fortunately, her job didn't require fancy clothes or makeup, so she washed her face, brushed her teeth and hair, and called it good.

Forcing herself to do a quick drive through at one of the fast-food restaurants, she ate a breakfast sandwich destined to sit in her stomach for hours. She arrived at Harper's place a little before nine. Whereas Stewart had a home, her master was into auto-repair shops. Though some might frown at his choice of living arrangements, this one was nice compared to his previous home.

With both a personal space upstairs and an area downstairs to confine Hellspawn before they were sold to the demon traffickers, it worked pretty well. Riley had come to appreciate it after learning this was Harper's way of commemorating his dead father, who'd been both a trapper and an auto mechanic.

Her master was still cranky this morning, so Riley collected the trapping orders and shooed her two newbies out before he barked at them.

She was used to his temper now, but there was no reason to encounter it more than needed. She was also thankful that both of her apprentices were still willing to continue their training. It could have easily gone the other way.

Once they were in her car, headed toward one of the private colleges in East Point, Kurt finally spoke.

"What's up? Master Harper was a bear this morning, at least more than usual, and you're looking as if you want to beat someone into the ground."

Oops. She hadn't wanted these guys to worry, but apparently she wasn't doing a good job hiding her anger. "It's complicated."

"It's because only two trappers showed up last night, right?" Kurt asked.

"Ah . . . yeah. Like I said, it's complicated."

"Not really," Richard replied. "You're a trapper. You were up against a Geo-Fiend. The others should have gotten their asses there to back you up. Any other action on their part is totally wrong."

"What he said," Kurt added.

These guys were going to be just fine. "Thanks. I appreciate that."

"This is happening because of last spring, isn't it? I mean, I don't know much about all that, but I've heard some of the trappers talking about it," Richard said.

"Yeah, a lot went down and I always seemed to be in the middle of it. There are some who can't handle women in the Guild. There always will be."

"That's bullshit. So how are you going to fix this?"

"I'm not," she replied. "Stewart and Harper will."

Kurt issued a low whistle. "This, I gotta see."

"You'll see it tonight. Wear your body armor. It's not going to be pretty. Nothing is more impressive than Angus Stewart on the warpath, and Harper's just scary any old time," Riley warned.

Once she finally found a place to park, they were out and headed toward the administration building.

"Let me guess—another Geeker to trap," Richard said.

"Yup. Techno-Fiends love college campuses. Why is that?"

"Lots of computers."

"What else makes this particular location a good choice for a fiend?"

Kurt pointed at a sign as they passed it. "Christian school. A chance to turn electronics to putty and flip off the church at the same time. Every fiend's dream."

"There you go," she replied.

"Have you heard anything from Jaye?" Richard asked.

"She texted me this morning and said she's hoping to be at the meeting. Her mom's lots better," Riley replied.

"Good. It'll be nice to have her back with us. She's cool." He nudged his fellow apprentice. "You should ask her out."

"Ah, I did. She turned me down," Kurt replied. "I like to think it was because her mom is ill. My ego can't handle flat-out rejection."

"I thought you were already dating someone," Riley said.

"We kinda broke up. My ex didn't like me being a trapper very much. Her family had 'objections,'" he said, using air quotes.

"Welcome to the wonderful world of trapping," she replied. "People adore you when you're hauling a demon out of their home or business, but they never want their daughter or son to date you."

"After last night, I can see why," Richard murmured. "And that Five wasn't even at the top of the demonic food chain. I can't imagine what an Archfiend looks like."

"Nearly your worst nightmare."

"And the worst is?"

"A Fallen angel. Because not only can they kill you, but they can seriously mess with your head."

Riley and her apprentices slowed their pace as they reached the front door of the administration building.

"You've really killed two Archfiends?" Richard asked.

"Yup."

"Then why aren't they making you a master?"

Before she could answer, Kurt cut in. "Let me guess. It's complicated."

"Very complicated."

And not likely to change anytime soon.

~~*

After taking care of the necessary paperwork, Riley and her charges were escorted to the computer lab by a young woman, probably an administrative assistant.

"Which computer?" Riley asked, looking at a roomful of desktop monitors.

The woman shrugged. "All of them."

Riley blinked. "It's not usually this bad. How long has this been going on?"

"A week. It took a while to get the okay to have you guys come fix them."

"That would be why," Riley muttered. "What kinds of things have been happening?"

"It started with weird blackouts, then the computers would come back on and all the icons would be changed to something different. Then it got really bad."

"Like how?"

"Twenty-four seven political ads. No way we could get rid of them."

"That is hardcore," Richard said, smirking.

"No, then it *did* get hardcore, as in pornography," the lady explained. "That *really* flipped out the administration."

That's why they finally called us. Riley looked back at the administrative assistant. "This'll take some time."

"Really? Can I watch?"

"No. It's safer if you don't. We'll let you know if we need anything."

Though the lady looked crestfallen, Riley shooed her out the door and shut it behind her.

"Always make sure the nosy civilians are out of the way," she said. "It's as important as getting all the right paperwork signed." Pointing down at the door's threshold, she added, "I need a line of Holy Water here to keep the Geeker from taking off."

"Have you ever seen one?" Kurt asked.

"Barely. They're only about a quarter of an inch tall. Personally, I prefer Magpies to these guys."

"Why?" Kurt asked, as he knelt and ran the line of sacred liquid where she'd indicated.

"You'll find out soon enough," she said, smiling over at Richard, who nodded in agreement. He'd been in on a Techno-Fiend trapping before, and it'd been wild.

"Done," Kurt said, recapping the bottle of Holy Water.

Riley scoped out the room. There was one door, a few windows, which were currently closed, and a ventilation register in the ceiling. Riley pointed at the register. "Put some on that thing," she said. "Richard, do the honors for the windows, will you?"

As her apprentices did her bidding, she stared at the sixteen computers. Where to start? She turned them on and fidgeted as each one fired up.

Their tasks completed, the guys joined her.

"What are we waiting for?" Kurt asked.

"We're waiting for the demon to say hello."

"Do they usually do that?"

"They do if she's around," Richard said.

As if in agreement, one of the computer monitors lit up.

BLACKTHORNE'S DAUGHTER

"Here we go," she said.

Chapter Five

More of the monitors came to life, each with the same "Black-thorne's Daughter" message. Then it changed.

HELL MISSES YOU

The message remained for a few seconds, then vanished in a sea of flames, blood-red and boiling like the center of a firestorm. Voices came out of the speakers now, the howls of the damned. She'd heard them before. Seen their faces. Feared she'd become one of them.

"Riley?" Richard nudged her. "You okay?"

She shook off the still-too-vivid memories and frowned at the monitors.

"Okay, this is war," she said. "Time to nail this little jerk." She beckoned the two apprentices away from the computers, then whispered her plan.

"Just give me some time to get it set up," she said.

They nodded their understanding.

Riley took a seat in front of the computer that had first displayed the message. She typed out a reply, trying to ignore the tormented cries that dug into her mind like razors.

IS THAT THE BEST YOU'VE GOT, DEMON?

The image faded away, replaced by one she knew all too well: the immense hall deep in Hell, the rebel angel Sartael in chains, the stench of brimstone, and the funk of hundreds of demons.

Lucifer, the Prince of the Abyss, clad in full armor, sat on his throne, his naked sword across his lap. His cruel voice promising her and the angel Ori eternal torment. He'd meant every word.

"Riley?" Kurt said.

His voice pulled her away from the scene, and she was grateful for that.

"Richard, can you come over here please?"

Her other apprentice joined them.

She jabbed a finger at the screen. "This is what Hell looks like, guys."

The two leaned closer.

"Holy shit," Kurt murmured.

"I second that," Richard added.

"This is why you never want to accept a demon's boon. One boon leads to another and then you find yourself in *that* place, forever."

"How do you know . . . " Kurt began. Then his eyes widened as the answer dawned on him. He pointed at the screen. "That's you! You were there."

"Yes, I was. The Fallen angel standing next to me used to be Lucifer's executioner. I sold my soul to Ori to save the world. But I got it back. Don't count on that happening to you."

Her two apprentices nodded in unison, their eyes still riveted on the monitor in mute horror.

"Okay, the geography lesson is over. Let's get this thing outta here."

Riley had to keep the demon occupied, or it would figure out what they were doing. As her apprentices moved from computer to computer, carefully pulling out all the cords and placing a line of Holy Water around each desktop, she set her fingers loose on the keyboard.

IF I'D KNOWN WE WERE SHARING PICTURES OF HOME, I'D HAVE BROUGHT A FEW OF MY OWN

A bizarre hissing sound came from all the remaining speakers as the screen shifted once again. This time, the image cut right into Riley's heart.

Two figures walked through the dark of Demon Central: her father and Beck. It was the night Paul Blackthorne never came home.

"No," she whispered. "Not this."

A rough laugh came over the speakers now, not one that a Geeker could make. Was another demon playing with her, using the smaller fiend as bait?

No matter how hard she tried, Riley couldn't look away. To her horror, it played out just as Beck had said: he and her dad being tag-teamed by a Five and a Three. They'd grounded the Geo-Fiend, but one of the pieces of swirling debris had cut through the magical shield, slamming into her father's chest.

His eyes flared in shock, then he fell to his knees, dying.

Oh my God.

Riley's breath tightened, pushing her closer to a panic attack. It was one thing to have someone tell her how it had happened, but another to see it play out before her own eyes.

As her father died, Beck held him, sobbing. Then he turned to take on the Three, to keep it away from the man he loved as much as Riley did. Beck battled with a ferocity born of grief. Of losing a friend.

By the end of the scene, Riley was crying. And furious. Her hand reached for the steel pipe in her backpack, wanting nothing more than to smash everything in this room.

"Riley?" one of her apprentices called out.

She forced herself to let go of the pipe. Looking up, she found two pairs of worried eyes watching her. She shook her head, wiping away the tears, then began to type again.

AND YOUR POINT IS? MY DAD'S IN HEAVEN. YOU LOST AGAIN. YOU WILL ALWAYS LOSE.

The noise from the speakers changed now, to the repeated thump of wings. It sounded like a legion of demons descending on them, but that wasn't possible. The image of a graveyard appeared, the one in Edinburgh where she'd killed the Archfiend.

"We're not going there," she said.

The scene played out, death by hideous death. Riley had just begun her sprint across the graveyard when Richard call out, "Ready!"

"Do it."

As Kurt ran a line of Holy Water around her computer, isolating the unit, Richard pulled out the various cables.

"Done," he said.

Riley inserted a special thumb drive into a port, activated the program, and watched as it sucked the mini demon into the drive. Richard pulled the power cord and the computer went dark.

"Tech is awesome," Kurt said, reminding Riley a lot of her friend Peter.

She dropped the drive into a sippy cup full of Holy Water and watched it sizzle away. End of Geeker. "Good job, guys. How's about we celebrate? The hot dogs are on me."

Though Riley doubted she could eat—not after what she'd seen—her apprentices liked that idea, eager to shake off the images of Hell. After packing up their gear, they exited the room ahead of her.

As she reached the door, she turned back on impulse. The computers were silent, devoid of electricity and one pesky demon. It'd been a good trapping, though her nerves were raw and her heart aching.

She'd have to ask Beck about what had happened here. No Techno-Fiend had the power to summon up those images. If it'd been Lucifer, he'd have shown up in person to torment her. He was like that.

Riley was about to turn away when all the monitors came to life at once, the Hellish flames flickering again. Which was impossible because the computers were unplugged and the Geeker dead.

YOU TOOK WHAT WAS MINE

The threat delivered, all the screens went dark with a snap.

"'You took what was mine?'" she said. She had no idea what that meant.

Shutting the door, Riley kept seeing her father's face the moment he knew he was dying, Beck's anguish, the Three tearing into him as he beat it off, then tore it apart.

"Hey," Richard called out. "Everything okay?"

No.

But she put on her game face, not wanting to spook these guys. They'd done a good job and needed her support, not her heartache.

Riley forced a smile, turned, and nodded.

"Let's get out of here. It's time to eat."

Chapter Six

Once they'd finished lunch and conducted the "postmortem" on how the trapping had gone, Riley set her apprentices free. With homework, of course, but they deserved the rest of the day off because they would have to be at the meeting tonight.

Though usually it was the masters who trained the newbies, that had all changed after the Guild lost so many trappers last spring. Now, journeymen trappers took up some of the slack, with a master's oversight.

Because Harper would remain Riley's superior until she made master, she called him and reported on how the run had played out.

"You ever hear of another demon using a Geeker to play head games with a trapper?" she asked.

There was a long pause. "No. What happened?"

After she'd relayed all the weirdness, Harper huffed. "That's how I can tell you aren't working for Hell. If you were, they wouldn't bother messing with you."

Riley wasn't sure if that was a compliment or not, so she let it slide.

"Got a couple Threes here that need to go to Fireman Jack," he said.

Fireman Jack was so named because he lived in an old fire station. He was a demon trafficker and happened to be gay, which, in the past, had sent Harper off into a major rage when she'd sold him some demons. Now he was telling her to do just that?

Huh. She doubted Harper was going to be putting Jack on his

Christmas card list, but it appeared he'd stopped being a raving homophobe. At least in her presence.

Miracles never cease, as her dad would say.

~~*

After delivering the Threes and chatting with Jack, who had always treated her well, Riley returned to Beck's house instead of her room at Stewart's. She'd spent more and more time here, probably because she missed the house's owner so much.

Once she'd fed Rennie, Beck's rabbit, she went to turn on her laptop. Then hesitated, as if whatever Hellspawn had tormented her at the college might have followed her home. Which was ridiculous.

Once the computer came to life, she wrote Beck a long e-mail about what had happened over the last few days, especially the trapping at the college. She avoided the news about the Grade Five trapping, how her and Reynolds had been on their own, left to hang in the breeze by some of the other trappers. Beck would threaten to rip several people's heads off when he got home. She smiled at the thought, realizing just how much she missed him. At least he'd be in Atlanta in time for Christmas.

Riley had barely sent the e-mail and curled up on her bed—hugging a pillow close as if it were her guy—when her phone rang.

"Hey, Princess."

His warm and deep voice hit all the right places.

Somehow she'd known he would call. "Hi, Den. Sorry I freaked out about the college trapping thing."

"I'd've done the same. That sure couldn't have been just a Geeker. They don't have that much power. You told Harper and Stewart about this yet?"

"Only Harper so far. Things are weird enough as it is."

Silence.

"You okay?" she asked.

"Just rememberin' that night . . . with Paul," he said, his

voice thicker. He'd never admit it, but she suspected there were tears in his eyes now.

"Everything that fiend showed me was of them losing," Riley said. "I escaped Hell, Dad's in Heaven, so they can't touch him. You're a grand master. They're failing and it's making them mad."

"This feels more like a Fallen's mind games than a lower level demon. If I hadn't chopped off Sartael's head, I'd swear this was him."

"Yeah." She shifted gears. "So how goes it in scenic Scotland?"

"Snowy and cold. I love this old house, but damn, I'd kill for some central heatin'."

She laughed. "Sorry to tell you, but it snowed here last night. It's still kind of pretty."

"Atlanta snow is one thing. Scotland's is another."

"More tests coming up soon?"

"Just finished one a bit ago. Now we're talkin' more about moral decisions and less about the history of the war between Heaven and Hell. You know, right versus wrong. How sometimes things aren't either one, but right in the middle. That's when it's a damned judgment call."

"My dad used to talk about that kind of thing."

"You'll know more about that when you become a master," he replied.

"As if. It's been four months and the National Guild has continued to blow me off all that time. Jackson made master right after he filed. Me? Oh no, I'm Blackthorne's daughter so I'm a troublemaker."

"So what's the plan?"

That sounded like Stewart, but it came with the grand master territory. They were adept at strategy and playing the long game. Mostly because that was exactly how Heaven and Hell played.

"Harper sent a letter to National, demanding they move forward on my application. He's been talking to other masters around the country and they're sending in letters too."

"You know, I'm beginnin' to like that old man more every day."

"So am I, but don't you ever tell him. Anyway, it'll get worked out eventually. They can't just turn me down and not look stupid."

"You might be surprised. Stupid is what they do best."

She smiled, sitting up now. "Not long before you come home."

No reply. Her nerves twitched. "You're still coming home on the twentieth, right?"

A brief pause. "Yeah. I was just . . . thinkin' of all the stuff I have to get done before that."

Riley exhaled in relief. His time in Scotland had already been extended once. She didn't think she could take it if that happened again.

I need you here.

"Look, I gotta go," he said. "Keep yerself safe. Tell the masters everythin' that's goin' on. They'll watch out for ya."

"I will," she said. He was using "ya" instead of "you," always a sign that he was upset. "Love you, Den."

"Love ya too, Riley."

Once she disconnected the call, she placed her phone on the nightstand, then flopped back down on the pillow. Something was up with Beck, but then, something was up with her. It seemed to be their thing.

Right before she closed her eyes, she set an alarm. Tonight was the meeting, and it wouldn't be good if the chief trouble-maker showed up late.

~~*

Close to sunset, Riley pulled her aged car into the church parking lot. Though she was better off financially now, she was still very careful with her money. The longer this car continued to run, the better. Her parents had taught her that frugality. They'd taught her a lot of good things, including that love lasts forever.

Her mom had died of cancer years before, and her father, just at the beginning of the year. Then he'd returned as a reanimate, but that wasn't like being alive. Soon it'd be the first anniversary of his death, and that was going to be tough. Especially since Beck would be back in Scotland by then.

Miss you guys. I love you.

Shouldering her backpack, Riley trudged toward the church as other trappers headed in the same direction. Some called out her name and she waved, while others ignored her as if she didn't exist. She wished her father were here. He always knew how to handle these people. Now it was up to her and the masters.

Over the years, the local Guild had met in a number of places, starting out at Six Feet Under, a local restaurant and bar. They'd quickly learned that the combination of alcohol and rampant testosterone wasn't ideal for conducting business. They'd tried out a few other sites before settling at the Tabernacle, a former-church-turned-concert-venue.

After a horrific demon attack, the historic building was history, along with a number of trappers. Now it was a makeshift shrine. Curiously, whenever anyone tried to buy the site to redevelop it, weird things happened: Paperwork was lost, funding dried up. It was as if Heaven (or Hell) wanted that ground to remain sacred.

Now the trappers shared a building with a fire-and-brimstone Pentecostal church. Since it was holy ground, there was less likelihood that Hellspawn would feel the need to set fire to the building. Or at least, that's what everyone hoped—especially the churchgoers, who were pleased to show their defiance of Lucifer by hosting the trappers. Riley might not believe everything their faith professed, but she respected their fight against evil.

She also knew she was way too pissed to be at this meeting. Actually, "pissed" wasn't the best word. "Livid" was closer. She'd been betrayed yet again. She had a right to expect that someone would watch her back as much as any other trapper, despite her "history" with Hell. But deep down, she wasn't the least bit surprised at what had happened. That hurt.

More than once, she'd risked her life for these guys, and

when it came time to do the same for her, some of them had turned their backs. That made her appreciate Jackson and Reynolds even more.

The other question still hung in the air: Why had a necromancer set her up? What would be the point? But before she could answer that, she had to settle matters with her own people.

Once inside the church, Riley headed down the long hall toward the meeting room. The bulletin boards along one wall displayed pictures from various missionary trips, along with notices about upcoming events, Bible-study classes, and free puppies. There was also a section of one board dedicated to the Trapper of the Month, as determined by the church members. Ironically, this month it was her.

Riley rolled her eyes at that as she entered the room where their meeting would take place. It had the usual utilitarian vibe: uninspiring paint color, long tables, folding chairs, etc. Of course, there was the picture of Jesus at Gethsemane on the far wall.

The church members always brewed fresh coffee for the trappers, and usually left little tracts on the chairs, in case any of them felt the need for religion. Some trappers were devout, representing various faiths, others not so much.

Riley had seen enough of Heaven and Hell to land somewhere in the middle. She knew angels existed—she'd made a bargain with one once—and she knew Hell was for real—she'd been given a personal tour of the place. Beyond that it got murky.

Various conversations died out the moment she entered the room. She did a quick count and found about thirty trappers here tonight. Some were friends; a few were her enemies. Often that feeling was mutual.

Riley carefully stepped over twin wet lines on the tile floor—a Holy Water circle laid down to protect the trappers from demon attack, even though they were on sacred ground. Traditionally it'd been only one line, but ever since the massacre at the Tabernacle they'd used two, and someone checked that the Holy Water was genuine. Lessons learned.

She greeted her apprentices, including Jaye, who was in her early twenties, with a slim build. Her red hair was shorter now, as if trying to deal with it longer was too much hassle, given all the other issues in her life. She wore her usual jeans and black turtleneck.

"How's your mother?" Riley asked.

"Better. She's at home now and in physical therapy." Jaye sighed. "I really need to get back to the trapping. I love her, but . . ."

"I know. Sick parents are a challenge. You love them, but they can drive you nuts," Riley said. She remembered that from when her mom had been ill.

"I think I can be back full-time right after the first of the year."

"Sounds good. I'll try to catch you up with these two as quickly as I can. But I won't cut any corners."

Mostly because cut corners could make for a very short trapping career.

The girl nodded. "I understand. I wouldn't want you to."

After chatting with the three of them for a few more minutes, Riley chose a seat near Reynolds. He gave her a quick smile and returned to typing something out on his cell phone. At the front of the room, Grand Master Stewart sat on one side of the podium. His expression, at least for those who knew him well, promised considerable unpleasantness. He caught her eye and delivered a solemn nod. Riley returned it.

Her own master sat on the opposite side of the podium. The scar on his face was pulled tight, a sure sign he was angry. Though he was now clean and sober, he was still one tough bastard, and no one relished getting on his bad side.

Jackson, the Guild's current president, took his place at the podium, and the group quieted down immediately.

"I'm calling this meeting of the Atlanta Demon Trappers Guild to order. We have a lot of business to handle." Even his tone was sharper than normal.

"The shit is gonna fly tonight," Reynolds whispered.

"About time," Riley muttered.

It was a good deal Beck wasn't here, or it'd be worse. Even distance didn't blunt his primal drive to protect her. If anything, it made it stronger, and any action that remotely resembled a threat to his fiancée sent him over the deep end.

Riley had learned not to tell him everything, which seemed wrong. But then, she knew that he didn't tell her everything either. As long as the secrets didn't overwhelm their love, they'd be good. It was a fine line they walked, and they both knew it.

The first portion of the meeting dealt with announcing new policies from the National Guild, which garnered the usual boos, as well as recognizing those trappers who had passed their exams to move from apprentice to journeyman. Clapping ensued when the names were announced.

"Go, Butler!" one of the trappers called out, and the new journeyman executed a short bow. Smiling, Riley joined in the clapping. She'd trapped with him and he was solid.

"Anything else we need to talk about before we get to the other part of the meeting?" Jackson asked.

Journeyman Kevin Remmers stood. He was a genial fellow, one of the five African Americans who were in the local Guild now. Riley always liked to trap with him because he had a great sense of humor.

"Had a run-in with a damned necromancer the other night," he said. "SOB summoned a Four."

Riley huffed. "No way could that go badly."

"Did you catch the dude's name?" Jackson asked.

"He refused to tell me."

"What color robe was he wearin'?" Stewart asked.

"Light brown."

Necromancers' level of magical ability was indicated by the color of the robe; the darker, the more powerful the summoner. The one Riley had seen in Demon Central had been wearing dark blue, so it wasn't the same one.

Summoning a Mezmer was a stupid move. You had to have a healthy respect for a fiend who could co-opt your will and make you its bitch. Or drain your life force like it was soda pop pouring out of a can. That was the problem with the spell slingers—they believed they had more power than they really possessed.

Even their most senior summoner, Lord Ozymandias, had learned that lesson. Unfortunately the lesson had cost lives, both civilian and trapper.

"If we can find the damned fool's name, I'll hand it off to Lord Ozymandias and he'll deal with the problem," Stewart said.

"What? Give the bastard a slap on the wrist?" a trapper called out. It was McGuire, who always seemed to have a rod up his butt.

"No, His Lordship will make sure the offender is a pile of smokin' dust," was Stewart's terse reply.

"He kills them?" another trapper asked.

"Aye. Once he's certain of the facts, the necro is history."

Reynolds whistled under his breath. "At least *we* don't do that kind of thing anymore," he whispered.

Want to make a bet?

These guys didn't know that one of the tasks of a grand master was to ensure that master trappers remained on the good side of things. If one went dark, as they called it, that master would die. If a grand master sided with Hell, same thing. There was no appeal. Often, "culling the herd" included journeymen as well. None of them were entirely safe if they sided with Lucifer.

"Anything else?" Jackson asked. Uneasy silence was his answer. The trappers knew what was coming and some seemed eager for a fight.

Harper shifted in his seat, scowling. As senior master and official head of the Atlanta Guild, it was up to him to take the first step.

"Last night we had a necro call up a Geo-Fiend in Demon Central. Then, he takes off." Harper leaned forward in his chair. "We had *our* people up against a Five, and a damned powerful one at that. I checked your work orders and there were *three* of you close enough to offer backup. So where the fuck were you?"

Oh yeah, he's pissed.

Silence was the answer.

"Don't think I'm going to let this drop," Harper warned.

"Same here," Stewart added. "This willna stand."

A chair scooted back, and Riley wasn't surprised to find McGuire on his feet. The man glared at the masters, apparently not intimidated.

"Why should we get in the middle of that? Blackthorne's kid can handle those things all by herself. She probably called the Five up anyway."

"No, that's not right," Richard began.

Riley looked back at him and shook her head, cautioning him to be silent. He didn't need any enemies this early in his career.

"Care to answer that, Blackthorne?" Harper asked.

All eyes swiveled in her direction.

"Yeah, I do."

It was time to make her case. Maybe she could convince some of these morons that she wasn't a threat.

Which would happen just about the time Lucifer and his demons built snow forts in Hell.

Chapter Seven

Riley rose from her chair. "I didn't summon that Five, because I'm not suicidal. Or stupid."

McGuire didn't reply, so she continued. "No matter how it got there, I expected someone to watch my back while I tried to ground it. Jackson and Reynolds did just that, but that's not enough of us to do the job safely."

She paused, her heart pounding now. "If we hadn't been lucky, there would have been three dead trappers last night."

"No big loss if one of them was you," McGuire muttered.

"What the hell is with this attitude?" Reynolds demanded, lurching up from his chair. His friendly, "I'm just a laid-back surfer from California" persona was gone.

"Even if I think you're a dick—and trust me, McGuire, I'm good with that—I'll watch your back because that's what trappers do. If we don't stick together, Hell wins."

"No way we can win if she's working with us," McGuire said, jabbing a finger at her.

Riley lost it. "You would have let Reynolds and Jackson die just because you can't handle me?"

"I didn't want them hurt, but they chose to back you up."

"Why do you have a problem with me? I've proved myself over and over to you guys."

"I hear you're playing house with the necromancers, learning magic. That's not what a trapper does. You have no right to be in the Guild. Never did."

"Even though I stood up to the Prince of Hell himself, I'm never going to be good enough?"

"Not when you're doing magic," the man retorted. A few trappers near him nodded. They seemed to have their very own "We Hate Blackthorne" cheering section.

"Riley," Stewart interjected. "Tell them why yer learnin' the spells."

She'd suspected the grand master would go in that direction.

"We don't need to hear excuses for why you're working with corpse stealers," McGuire replied.

To her surprise, Riley actually grinned. "You know, I kind of like that description. Remind me to use that down the line."

She didn't like where she was standing, so she moved to the front of the room. In the back of her mind, she could hear Beck telling her to "own these bastards." She wasn't sure that was possible, but it was worth a try.

"Some of you know I flew over to Scotland at the end of October, for my birthday." The best part of the trip filled her mind and she held up her left hand, displaying her ring. "Beck and I got engaged there." She lowered her hand. "But it didn't go right at first. I walked off the plane and got kidnapped by a bunch of necromancers. They used me as bait to summon an angel. The problem was, only the lead necro knew he was actually calling up an Archfiend."

"Shit," someone muttered from the crowd.

"The demon killed three people."

"Good riddance," McGuire said.

"Easy to say if you didn't watch them die," she replied, glaring at him. "I thought it was over, but the necro who had set up the whole scheme came after me. She tried to make me cut my own throat so she could summon a Fallen angel."

A low whistle came from Reynolds.

"I was able to break the spell. How I did it, I don't know. But if I hadn't, I would have killed myself, and Beck would have had no way to stop me. Then he and Grand Master MacTavish might have died as well."

There was silence now, except for the occasional drip of the faucet in the corner.

"Tell them who is teachin' ya," Stewart urged.

"I'm working with Mortimer Alexander. He's the necro who fought with us against the demons in Oakland Cemetery. I'm also training with Ayden, the witch. She was in the cemetery battle too." Riley swallowed hard. "I don't really like magic. I respect those who do it, at least if they don't hurt anyone, but I never wanted to learn the stuff. What happened in Scotland proved there would *always* be someone who would want to use me because of my . . . history . . . with Heaven and Hell."

"Then quit," McGuire said. "Give it up. They won't bother you then."

"It won't work that way," Stewart replied. "Because she's dealt with Heaven's angels *and* with Lucifer, she's the ultimate bait. Every necro with a taste for power wants ta use her ta gain even more power."

"There has to be another way than magic," one of the trappers said.

"Not if I want a future," Riley said. "Not if I want to get married and have kids like everyone else. I have to learn how to protect myself. Being a trapper helps, but the only thing that will stop these guys is knowing protection spells. That's why I'm doing this."

"What keeps you from turning on us?" a voice called out from the back of the hall.

She looked the trapper full in the face. "What keeps you from giving up your soul to Hell?"

The man glared at her. "I wouldn't do that."

"Well, I'm not going to turn on you guys, even if you hate me. I'm doing this for my dad, because he's not going to be here to walk me down the aisle or play with his grandkids. If that's not good enough, you can just get screwed, because I'm going nowhere."

She returned to her chair, shaking less than she'd expected.

"Any questions?" Harper asked.

"She can still go bad on us," McGuire warned.

"If she does, Stewart and I will take care of the problem."

"How?"

"Given what Riley's been through," Stewart said, "the International Guild has assigned me the task of keepin' an eye on her. As has the Vatican, I might add. If she goes dark, she's done for."

"What are you going to do, send her to bed without her supper?"

Stewart glared. "Apparently yer not aware that grand masters have the right ta summarily execute anyone we feel is a threat ta the balance between the Light and Dark. A journeyman wieldin' magic who goes dark, one who has had contact with Lucifer before? There will be no other judgment than death."

"Jesus," someone behind her muttered. "That blows."

Welcome to my world. She would always be under someone's scrutiny. Screw up, and she was in deep trouble.

"That good enough for ya, McGuire?" Stewart demanded.

A low grumble.

"I dinna catch that."

"Yeah, for the time being. I still don't trust her."

"I don't give a damn if you trust Blackthorne or not. The next time she or any of our people call for help, you'll be there," Harper snarled. "If you're not, I will personally bust your ass right out of the Guild, right after I beat the living hell out of you. Got it?"

"Yeah. Got it." The man sank down in his chair, glowering at her.

Oh boy.

The meeting ended shortly after that, though tensions still ran high. Riley didn't exactly sprint out of the room, but she didn't loiter either.

Reynolds called after her as they reached the parking lot. "You okay?"

She shrugged. "It was supposed to be easier. Get past the apprenticeship, become a journeyman, and then it's a smooth coast to becoming a master."

He chuckled. "You actually believed that?"

"Not really, but I kinda hoped some of it was true. Thanks

for standing up for me in there."

"My pleasure," he said, smiling. "The next time a Five comes after me, I want to know I'm covered." A car horn honked and he looked over at a shiny Toyota; his smile grew broader. "Got to go. My hot date awaits."

Reynolds took off at a lope toward a pretty blonde. They kissed through the open window.

Glad you have a real life, dude.

Maybe someday she'd have one too.

As Riley unlocked her car, her cell phone pinged.

HOW DID IT GO?

She blinked. She hadn't told Beck what had happened the night before, or that the meeting was anything but routine. That meant either Stewart or Jackson had ratted her out.

There was no way to hide it now.

AS GOOD AS IT COULD HAVE. MCGUIRE IS STILL AN ASSHAT.

U WANT ME TO POUND HIM WHEN I GET HOME?

"Tempting," she muttered. But that wouldn't do.

She typed back, NO NEED. MAYBE I'LL TURN HIM INTO A FROG OR SOMETHING.

JACKASS. LESS MAGIC.

Riley laughed, desperately needing the release. I LOVE YOU SO MUCH.

LOVE U TOO. SEE U NEXT WK. GOTTA GET TO BED NOW.

GOOD NIGHT!

NIGHT, PRINCESS.

Riley checked the time—it was close to eleven in Scotland, which meant he'd stayed up late just to chat with her. Given his heavy academic load, that was a sacrifice.

I so don't deserve you.

Since it was just a little after six here, the Grounds Zero Coffee Shop—home of the best hot chocolate in the city—was still open. She had just enough time to fuel up before she headed to Mort's for another lesson in defensive magic.

Given the way things were playing out, she'd better be a quick study.

Chapter Eight

Mortimer Alexander lived in Little Five Points, often called L5P by the locals, a part of Atlanta that was home to a significant number of magic users, both witches and necromancers. It had a New Age feel and Riley had grown to like the area more with each subsequent visit.

Though they both employed magic, the witches and the summoners did not always make good neighbors. Most of the time they ignored each other. Other times, there was open hostility and magical feuds, which never made much sense to Riley. What was all the fuss about?

Her dad had once described the acrimony as being like the rivalry between Georgia Tech's and the University of Georgia's football fans; it was just a thing, and you learned to live with it. Except rabid football fans didn't sling spells around like confetti.

Back when Riley's friends Ayden and Mort had first begun to work together, their relationship had been like that of two annoyed porcupines: lots of prickly moments. After the horrific battle at Oakland Cemetery—and what could have easily become Armageddon—the two magical folks had grown to respect each other. That still didn't stop the sniping, but at least the verbal fencing was good-natured now.

As Riley pulled into a parking place, a horse-drawn carriage trotted by. There were fewer of them now, as gas prices slowly sank from a high of over ten dollars a gallon. Currently at just below eight fifty, it seemed like a bargain. Though the carriages were quaint, no one would miss the horse droppings in the streets.

Mort lived on Enchanter's Way, which was aptly named as it had a big metal arch over the entrance to the street, and that arch was enchanted. Since metal meant money to thieves, the spell was a smart move. Otherwise, the arch would be long gone.

More an alley than a street, Enchanter's Way was lined with small businesses and homes, the majority of the latter belonging to the magical folk.

Riley stuck her nose in at the Bell, Book, and Broomstick to see if Ayden was working, and was pleased to find her arranging crystals on a long glass shelf. As if knowing she was being watched, the witch turned toward her, and a smile came immediately. Ayden's curly auburn hair was up in a loose bun, and she was wearing a blouse and long skirt that would have been at home in a Renaissance faire.

"There you are," she said. "You've been pretty quiet the last few days."

"Yeah. It's been . . . rough."

Ayden's brow furrowed. "Trappers bothering you?"

"Yeah, it's getting worse." After a quick check to make sure there was no one else in the shop, she unloaded the story of the last two nights while Ayden's frown grew more pronounced.

Riley was instantly enveloped in a hug that fed good vibes through her, courtesy of her friend's magic. Ayden could wield both soft and tough love with the best of them.

The embrace ended and the witch studied her closely. "You down this way to see the Magical Mort?"

"Yup. We have a lesson."

"Good. Just remember, the summoners don't know everything."

Riley chuckled. "Funny. He said the same thing about witches."

"He would."

Ayden walked over to the counter, fished around, and returned with a small bottle of oil. "Use this for clarity. And balance. As usual, your aura is all wonky."

"Thanks. How much do I owe you?"

"On the house. We still up for a lesson tomorrow night?"

"Sure are." Riley might not like magic, but she really liked the people who were teaching her. "You doing okay with the other witchy people?"

Ayden sighed. "Not everything is kosher with some of them right now. Lots of . . . drama while the most senior witch is out of town. Not exactly sure what that's all about."

"Maybe it's something in the water," Riley said. "I should go. Don't want to be late. Thanks for the oil."

"Send my regards to Mort," Ayden said, delivering another hug.

As Riley turned away, she couldn't help but notice that the large tattoo covering her friend's upper chest was of a thunderstorm over a spooky graveyard. Since the tattoo changed on its own, acting like a fleshy oracle, that wasn't a reassuring omen.

Farther down the alley, Riley paused in front of a collection of mailboxes. They were placed on a wall, some higher, some lower, many requiring the owners to climb to collect their junk mail. Each had its own decoration and Mort's was graced with a pinwheel, which spun in the light breeze. That one, in particular, always brought a smile.

His front door was purple and a plaque next to it indicated he was the Summoner Advocate for the city, which meant he dealt with internal necro conflicts as well as preventing the public from demanding they all be burned at the stake. It was a tedious job, but he did it well, though his fellow summoners never gave him any respect for his efforts.

Mort's nephew answered her knock, then leaned up against the doorframe, checking her out. Alex was about her age and liked to hit on her, despite the engagement ring. At first, she'd just ignored him, but when he'd persisted she'd mentioned her fiancé, the one who'd *killed an Archangel*. Once that phrase sank in, Alex ramped down his come-ons, no doubt figuring if he kept it up, he'd be meeting Beck and not in a good way.

"My favorite part of the week," Alex said, delivering his bad-boy smile. It was pretty good as those went, but he had nothing on Riley's guy. Beck's smile could make a convent of nuns go rogue.

"Hi. How's it going?" she asked.

"Good. Climbed Stone Mountain today. Not as easy as I thought it would be."

Riley couldn't help but smile. Alex was really nice, and if Beck hadn't already claimed her heart, he'd probably be on her radar.

He closed the door behind her and locked it. "His Magicness is in his office, like always. Fair warning: I think he has something different lined up for you tonight."

"Oh goodie," she said. The last time Mort had done something different, she'd left with a section of scorched hair and first-degree burns on her fingers because her magical "control" wasn't anywhere near what his was. "As long as it has nothing to do with demons, I'll probably do okay."

"So you say now," he replied. "When do I get to meet this big bad dude of yours?"

"Pretty soon. Beck's flying home for the holidays."

"Is he the jealous kind?"

"Yeah. Definitely."

"Lifts weights?"

"Yup, and ex-military."

"I was afraid of that," Alex said. "I think I'll just continue thinking you're off limits, okay?"

"Smart move."

Riley negotiated the hallway to the curiously circular room that served as Mort's office. It was brick, painted white, with skylights to help bring in the outdoors. The necromancer sat at his desk, which was really a picnic table. For once, there were no books stacked on it.

"There you are," he said, beckoning her forward, smiling.

Mort was a short and round fellow, with a good laugh and sharp mind. At one time, he'd been a mortician and somehow had migrated into the corpse-summoning business. Of all the necromancers Riley'd met, he was the most moral of the lot. He never pressured anyone to raise their dead family member, never played tricks on them. He had put his life on the line repeatedly, when it mattered most.

"Alex said you have something special for me this time."

Mort waggled his eyebrows. "Levitation."

"You're serious?"

"Yes, I am. But first, tell me about last night. Stewart called this morning and said I should ask you about it."

Riley gave him the quick and dirty version of the events, and by the end, Mort's brows were furrowed so deeply they had to hurt.

"Describe the summoner," he said crisply, all trace of humor gone.

When she did, he shook his head. "He doesn't sound familiar. Of course, he could have been using a glamour to hide his identity."

Riley hadn't considered that, which was dumb since she *was* studying magic. "How would I know?"

Mort thought for a moment, then nodded. "Let's set the levitation aside for this session, and I'll show you how to see through someone's glamour spell. How about that?"

"Works for me." Because the times she'd need to know how to levitate would probably fall into the almost-never category. Well, except for when she was trapping Geo-Fiends.

"I'll call Ozymandias after our class, let him know what's going on. We do *not* need bad relations with the demon trappers."

"Too late. Some of them hate you."

"Well, there are some of my people who don't like the trappers. In fact, they rate them as untrustworthy as witches."

"Wow, that bad, huh?" she jested.

"Yes," he replied. Except he wasn't joking.

Okay then.

Mort took a deep breath. "Glamour spells are sometimes simple, sometimes complex. It depends on how much you want to hide. Sort of like whether a woman puts on a wig to change her appearance or goes for a complete makeover."

"That bracelet you gave me last spring—it was a glamour spell, a pretty complex one, right? It made me all goth with lots of piercings and weird hair. Which rocked, by the way."

"That one was complex. We'll start with you recognizing and busting the simple spells and work up."

"So how do I do that?"

Mort grew pensive. "How do you know when not to trust some man you meet on the street?"

She thought that through. "Ah, something doesn't feel right. I get creeped out, you know?"

"You've learned to trust that instinct?"

"Most of the time." Except when it came to a certain Fallen angel who had totally waltzed past her defenses. But then, Ori's charm had been one of his best weapons.

"What if this guy you meet is wearing a clerical collar?" Mort asked.

"A priest? I'd be more likely to think him trustworthy than a guy in a ratty T-shirt, covered in tattoos."

Mort nodded. "Most people ignore their sixth sense, the internal warning that insists 'something's not right here.' They figure they're wrong, or being paranoid. Trusting your instincts is one of the first things young children should be taught to avoid sexual predators. The same applies here." He paused. "Except we're going to enhance your intuition with a bit of magic. A powerful glamour is hard to break, but you'll be able to discern a simpler one fairly quickly."

"Powerful like Ozymandias's whirling-leaves trick?" Now that her father's body wasn't in the necromancer's possession, and his soul was in Heaven, Riley had to admit that the high lord's magic did kinda rock. Not that she'd ever tell the creep that.

Mort nodded solemnly. "Lord Ozymandias is very skilled at spellcasting glamour and illusions. I'm thinking once you have the simple spells down, it might be good for him to teach you how to crack the stronger glamours."

There he goes again. Ever since she'd asked Mort to help

her learn magic, he'd insisted that she should spend some time with Ozy, as she called him. So far, she'd resisted that, mostly because Ozymandias had used her dead father to gain his own freedom from one of Hell's Archangels. Even though her father had agreed to help, moves like that didn't win you friends.

Mort read her expression. "I know you don't like him, but Ozymandias is the best at this kind of stuff."

Riley mumbled under her breath about how she'd rather play tag with a rabid wolf.

Mort grinned. "There's a lot of similarity. But first, close your eyes and wait for me to tell you when to open them."

She did as he asked. She heard him leave the room, and as time passed, boredom set in. To keep herself occupied, she began figuring out exactly how many hours were left until Beck arrived at the airport. One hundred and forty-four. She began working on how many minutes when Mort returned.

"Okay, you can open your eyes."

Three things sat on the picnic table in front of her: an orange, a lizard, and a bowling trophy. The lizard flicked its tail, each eye swiveling in a different direction at the same time.

Riley leaned forward. "Is it real?"

"Depends. Is it a veiled chameleon, or is it an illusion?"

She frowned and tried to use logic to solve the problem.

Mort shook his head. "You're going about it wrong. You're thinking, 'Does he have a pet lizard?' You should be asking, 'Does the lizard feel real?'"

Riley cocked her head. The thing looked real. It had scales, swiveling eyes, all the telltale reptile stuff. She knew a bit about the creatures because her friend Peter'd had a chameleon when he was young, and he'd insisted on regaling her with all the details about its everyday life.

The reptile crawled across the table; when it reached the edge, Mort scooped it up and put it back in front of her. "What's the verdict?"

"I think it's real."

"Okay. What about the orange and the bowling trophy?"

She studied each of those in turn. Her eyes kept going back to the trophy for some reason. She pointed at it. "It feels wrong."

"Let's find out if your instincts are right."

The trophy changed into a can of soda, the lizard vanished entirely, and the orange stubbornly remained a fruit.

"Ah . . . crap."

"The orange was what it claimed to be," Mort explained. "The soda was hidden by glamour, and the lizard was pure illusion."

Riley groaned, a dull headache forming behind her eyes. "How do I tell the difference between glamour and illusion?"

"You already did. You zeroed in on the trophy instinctively, knowing something wasn't quite right about it."

"But the lizard looked so real."

"That's because I'm very good at magic. Still, you want to know how to tell if it's fake or not."

"How?"

"Be better at magic than I am."

This time, her groan filled the room. "Yeah, right. That should be a snap."

Mort grinned. He rolled the orange over to her. "Let's start by teaching you how to make this look like something else. Once you understand the process, you'll have a better chance at recognizing when someone else is doing the same thing."

Now we're getting somewhere.

Chapter Nine

Denver Beck yawned, covering his mouth with the back of his hand as he walked down the manor's long hallway to score some breakfast. He'd stayed up later than normal so he could text with Riley. After that, his anger at what was going on back home had made sleep difficult.

At dawn, he'd loaded up his backpack and gone for a run in the snowy hills, trying to burn off that anger. It'd helped, somewhat, but he was still pissed off and likely to stay that way. At least until he had a private chat with the dickheads who had left Riley unprotected.

How the hell could they do that to her?

Beck shook his head, trying to clear his mind. He had a full day of studies in front of him, and he couldn't do much for his girl at the moment. Once he got back to Atlanta, things would change. He'd make sure they did.

He hurried down the long staircase, past the pictures of various grand masters from over the centuries. One of these days, his portrait would be there among the rest.

Beck walked faster, trying to keep warm. He'd grown to love this place, but this morning was chilly, even by Scottish standards. Southern born and bred, his body didn't like the cold. He'd even had to buy a pair of insulated long underwear, which had drawn some good-natured chiding from his superior, Grand Master Trevor MacTavish.

Beck nodded at one of the maids as he reached the room used for informal meals, just off the kitchen. Unlike the main dining room, there was no weaponry on the walls, no bold messages of intent other than *"it's time to eat."*

The table was old, like everything in this place, but sturdy and well built. MacTavish was already seated at it, his plate filled from the selection on the sideboard.

"Good mornin', lad. Yer later than usual," he said. "Been out for a run?"

"Yeah, I needed to blow off steam," Beck replied, moving to the sideboard and picking up a china plate. "I was up late last night textin' with Riley."

"Everythin' all right with ya two?"

"We're fine," he said. "Just missin' each other."

"Aye, I know how that goes. Ya'll see her soon enough."

Beck turned his attention back to the food, a classic Scottish breakfast. This morning he loaded up on four eggs, a mound of bacon, three link sausages, sautéed mushrooms, half a broiled tomato, and baked beans.

As he sat next to the other grand master, MacTavish chuckled. "I wish I could eat that much nowadays. Enjoy it, because soon age will catch up with ya, and so will yer waistline."

Not that MacTavish had an inch of fat on him.

Beck nodded, pouring himself a cup of coffee, then retrieved two slices of brown toast from the rack.

"I hear things are gettin' unpleasant in Atlanta," MacTavish said.

Beck looked over at the older man. "Stewart called you?"

"Aye, early this mornin'. He said someone's stirrin' the pot in yer hometown. He's unhappy about how things are playin' out. It's good yer goin' back ta the States soon." MacTavish took a sip of his tea. "Be sure ta let us know what's happenin' there. Lucifer has taken far too much interest in Atlanta of late."

"I'll send you regular reports. Hopefully things will settle down once I'm home."

Voices at the door brought Beck's head up. Grand Master Jonah Kepler, the archivist, had a visitor at his side, a man Beck hadn't seen since the big battle in Atlanta.

Beck blinked in surprise, then broke into a smile.

Elias Salvatore, the head of the Vatican's Demon Hunters, smiled back at him. He appeared in good health—all dark hair and badass attitude, dressed in navy trousers and a navy turtleneck with the Demon Hunters emblem over the left breast. His goatee was precisely trimmed, as always.

"Elias!" Beck said, shoving his chair back. "It's good to see you!" They'd formed a bond last spring when all hell had broken loose, literally.

"Same to you, my friend. I had Vatican business in Edinburgh and I remembered you were here, so I wrangled an invite to breakfast."

There had to be more to it than that, and they both knew it.

As Elias reached the table, they shook hands, then slapped backs. The demon hunter sobered, giving the senior master a respectful nod. "Grand Master MacTavish."

"Captain Salvatore. It is good ta see ya again. Come, have some food. Tell us what it's like in the Vatican nowadays."

"Like you don't know already."

MacTavish smiled right back. "Not much changes in that regard. It's the same here as well."

"We are slaves to tradition," Elias replied.

"Jonah? Ya joinin' us for breakfast?" MacTavish asked.

Kepler shook his head. "I have research that needs to be completed this morning." He left them, shutting the door behind him.

"He's looking good," Elias said, once the man was out of earshot.

"Stayin' well. At his age, that's a blessin'," MacTavish said.

As Elias filled his plate, he paused and looked over at Beck. "I had a chance to talk to Simon Adler at Pluscarden Abbey about a week ago. He said you'd been up to visit him."

Simon had been Riley's boyfriend, at least until he nearly died at the hands of a demon and then became a pawn of Hell.

"Yeah, we met for supper," Beck replied. "He's definitely gettin' his head screwed on right." He paused. "Simon was very closemouthed about what he'd been up to the last few months.

You happen to know?"

"I do, but I'm not at liberty to speak about it," the hunter said, sitting at the table. "I'm sure he'll tell you soon enough."

Now that's interestin'. "I'm happy to see he's got another chance. Not many have after an Archangel gets done with them."

"Amen." Elias bowed his head, said grace, and then they ate in silence for a few minutes.

Once their guest's plate was empty, MacTavish leaned back in his chair, arms crossed over his chest.

"So what brings ya ta our doorstep, in particular?" he asked.

Elias took a long drink of his coffee before answering. "The Vatican has heard rumors that things are becoming unstable in Atlanta again."

Beck didn't take the bait. From the corner of his eye, he caught a faint nod from MacTavish. Learning patience had been the master's mantra since Beck had arrived at the manor house. It had been a tough lesson to learn, as he'd always been the kind to grab someone around the throat and demand answers.

Elias must have realized his silence wasn't working and he sighed. "Grand Master Stewart sent us a report that has my superiors worried. I suspect you know what that report contained."

"That Riley's studyin' magic," Beck said. "Stewart explained why, too." He'd seen a copy of the report. Fortunately, Riley wasn't aware he was in the loop, and he wasn't sure he'd ever tell her.

"There are those in the Holy See who are not pleased by this information," the hunter continued. "They fear her connection with Hell, paired with the magic, will only lead to trouble. They are nervous about this new development."

"But yer not," MacTavish said, leaning forward with both elbows on the table. "Why is that?"

"I've spent time with Riley. She possesses a good heart, a strong moral compass, and she's tough as nails." Elias looked over at Beck now. "We've fought together. I know she's not going anywhere near Hell, no matter what Lucifer or his demons offer. Other than Father Rosetti, my superiors don't know her. It's hard to see inside her bright soul when all you're doing is judging her from a report."

Beck inclined his head in thanks. "So how do we get them to know her better, so they'll leave her alone?"

"She could go to the Vatican," Elias suggested. "But then some might not allow her to leave. Not all in the Holy See have an open mind about such things."

"So your visit is more a warnin' than a social call?" MacTavish asked.

"No," Beck said, before the demon hunter could reply. "I think this is a heads-up that things could get worse if we don't keep an eye on them."

"That's it entirely," Elias said. "My superiors know I'm visiting you, but they assume I came here to talk about demonic hotspots, not about Riley Blackthorne."

"And Father Rosetti?" Beck asked.

"He was the one who suggested I be candid about the problem, so you can determine a way to short-circuit whatever is going on in Atlanta."

"Riley is not causin' the problems," Beck insisted.

"Rosetti and I know that, but others don't. We figured, what with Christmas coming soon, you might be headed home. Maybe you can find a way to spread some oil on the water, as it were."

"Indeed," MacTavish said. "I'm pleased that the hunters and the grand masters are workin' tagether more than before. I'm sure Hell doesn't appreciate it, and anythin' that annoys Lucifer is fine by me."

Elias nodded his agreement. "Ironically, it was Riley's situation that brought us into more contact. Stewart's reports to the Vatican have been concise, thorough, and unbiased. I've read all of them, and I can tell he's pulling no punches, which can't be easy given the situation."

"I don't envy him," Beck murmured.

Especially if something went wrong. It was as much Stewart's life on the line as Riley's.

"So where are ya off ta next?" MacTavish asked.

Elias set his napkin aside. "Things are heating up in Croatia, so I expect the team will be headed there in a few days. I had hoped for some time off over Christmas, but that wouldn't be Hell's plan at all. They love to stir up trouble this time of year."

"Well, yer doin' good work nonetheless. Celebrate Christmas where ya are," MacTavish said.

"We always do."

"Is Rosetti still workin' with the hunters?" Beck asked.

"Part-time. He has . . . new responsibilities now."

Which, clearly, Elias wasn't going to explain.

"All right, I'll let you know what I find out in Atlanta," Beck said. He trusted the man, and he knew that any information he shared would go to Father Rosetti, who seemed to carry a fair amount of weight in Rome.

"I appreciate that." The demon hunter rose. "Thank you so much for breakfast, gentlemen. Have a very merry Christmas and a blessed New Year."

The sentiment was returned, and then Beck escorted him to the manor's front door. As they stepped outside into the crisp air, Elias asked, "So, this grand master thing, is it all you thought it would be?"

"I've always liked trappin' demons. Now, I know there's so much more to it than that. The whole Grand Game, how we humans are stuck in the middle of it. How easily it could go wrong."

Elias nodded. "I remember what Riley said during the battle in the cemetery, when she stood between the Prince and the Archangel Michael." He looked into the distance, as if picturing the scene. "She said mortals were created to balance the Light and the Dark. That we were in the perfect position, not the angels in Heaven or the demons in Hell."

Beck nodded, remembering that moment as well. The immense courage it had taken to stand between those eternal foes.

Elias looked over at him now. "Keep Atlanta from boiling

over, no matter who is causing the trouble. My superiors' patience is thinning."

"Do you think Hell has somethin' to do with that? Yer bosses' lack of patience?" Beck asked bluntly.

Any other representative of the Holy See would have felt insulted, but Elias was pragmatic. "I'm not sure. I'll find out."

They shook hands. As the demon hunter drove away, Beck found MacTavish waiting for him just inside the manor's entrance.

"Is it possible Lucifer's infiltrated Rome?" Beck asked.

"It's entirely possible." MacTavish hesitated for only a few seconds. "Start packin', lad. We'll see if we can get ya an earlier flight home. It's time ta put all yer trainin' inta practice."

Chapter Ten

Riley's mind wasn't playing fair; Mort's Latin homework required more attention than she was willing to give it. The noise of Grounds Zero, usually comforting, just jumbled her thoughts.

Part of the problem was the headache she'd endured since last night's magic session. Two hours of trying to make an orange look like a banana had done that to her. Mort had said there'd be fewer headaches once she didn't have to work as hard at casting a glamour spell. Couldn't come soon enough for her.

Still, after those two hours of practice, she'd come up with a scrawny banana-like object all on her own. Then she did it three more times.

The other issue was Mort's solemn announcement—perfectly timed as she was leaving his house, so she couldn't ask a ton of questions—that there was an "event" she must attend to become an official member of the Summoners' Society. That he really couldn't keep teaching her magic without it. When she asked if this involved a blood sacrifice, he shook his head, but she got the notion that this thing was going to be pretty serious.

Hence the continued headache. If she wanted to make one fruit look like another or figure out who was summoning Grade Five demons just to mess with her, she had to be part of their society. As if already belonging to one organization that didn't entirely trust her wasn't enough.

To make things worse, she was on call later tonight, but what if some idiot necro summoned another Five? The job was terrifying enough without worrying if you had backup. The other trappers on duty this evening were mostly friendly, but she never knew when loyalties might shift, which happened more often than was good.

Riley dropped her pen and took another sip of hot chocolate. Thank God that was the one thing that never failed her. As she set the cup down, she heard someone clear his throat. She looked up and gasped.

"Simon?"

Her ex-boyfriend stood near the table, smiling. His bright-blond hair was much longer, curling down on his collar, and his eyes were as blue as she remembered them. He wore jeans, a black shirt, and a heavy coat.

"Riley," he said, opening his arms wide.

She slid out of the booth and walked into those arms without hesitation.

They hugged, hard. There'd been a time when she'd hated him for what he'd done to her, but now that anger was gone. Simon had endured a test that would have broken most mortals.

"I have missed you so much," she said into his ear.

"I've missed you too," he replied.

They broke the embrace and she smiled up at him. "When did you get back in town?"

"Last night. I hoped I'd find you here. I can't stay long. I promised the 'rents I'd be home in time for supper."

Riley waved him over to the booth.

"Let me get some coffee first. You need a refill?"

She shook her head and he set off for the front counter.

"Simon's back," she whispered. From the look of him, he was doing well. Fit and healthy. There was a fire in his eyes now, and that made her wonder who, or what, had put it there.

He returned to the booth with his drink. After he sat, they just stared at each other for a few moments.

"Beck said he saw you a while back."

Simon nodded. "He looks different. Older. Comes with being a grand master, I guess."

"I still can't believe he killed an Archangel." Suddenly nervous, Riley took a drink of her hot chocolate. "Are you coming back to work as a trapper?"

He shook his head. "I've got another job now."

"Oh. What are you doing?" she asked.

Simon looked around, then lowered his voice as if what he was about to say was a state secret. "I'm a lay exorcist for the Vatican."

She blinked. "You cast out demons? For real?"

"For real. The trappers do a good job capturing the fiends, so do the hunters, but there is a need for personal exorcism, and there just aren't enough priests to go around. At least not those trained to handle this kind of thing."

"Wow. A genuine exorcist. Not like those girls who tried to cast out my devils last spring."

He nodded, smiling at the memory. "It's . . . a new organization within the Vatican, and I was invited to be in their first training course."

"Because of what you went through?" she asked, quieter now.

"Exactly because of that. Father Rosetti is heading the group."

"Rosetti, huh," she said.

The priest had been sent to Atlanta to determine if she was working for Hell, and they hadn't trusted each other. By the end of the battle at Oakland Cemetery, Rosetti knew she wasn't a threat. In fact, she kind of liked the guy, even though he was the Vatican's watchdog.

"He said to send his regards."

"That's nice of him. I never figured he liked me," she said, shrugging. "You got hand-picked, huh? That is awesome, Simon."

That comment earned her a smile. "Trust me, there was a *lot* of psychological testing before I was accepted."

"Did they break out the papal Holy Water?"

He nodded. "Passed that test too."

"I didn't the first time around," she admitted. "I really kinda blew Rosetti's mind with Hell's mark on one palm and Heaven's on the other." She looked at the crown on her left hand. "I'm down to just one now."

He nodded his understanding. "Luckily it's Heaven's."

She agreed. "Thanks for writing me. It helped knowing you were doing okay."

"It was life changing journey. I visited so many places, talked to so many people. All of them had their own personal faith, and they shared with me how they view their god. Or sometimes a goddess or gods, depending on who I talked to."

"Beck said something about spending time in Pluscarden Abbey at the end of his training. Is that why you were there? To straighten things out in your head?"

"Yes. I needed to get my heart and my head in the right place. The actual exorcism training took nearly five months. It was nothing like I'd imagined," he said, his eyes not meeting hers now. "No surprise—I seem to be good at blocking demonic bullshit, so now I'm an exorcist. I don't think that's what Lucifer had planned."

Bullshit? The old Simon would have never used that word. She couldn't keep the grin from filling her face.

Riley took his hand and squeezed it. It wasn't soft like before, but had calluses now, like he'd been doing heavy labor. "I'm so glad you're back." He'd know she meant more than just being in the city.

"Thank you. What happened between us is one of my biggest regrets."

"No, I don't look at it that way," she insisted. "It made us both what we are today."

"God's will and all that?" he said.

"That's how I see it, no matter how much it hurt at the time." She paused to take in more hot chocolate, caught by the strong emotions between them. Almost like the love between a brother and sister. "What about your parents? Are they good with this new job?"

"Mom doesn't like the idea, but Dad is all for it. They'll adjust." He took a look at his phone to check the time, then winced. "I better be going. She'll have my head if I'm late. Amy's coming by with my nephew. He was born while I was gone."

His sister had been pregnant when Simon was lying in a hospital bed, dying. Because of Riley's bargain with one of Heaven's winged messengers, he was alive to meet the little boy. It was hard to fight back the tears.

"That's great, Simon. Say hi to Amy for me. Oh, and once Beck gets home, you should come over for dinner."

"I'd be happy to. When's the wedding?"

Everyone asked that question, and she didn't have an answer.

"I'm not sure. I'm . . . still adjusting to the idea. It's not that I don't love him, but with so much else going on . . . "

"Don't put it off. You know how precious every day is, how little time we have in this world."

He was right.

They both rose at the same time.

"I've been studying magic with Mort and Ayden," she said. "I really had no choice."

She'd expected Simon to stiffen, to pull back from her. To retreat behind his fortified wall.

Instead he just nodded. "Beck told me what happened. I still don't like magic, but I understand why you're doing it." He hugged her again, and then he was out the front door of the coffee shop, leaving behind a lot of memories. Some were good, some bad. But all worth it.

"Thank you for letting him find his way back," she murmured as her eyes rose to the ceiling. "He'll be an awesome weapon against the darkness."

Which had probably been Heaven's plan all along.

Chapter Eleven

It was nearing seven-thirty in the evening when Riley hustled up the path in Oakland Cemetery on her way to "class" with Ayden. Why her witchy friend wanted to meet *here,* she didn't know. The place held so many vivid memories it was hard to handle them all. Ayden knew that. But then, the witch never did anything without a reason.

The chilly night made Riley's breath cloud, and she regretted having left her gloves in the car. The snow had remained, settled around the graves like melted frosting. Above her, through the naked branches, the stars shone. In the spring, the cemetery would come alive with blooms. Now it appeared to be hibernating, resting up for the coming year.

As she drew close to the bell tower, Riley caught sight of a ring of twinkling lights farther down the path. A quick glance at her phone indicated she might have enough time to check it out. If she was lucky, inside that ring would be the cemetery's guardian angel.

Instead of bearing left toward the Blackthorne mausoleum, she kept going straight. Farther up the path she found Martha in a lawn chair in the very center of the circle, knitting something or other. She looked elderly, in old-lady garb—including orthopedic shoes—though Riley had seen the angel's real appearance after the big battle.

Martha smiled warmly as she approached. "Ah, there you are. I was hoping you'd come by to see me. How have you been?"

Riley stopped about five feet away from the ring of candles, the sacred circle that kept necromancers from stealing the body in the new grave.

"I'm good. Well, sorta good. It's getting crazy again."

"So I hear. And you're engaged now," the angel said, pointing at Riley's ring. "A grand master, no less. Well done. You've chosen wisely."

"It's more my heart's doing than anything," Riley admitted.

"Which is why it was a wise decision."

"So how goes the angel business?"

Martha shrugged, rising to her feet. Then she stretched. "Same old, same old. Lots quieter since last spring. But I'm thinking that's going to change pretty soon."

"Any hints you can give me so I don't end up dead?"

"Nothing is what it seems," the angel replied.

"Like that's any different than normal?"

"In this case, that's the new normal." Martha looked off into the distance. "Your witch friend is starting to get anxious."

"That, I wouldn't doubt. I better go see her. Stay well, Martha."

"You too, Riley Anora Blackthorne."

Riley cut back toward the road that led to her family mausoleum. The night the trappers were attacked at the Tabernacle, she'd taken refuge here in case the demons went on a rampage. Beck had joined her, injured and ill. She still remembered him lying next to her, stroking her hair. Now she knew it had been the start of something between them. Something that had turned into love over time.

As Riley moved closer to the mausoleum, the moonlight cast shadows over the structure, the spire jutting toward the sky and stone gargoyles perched on all four corners of the roof. The fifth gargoyle, the one facing east, sat alone.

Ori.

The handsome rogue who knew just what to say and how to step in when she and Beck were at odds. He'd been her first lover, a Fallen angel who'd sought her soul in a misguided quest to keep her safe. Now Ori was dead, watching the sunrise every morning, savoring the light he craved. His sacrifice had given her a future with the man she loved.

"I hope you're at peace."

Ayden sat on the steps of the mausoleum, frowning. "You're late," she said.

That was unusually curt. "Not by much. Since when do you worry about time?"

"Tonight I do."

This wasn't the Ayden she knew. Riley stopped a few paces away, judging the situation. Was this really her friend? Or had Mort's glamour training just made her question everything she saw?

"So what's wrong?" she asked, buying time.

"Lots. But right now, let's get your lesson done."

"And I know you're Ayden because . . . ?"

The witch's trademark eyebrow raise sealed the deal.

Question answered. "Does what's wrong have something to do with you training me? Are some of the other witches not liking that?"

Ayden cocked her head. "Goddess, you're too perceptive nowadays. I used to be able to get stuff past you, but not now."

"If the trappers are giving me crap, I figured it was a good bet the witches were doing the same to you. What's their problem? I would think they'd like to have a trapper on their side for a change."

Ayden tapped the stone step next to her and Riley joined her.

"Often, witches do things that are counterproductive to their own self-interest. Just like everyone else."

"Do you want to keep training me? Because I can back away and maybe it'll take the heat off you for a while."

Ayden's brow furrowed. "No. If you're being trained by a summoner, you really should learn from a witch, too. Your magic must be balanced. For anyone else it wouldn't matter, but for some reason, it's important for you. I really can't figure out why."

"Would it help if I talked to your people?" Riley offered.

"Not sure. Let me think about that."

"Okay, then what are we doing tonight?"

Ayden straightened up, slipping into teacher mode. "Learning how to feel the magic of a place or a person."

"Why would I need to do that?"

That earned her a sidelong glance. "Because it's what you need to learn?"

"Ah, got it." When her friend was in one of these moods, it was best to just go along.

Ayden walked down the steps, then stopped in the middle of the area where Riley had once sat vigil for her father. She waved Riley down.

Once she was in place, the witch said, "Close your eyes. Tell me what you feel here."

Riley did as ordered, trying to calm her mind enough to pick up any sensations. At first, there was little more than a jumble, too many memories.

"Clear your thoughts; that will help."

Riley tried, and slowly, little threads began to appear in her mind. A white one, flowing softly in the nonexistent breeze, coming from the two graves behind her.

"What do you feel?" Ayden asked.

"My parents. I feel their love for each other. And for me."

"What color is that love?"

Clearly Ayden had known Riley'd be able to see the threads in some way. "It's white. Pure white."

"As it should be," Ayden replied.

Another thread, silvery gray, led to Ori. That made sense, as he was a mix of the Light and Dark.

"Ori. He's here as well." She felt another one. "Blue. That's Beck. He's really strong. Maybe because he's deep inside my heart."

"And because he was here in the cemetery at emotionally difficult times. We all leave a bit of ourselves behind in cases like that. What else?"

"I sense you. You're a vibrant green." Riley opened her eyes to find her friend smiling.

"That's a good start, but there's more around here. Let's rest a bit because you seem really tired."

Riley didn't dare admit that her weariness was courtesy of a certain necromancer's lessons, as that might set off the witch.

"What is Mort teaching you?" Ayden asked, as if hearing her thoughts.

"Illusion spells. How to tell if someone is using glamour. Trying to teach me how to make an orange look like a banana." She waited for the negative reaction, but instead she received a nod of approval.

"Good. That way you can tell who is what and vice versa."

Ayden was even more cryptic than usual this evening.

"So close your eyes and try again," the witch said. "See what else you can sense."

Riley sat on the cold ground. She could fetch a blanket from the storage box in the mausoleum, but that would be too much effort.

Closing her eyes, she picked up those few threads again and then began to feel others. They were more like vibrations than actual threads of energy, and many were very old, no doubt from the dead buried around them. One vibration was drawing closer, and it felt different from the others.

"Necromancer," Riley said, opening her eyes. And she knew exactly which one.

"What is *he* doing here?" the witch muttered, even before the figure came into view.

"Probably wanting to talk to me. I'm really popular right now."

This time, the high lord of the Atlanta summoners didn't blow up in a whirl of leaves like he had in the past. Instead, Ozymandias walked along the path just like anyone else, his black cloak flowing behind him, staff in hand. Ayden frowned, crossing her arms over her chest.

The necro halted about ten feet out, gazing first at Ayden and then at Riley. "Witch," he said.

"Summoner. What brings you here?"

"Her," he replied, gesturing toward Riley.

"Told you," Riley said to her friend. "What can I do you for, Ozy?"

Ayden groaned at her disrespect.

"I made a trip to Demon Central this evening," he said. "I checked out the site where you encountered the Geo-Fiend. I felt a blended kind of magic, part summoner, part witch, part unknown."

"We don't call up demons," Ayden said.

"Because if you do, the witch usually ends up dead," Ozy replied.

"That's the main reason," Ayden replied. "We leave that nonsense to your people."

Riley jumped in. "Could it be a rogue summoner?"

"Potentially," he admitted. "Still, the magic felt confused in some way, darker than what I'd expect."

"Who else could do that kind of spell?"

"There are a number of people," Ayden said, her attention still on the necro in front of them. "Shamans, Voodoo priests and priestesses, Druids."

"So it might not be either of your people," Riley said.

"That doesn't follow," Ozymandias argued. "The reason a demon was summoned was to bring you to that site and, most likely, ensure you were dead or injured. The only people who might want that to happen are either summoners or witches."

Riley looked over at her friend. "Is he right? Do the witches want me hurt?"

Ayden issued a long sigh. "There are those who are not happy with you or the trappers."

"Not being happy with me is one thing. Calling up a Five to kill me is another."

"I agree. I don't think it's gone that far, but anything is possible."

"Any chance you can get these people to back off?"

"If I get further involved, this is going to get worse," Ayden warned.

"You're already involved," Ozy said. "You crossed the line when you fought with the trappers and Summoner Alexander during the battle. You can't unring that bell, witch."

"I know!" Ayden snapped. "I wouldn't want to. I had as much right to be there as any of the others."

"Nevertheless, your people don't agree, do they?"

She shook her head. "I was told it wasn't our fight. Some of them naively believed that when the demons finished killing all the trappers and hunters, they'd just stop. Not sweep through the city, slaughtering everyone they found, us included." She glared at the necromancer. "A hell you unleashed on us."

To Riley's surprise, Ozymandias issued a contrite nod. "I remember that fact every day of my life. My greed for power got people killed. Innocents who would otherwise have been safe if I'd done my job."

"Well, when you put it like that . . . "

Ozymandias half turned, as if he'd heard something. "We have company. Witches."

Ayden nodded. "They're waiting for me."

"Why?" Riley asked.

"I was warned not to train you any further."

"So you blew them off?"

"It's not their decision. They've overstepped their authority."

Ozymandias gave a respectful nod. "You know, witch, I rather like you. You have a backbone. I can, if you wish, transport you out of here and they won't know where you've gone."

Ayden shook her head. "They'll catch up with me sooner or later. I've been expecting this."

She turned to Riley and gave her a hug. Then she pressed a small embroidered bag into her hand. "There's an amulet inside. Wear it at all times, even when you're sleeping or showering."

"Okay, now you're spooking me."

"Not my intention. This will enhance the spells Mort is teaching you. In time, you won't need it, but right now you do."

"Excellent. I was thinking of something similar," the necromancer said, clearly pleased. "I'll leave you to it. Miss Black-thorne. Good evening, witch."

Ozymandias vanished.

"He wasn't really here, was he?" Riley asked. "That was a sending. It's why he felt more like a vibration than an actual energy thread."

Ayden nodded. She looked off into the distance. "You should wait here until I'm gone."

"Not an option."

Her friend sighed. "Goddess, you're stubborn."

"Learned from the best, my friend."

Chapter Twelve

They didn't speak on the way out of the cemetery, and that only made Riley worry more. Ayden must have known what they were facing, but she made no effort to spin up any magical protection. Which meant she was trying not to turn this into a war.

Three witches waited for them just outside the cemetery entrance, and there were no smiles with this bunch. Though Riley would have expected the classic maiden-mother-and-crone configuration, these ladies were all in their mid-forties. In other words, about Ayden's age. Each wore a thick black cloak that reached the ground. At least the necros had some sense of color.

"*When shall we three meet again?*" Riley said, quoting from one of her favorite Shakespearean tragedies. "*In thunder, lightning, or in rain? / When the hurly-burly's done, / when the battle's lost and won.*"

The witches' scowls grew.

"Not fans of the Bard? That is so disappointing."

Ayden shot her a look. "Being a smartass is not a good idea right now."

"If they don't want to be compared to the crones in *Macbeth*, maybe they shouldn't go around in groups of three. "

The witch in the middle, a blonde, stepped forward, making a point to ignore Riley.

"Ayden."

"Morgaine."

Morgaine? As in Morgan le Fay from the legend of King Arthur? That wasn't very original.

"You are in the company of the demon trapper. I warned you

about that," the woman continued.

"You have no authority over whom I see, or teach," Ayden replied. Her voice had an icy chill that Riley had never heard from her before. The kind of tone that said these two had crossed swords, or magic, repeatedly.

"Then you leave me no choice but to move forward."

"Move forward on what?" Riley asked.

Morgaine shot her a frown. "None of your concern, trapper."

"Actually, it is my concern. Ayden is a dear friend of mine. Now, there are those who say I shouldn't be hanging with a witch. Me? I don't care. If you treat me decently, I'm your friend." Riley paused for effect. "But if you hurt my friends, you make an enemy. *For life.*"

Morgaine laughed, though the other two witches appeared uneasy.

"You do not scare me, child."

"Why is it every time someone wants to insult me, they call me a kid? You can't come up with anything better than that?"

"Riley . . . " Ayden warned.

"I know. I'm getting in her face because she's pissing me off."

"It is not wise to train one of you in magic, even if you did have any talent. Which you don't. Your kind just stirs up trouble, demonic trouble," Morgaine countered.

"If you think the fiends wouldn't be here if not for us trappers, you're wrong. Lucifer will keep feeding Hellspawn into this city until the end of time." Riley took a step closer to her. "Your kind is supposed to keep the innocents safe. Except for Ayden here, you've been doing a damned poor job of it."

Her friend sucked in a breath, telling Riley she'd gone too far. The spell came out of nowhere, swirling around her, locking her feet in place. Riley tried to break free, but it only made it worse, as if every cell in her body was on fire.

"Don't fight it," Ayden said. "It won't hurt you."

Morgaine frowned. "You are ordered to cease any interaction with this trapper from this point on. Any infraction will be dealt with severely."

"What does Rada have to say about this?" Ayden asked.

"She's out of town," one of the other witches muttered. From her tone, Riley got the impression that she was hoping this Rada person would return soon.

"While she is gone, I make the decisions," Morgaine said.

That flew in the face of what Riley knew about witches. They were independent as cats and only came together in a coven when they had heavy-duty magic to perform. Since when did Atlanta have some sort of head witch?

Ayden gave her a quick look and sighed. "We'll settle this when Rada returns."

"So we shall," Morgaine replied.

"Keep practicing your lessons and do *exactly* what I told you to do," Ayden said.

The amulet.

"I will. You be careful." *Because I don't trust this woman.*

"You'll release her after we leave?" Ayden asked her fellow witch.

"Of course," Morgaine replied, but the answer came too quickly.

As her friend walked away with the others, Riley used some choice Hellspeak curses. One of the other witches looked over her shoulder and mouthed, "Sorry."

Tell me about it.

Once they disappeared from sight, Riley waited for the glue-the-trapper-to-the-pavement spell to dissipate. It didn't. Morgaine had lied.

"Oh come on, you're kidding me," Riley said, struggling against the binding as sweat popped out on her forehead. They were going to leave her like this? At least she could reach her phone, but who should she call? Certainly not one of the trappers, not even one she trusted. She'd never hear the end of this. *Maybe Mort . . .*

"Now, this is fun," a voice said.

She knew immediately who that voice belonged to and had

prayed, repeatedly, that she'd never hear it again. Her prayers were not answered, as Lucifer, the Prince of Hell, appeared on the road in front of her. Tonight he was rocking the mysterious look: black slacks and black turtleneck, his bright-blue eyes set off by black hair that reached his collar.

Riley twisted in the spell, trying to get free, but it didn't help. *Damn witches.*

"If you'd like me to assist . . . " he began.

"Don't bother, I know the drill. No, I'm not willing to give you my soul so I can get free."

"Am I that predictable?"

"Ah, yeah," she said.

"I wasn't even going to make the offer. Part of me is amused seeing you stuck here like a helpless fly on sticky paper," Lucifer said, his tone smooth and low.

It was the opposite of the voice she'd heard in Hell, when she'd stood in front of his throne and been threatened with eternal torture.

"What brings you here?" she asked. "Things dull down in the fiery pits?"

"Just checking up on how my favorite demon trapper is doing."

"Fine. I'm taking a rest at the moment."

He laughed. "I've been keeping an eye on your fiancé too. Denver Beck is doing well, and it appears the grand masters are very pleased with him. I'm still annoyed he didn't accept my offer when he was in my domain."

"You win some, you lose some." *Why are you here?* Only then did she remember he could read her thoughts.

"I'm here because I was bored. It's been rather quiet since I purged Hell of my enemies. My remaining servants are too scared to try any new intrigues." He sighed dramatically. "I so hate demons. They're either incredibly stupid or too cunning for their own good." He waved off her next comment. "I know, I know, if I'd stayed in Heaven, I wouldn't have to put up with them."

"You wanted freedom, you got it. The demons are the price you pay. So really, why are you here?"

"In the next few days, your life is going to change. It is not a change I'm happy about, but events are already in motion, so I figured, why not let it play out?"

Her blood chilled. "Events like what?"

"You'll be offered an opportunity. It'll be challenging. Still, it'll make both our lives a lot more interesting."

What is he going on about?

"You'll know soon enough," Lucifer replied, once again having heard her thoughts.

"What if I walk away from whatever this is?"

"Part of me is so hoping you don't," he said, smiling.

That smile made the hair on the back of her neck rise. He waved a hand and the witch's spell cracked apart like an egg.

"Choose wisely. And please send my regards to the new grand master. I'm so looking forward to breaking his will. One day, his soul *will* be mine."

Before she could respond, Lucifer vanished, much like Ozymandias had. The comparison made her twitch as she shook off the effects of the spell.

A new opportunity?

His Infinite Darkness had to be playing with her head. *Again.*

She glared into the distance, hoping Ayden was going to be okay. Right now there was little she could do, but down the line she'd know how to fight Morgaine's spell.

Then there will be payback.

Chapter Thirteen

Though it was late—nearly half past eight—Riley knocked on Mortimer's door. And waited. Then knocked again. Finally it cracked open to reveal the summoner himself. Alex must have been out for the evening.

Mort took one look at her, then waved her in.

"I'm sorry I'm here so late."

"No problem. He said you would probably be dropping by."

The "*he*" was no doubt Ozymandias.

Mort guided her not to his office, but to the living room in the back of his house. It was comfortable and unpretentious, like him.

Riley plopped down on a tan sofa and was immediately colonized by Orson, Mort's big black cat. Orson was a recent addition and had settled right in, as if this were his home and Mort merely a renter. In short, typical cat behavior.

As she scratched Orson behind the ears, she found herself staring at the feline, puzzled. Something didn't seem right about him.

Mort took a seat in a brown, plaid recliner. A half-empty glass of beer sat at his elbow, with a copy of *Necromancers Quarterly* nearby. It seemed she'd interrupted his quiet time.

He smiled over at her confusion. "So what do you see?" he asked, gesturing toward Orson, who was purring in a steady rhythm as she continued to stroke him.

"A cat." Riley concentrated, trying to sort out what felt wrong. To her astonishment, Orson's coat shifted from black to tabby. She looked up at Mort. "Glamour? Why?"

"Because everyone expects my cat to be black."

Which meant that all the times she'd petted Orson, he'd not been what she'd thought. She wore Ayden's amulet now. Had that helped?

"Okay, that's creepy. How do I know what you look like, for sure?"

He smiled. "I promise I am what I appear to be. Now tell me what happened with the witches."

Riley brought him up to speed on Ayden, Morgaine, and the spell.

"Morgaine left you bespelled in the cemetery?" Mort asked, his voice harder than usual.

"Yeah." Then she told him how she'd gotten free.

"Oh God. I'd hoped *he'd* forgotten about you," Mort said.

"The Prince never forgets anything or anyone." She hesitated. "I know it's not right to learn magic when you're angry, but I'm sick of this. I need to be able to protect myself from asshats like Morgaine."

"I agree. I'll teach you an elementary protection spell before you leave tonight. Wear the amulet Ayden gave you. It'll help."

She hadn't mentioned that to him. "You felt her magic, didn't you?"

"Easy to do once you know what to look for." He gestured toward the cat. "You can see it works, even if the amulet doesn't give you a clear picture of what's behind the glamour."

"Will they hurt her?" she asked, because that was her greatest fear.

He saddened. "I'm not sure. I don't know witch politics that well. It's my guess that she has a history with Morgaine, and somehow you've got that feud going again. You do have a tendency to unsettle the status quo."

"I don't try to. Honestly."

"I know, but you still do. I'm not saying that's a bad thing." Mortimer rose from his chair. "How about I make some popcorn, and then I'll teach you that protection spell. Sound good?"

"Yes. Thanks."

After he'd left the room, she closed her eyes and opened them again. The cat was back to being black. Apparently if she didn't concentrate, the glamour reasserted itself.

What else am I not seeing?

Riley left Mort's place full of popcorn and hot chocolate, and with her mind full of a protection spell. As she made her way to her car, she dialed Ayden's number. The call went directly to voicemail.

"Hey, let me know if you're okay. I'm worried."

It was only then that she noticed she had a voicemail from a couple hours earlier, just about the time she'd been mouthing off to Morgaine in the cemetery. It was from Beck; for some reason she hadn't heard the call.

Riley pushed the play button.

"Hope you get this. I'm just about to leave New York. My flight arrives in Atlanta at ten thirty-five tonight. Sorry I didn't tell you ahead of time, but I flew standby and I didn't want you gettin' yer hopes up. Looking forward to seein' you soon, Princess. Love you."

Riley stared at the phone. "Tonight? He's home *tonight*?" She checked the time. "In an hour?"

Beck wasn't supposed to be in Atlanta, so all her plans to have the house in perfect condition were no longer an option. No chance to have her hair curled and her nails polished. Her fiancé was almost here, and if she didn't hustle, he wouldn't find her waiting for him.

Riley sprinted for the car as if her life depended on it, cursing for the second time in one day. Just once, why couldn't things go the way she'd planned?

~~*

It had been three years since Denver Beck last flew into Atlanta's airport from overseas, when he'd come home from the Army. Two people had been waiting for him that time: Paul Blackthorne and Paul's young daughter, Riley. He still remembered the hand-lettered sign that said WELCOME HOME, DENVER! and the twin shouts of joy when he'd first appeared out of the crowd.

Tonight the crowd noises were pretty much the same, though they didn't spook him as much as they had back then, when he was fresh from a war zone. This time, the sounds spoke of home.

Riley would be here, if she'd gotten his message in time. It'd been so long since he'd last held her, last seen her walking to her plane, proudly wearing his engagement ring.

It was a big step forward—a wife, maybe children someday. Becoming a grand master. So much had changed in these three years, he found it hard to believe. Moments like this brought it into sharp focus.

Beck adjusted his backpack, then rolled his heavy suitcase along. His eyes searched faces and when he found the woman he loved, his breath caught. Up on her tiptoes, Riley was searching for him as well, her brown eyes bright, her soft hair hanging loose around her shoulders, just the way he liked it. She wore his favorite bright-blue sweater and jeans, the demon claw necklace visible at her neck. For just a second, he swore he saw Paul standing next to her, though that wasn't possible.

Beck could tell the instant Riley spied him—she bounced up and down and called out his name. Weaving her way through the crowd, she waited until he was free of the security area and then she sprinted to him, her hair flying behind her. He caught her around the waist, and pulled her tight against him. Their lips connected with a longing that spoke of too many weeks apart.

She was warm and soft and all his.

"Get a room," a man joked as he passed them.

Beck laughed. "Plan on it!" he called back, then kissed his girl one more time. She smelled of light perfume and popcorn.

Riley cupped his face, looking deep into his eyes. "You're really here," she said. Then she took hold of his arm, as if she couldn't bear not to touch him. He knew how that was.

"I'm sorry I didn't call you," he said. "I had short connections in Amsterdam and in New York. I was lucky to get a flight home at all today. I think MacTavish called in some favors."

"I'm happy you're home, but why the change in plans?" she said.

"Because I couldn't wait to see you." Which was the truth, and a way to keep from explaining the other reason, the one that involved the Vatican. At least for now.

"So how's my rabbit doin'?" he asked, wanting to deflect her curiosity.

Riley gave him a quick frown, as if she knew what he was doing. "Rennie's good. She'll be so happy you're home."

Beck smiled at the thought—even his bunny had missed him.

"You don't have to go back early, do you?" she asked, concern in her voice.

"No. Still headin' back on the thirty-first."

Riley's smile lit up. "Okay. You're home longer. I can deal with that."

He'd hoped she'd see it that way. "MacTavish said I've been doin' really good and that I need some down time. Of course, I'll have some studyin' to do while I'm here, but we'll have time together."

"I can help you. At least, if it's something that I can know about."

"It is," he said, although he couldn't share everything. It was the way of a grand master. To keep their sanity, there were things the world, and Riley, didn't need to know.

"I love you," she added, rather solemnly.

He ducked down and stole a kiss. "And I love you. Now get me home. All this travelin' has worn me down."

Beck rolled his suitcase along behind him, refusing her offer to help. The moment he stepped outside the South Terminal, he took a deep breath. Atlanta in December. A little chilly, but nothing like the Scottish Highlands. He took another deep breath and sighed.

Georgia. I'm really home.

Originally it had been his plan to spend the next few weeks not worrying about demons or Hell or whatever devious schemes they might be concocting. Time to live, love, and laugh with the one person who was the center of his universe, the young woman who had agreed to be his wife.

Beck still planned on doing most of those things, but Elias's visit to the manor house had told him his job would always weigh him down, always cut into his happiness. He'd been warned about that, but here it was, up close and personal.

As Riley drove him home, Beck listened to her talk about everyday things, how she'd gotten a B⁺ in her Latin class and how her friend Peter was on a ski trip in Vermont. MacTavish had once pointed out that when women were nervous, they would talk through that unease, whereas guys tended to clam up.

Riley could have said anything—even read to him from a fast food menu—and he wouldn't care. It was hearing her voice again that mattered.

What she didn't say caught his notice as well: not a word about her magical studies or how things stood with the demon trappers. He suspected the studies were going fine—Riley was a quick learner—but that the issue with the trappers was festering like an untreated wound. He also caught an undercurrent of tension, as if something else had happened and she wasn't ready to tell him about it yet.

Tempting as it was to drill down on all that, Beck knew it was best to let her reveal it in her own time. She wasn't a kid anymore and he respected her too much to treat her as one. He'd done that before and it had blown up in his face more than once.

Instead, he went with safe topics. "Stewart doin' okay?"

"He's good. He really misses you. So do Jackson and the other trappers. They're really proud of you."

Some of them maybe, but not all. Some would resent that he'd become a grand master, envious that he'd somehow managed to kill a Fallen angel. Some of the trappers would never trust him, no matter what he said or did, because he now held the power of life or death in his hands.

"I changed some stuff around at your house. I hope you're okay with that," she said.

"It's yer house too, you know."

"No, not yet, but since I was living there part time I thought . . . well . . . "

"I'm good with whatever you did."

That earned him a relieved smile. Judging from her reaction, whatever she'd done meant a lot to her.

Riley drove past the usual turn for his house. "I thought you'd like to see some of the Christmas lights," she said, by way of explanation.

Caught up in his studies, he'd almost forgotten about the holiday, at least until the nine-foot Scots pine Christmas tree had gone up in the manor house. He'd made a prompt trip to Edinburgh to pick out Riley's presents and had already shipped most of them to Stewart's house. A few were tucked into his luggage. He couldn't wait for her to open them.

Now, as Beck looked around, he found that a number of houses had their holiday lights up, glowing in the late night. Had there been Christmas decorations in years past and he'd just never noticed them?

Maybe so. It wasn't the kind of thing a poor boy from South Georgia would care about, not when he was more concerned about food and keeping a roof over his head. It had taken every bit of luck and long hours just to be able to make the house payments.

Now it was different. As a grand master trainee, he was earning a decent salary. He wasn't wealthy, but he was better off than he'd ever been. But money was only part of it.

Beck looked over at Riley, knowing she was the sole reason he was appreciating any of this. She'd opened his eyes to so many good things in life, like sunsets, the joy of sharing a kiss on a rooftop as the city lights came on one by one. The simple act of loving.

All because of you.

Riley slowed the car to a crawl. "What do you think?" she asked, waiting for his reaction.

He studied the nearest house out his side window and nodded

in appreciation. White curtain lights draped along the porch railing and down both sides of the stairs. A large green wreath hung on the door, and the main window was framed in twinkling lights. Even the mailbox had a red ribbon and greenery. The place looked great.

"Real pretty," he said.

"Welcome home, Den."

Beck's mouth dropped open. This was *his* house?

The moment Riley pulled into the driveway, he was out of the car. He strode to the middle of the front yard, barely aware of the snow in the grass. Hands on his hips, he stared in astonishment. He'd always kept the place nice—he was "house proud," as his grandmother would say—but this was even beyond that.

Riley joined him. "Do you like it?"

"It's so . . . " *Like a real home.* Something he'd never had as a kid, but something their children would have, if they raised any.

Beck felt his eyes grow moist. He could feel Riley watching him, and he pulled her into his arms, hugging her tight. He set his chin on top of her head.

"I love you so much," he said.

"All because of a few Christmas lights?" she joked.

"Yeah, just because of that," he said, knowing there was a world of words he wanted to say but didn't know how. "Now, if they'd been another color, I might have changed my mind."

She laughed and pulled out of his arms. "Riiight. Come on, Rennie is probably going nuts. I made her this big exercise pen so she could hop around more. She really likes it."

"She talks to you now?" he jested.

"All the time," Riley replied, winking. "Just like she used to talk to you."

He laughed and hugged her again, then spun her around in the air.

"God, I have missed you."

"I'm sorry I'm not dressed up. I got your text right before you landed. I wanted to be all pretty and—"

He caught her chin and brought her eyes up to meet his.

"Doesn't matter what yer wearin', to me yer the most beauti-ful woman in the world. You understand?"

She nodded, her eyes filling with tears.

"Now that we've got the neighbors wonderin' what the hell we're up to, let's get inside."

After Riley disabled the alarm, he set his luggage just inside the door and waited as she flicked on the lights. Things *had* changed. She had moved the front-room furniture around, and it looked better than it had before. A large space was open in one corner; when he asked her about it, she grinned.

"I left room for a tree. There's a place outside of town that sells them. We can cut our own so it's not as expensive. Not that I know how to do that, but I figured you would."

Beck felt a smile forming. "Sounds like a plan. We had a Christmas tree in our barracks in Afghanistan—it was a little scrawny thing—but I've never had one of my very own before."

Riley blinked at him, looking stunned. "Never?"

"No." His mother hadn't been into that kind of thing—too busy drinking. Once he'd had his own place, he'd never bothered.

Now it all seemed to matter.

"That's sad, Den," she whispered, taking his hand and squeezing it.

That was the downside of this new life—the realization of how much his old one had sucked. How easily this one could vanish if Riley wasn't at his side.

"So where is that rabbit of ours?" he asked, trying to sidestep the familiar ache in his chest.

"Right this way," she replied, tugging him along.

Chapter Fourteen

Despite the fact that Riley hadn't been able to put all her plans in place before Beck arrived home, it didn't seem to matter. He'd really liked what she'd done to the house, and he'd had a great reunion with Rennie.

Then he'd grown far too quiet. Some of it was jet lag—she remembered that from her trip—but it seemed deeper than a time zone change. It made her worry that maybe things weren't right with him. Would he have told her if something was wrong? Maybe not. Beck could hold back things when he wanted.

Just like me.

Though she rejoiced that he was home early, she couldn't help but wonder why. Had he finished his studies ahead of schedule, or was it because of what was going on with the trappers? She suspected it was the latter, and that made her nervous.

It was only later, when Beck joined her in bed, that she asked him what was wrong. He didn't answer right away, just held her close and stroked her hair like he was trying to memorize every strand.

"Nothing is wrong," he replied. "So much is right, it scares me. I realize how easy it would be to lose it all."

"We're together. That's all that matters."

"I know. I love you," he replied. "That will never change."

Then Beck kissed her, and from the power of that kiss and his urgent touch, she knew sleep wasn't going to come anytime soon.

"I dreamed of you every night," he whispered in her ear as he stroked her. "Of what it would be like to make love to you."

"Tell me what it was like," she said.

"No. No more dreams. Tonight, this is for real."

~~*

Riley woke to the warmth of her guy sleeping next to her, and that brought a lazy smile at the memory of their lovemaking. It had been as passionate and satisfying as it had been in Scotland. And even before that. They were lovers, both in body and in spirit. All her concerns about whether things were still good between them had been needless worrying.

She turned her head to check the clock on the nightstand. A little after three in the morning. What had woken her?

"I like being home," Beck murmured, tightening his grip on her. "For a lot of reasons, not just the main one."

"Being warm?"

"Yup, that's one of them. Then there's the other one."

"You are such a guy."

"I didn't hear you complainin' about that earlier."

Before she could answer, her cell phone rang.

"Yer kiddin' me," Beck mumbled.

She rolled away from him and answered the call.

"Riley? It's Jackson. I just got a report of a Three running around Piedmont Park. Kurt's working with me tonight, and I'd like to take him out to trap it. We need some backup. You up for that?"

"Oh . . . " she yawned. "Okay, sure. I'll be there in a few." She placed the phone back on the nightstand and yawned again.

"You didn't say you were on call," Beck said, sitting up.

"Sorry, I forgot. You sort of distracted me."

"Let me guess. You scheduled yer time off for when I was plannin' to be home, and I screwed up those plans."

"You got it." She leaned over and kissed him. "I am not complaining."

Riley rose and stretched. As she began pulling on her trapping clothes, Beck dug around in the closet and found an old pair of jeans and a heavy shirt.

"You can stay here," she said. "It'll be fine."

"Nope. I wouldn't be able to sleep anyway. Who you trappin' with tonight?"

"Jackson. He's got one of my apprentices with him. We've been switching the newbies around between a few of us, trying to show them different trapping techniques."

"Smart."

By the time Riley reached the front door, coat on and backpack in hand, Beck had pulled his own trapping bag from the front closet. He added a few spheres and chose one of the steel pipes he favored. In his jeans, leather coat, and baseball cap, he looked just like the trapper she remembered.

"You sure you want to come with me? You have to be really tired."

"I haven't trapped in a couple months. Wouldn't miss this for anythin'."

"Okay, your call. I got the bait, so let's go kick some demon butt, Backwoods Boy."

"Yer on, Princess."

~~*

As she drove north from Beck's house, the traffic was light. In a few hours that would change, but right now it was deserted, except for a few brave souls out doing lord knew what.

When she looked over, she found Beck dozing against the window, which meant he was totally exhausted but not about to let her out on her own. That protective behavior alternately annoyed her and made her love him even more.

He still hadn't given her a good explanation for why he was home early. But she hadn't told him about Lucifer yet, so they were even in the secrets department.

When she pulled her car up next to Jackson's pickup, Beck woke with a mighty yawn. Gear in hand, they set off for the two trappers waiting for them by the park's entry gate. Riley gave

Kurt a nod and he returned it, but she could see he was spooked. After that Five in Demon Central, she couldn't blame him.

Jackson grinned. "Is that you, Mile High?"

"Sure is."

Riley knew Beck didn't like the nickname, but what else would they call him, when his first name was Denver? The two masters slapped each other on the back, then did a little play rough-housing.

Guys. They're so weird.

"I didn't know you were back in town," Jackson said, still smiling broadly.

"Just got in a few hours ago. You, dude, are why I'm not in bed cuddlin' with my pretty lady."

The master shook his head. "Hey, blame the damned demons."

"Speaking of which, where are they?" Riley asked, keen to get this run completed.

Jackson pointed toward the nearly two-hundred-acre park. "Somewhere out there."

She groaned.

"Hey, Kurt. How's it goin'?" Beck asked.

"Good, I guess. Welcome home." They shook hands.

"You'll be fine tonight. Stick close to us and do whatever these two tell you. I'm just ridin' shotgun on this one."

Riley smiled to herself. Beck had always been supportive of the apprentices, but now she could hear the confidence in his voice. The strength. His time in Scotland had taken the raw essence of a good man and made him even stronger.

She pulled out a bag of bait, tossed it at Beck, then removed one of the Holy Water spheres. "I'm ready. You guys done gossiping?"

"Somebody's crabby tonight," Jackson said.

"Not my fault. I did my best to put a smile on her face," Beck replied.

Muttering under her breath, Riley walked to the gate. She pushed on it and it swung open. "So where's the guard?"

"He said he was going to take a long break. If he's smart, he's hiding somewhere. That's what I'd do if I were him," Jackson replied. "You taking lead on this?"

"I thought you were," she said. The whole point had been for Jackson to show Kurt some of his trapping strategies.

"Go for it," he said. "Since I pulled you out of bed, you might as well have all the fun." And she'd get a bigger cut of the trapping fee.

Riley gave in. "Okay, Kurt, you're with me. These guys will watch our backs."

As she and her apprentice set off, Jackson and Beck fell in step on either side of them. Fortunately, the moon provided adequate light for them to see their way.

"Remember when I said that the Threes are leaving Demon Central, going farther north?" she said. "This is a good example of why clearing Five Points is a bad idea."

"I'd think it would be easier to hunt them down there because there are fewer places to hide," Kurt replied.

"It is, but demons are creatures of habit. Get them out of their natural habitat and they become unpredictable."

"Much like humans," Jackson added.

He had a point.

"So once we find this thing, tell me how you're going to trap it."

Kurt took a deep breath, his voice indicating his nervousness. "Once I see it, I wait until one of you guys tosses the bait to distract it. While it's eating, I try to hit it with a Holy Water sphere."

"What if you miss?"

"If I have time, I throw another one."

"And if you don't?"

"I use my steel pipe to keep it from ripping me up while one of you hits it with a sphere," he replied.

"Which is why you *always* have a backup with you," Beck said. "Right, Riley?"

He just had to go there.

Riley grimaced at the memory. "Totally right. Never try to trap one of these things on your own, or your chances of dying go up dramatically. Like nearly one hundred percent. I speak from experience."

Kurt stared at her. "For serious?"

"Yup."

"Did you trap it?"

"Yup. Then two losers stole the demon from me. I almost died and had nothing to show for it."

"What if I don't know it's a Three until I get to the location?"

"Then step away and call for help," Jackson said. "For instance, like tonight. We got far too much ground out here to search without extra pairs of eyes."

Kurt fell silent now, but Riley swore she could hear his mind churning, working through all he'd been told.

As they searched, Beck and Jackson chatted back and forth, but she tuned them out, listening for anything that would help her locate the Gastro-Fiend. And she failed.

~~*

An hour later they'd circled back toward where they'd started, cold and annoyed. Riley felt bad for Kurt, who had gotten himself all nerved up for this run, and now it looked like it was a bust.

"Where is the damned thing?" Jackson muttered.

"Probably in bed. Like we should be," Beck said.

Where did demons sleep in a park? There weren't any holes.

Was it possible to use what Ayden had taught her to find the demon?

Couldn't hurt to try.

"Give me a second, guys," she said, halting. Riley closed her eyes and attempted to pick up any of the threads around her. Initially all she could feel was Beck's bright blue. Then she slowly expanded outward and found Jackson's muted green and Kurt's pale orange.

So why can't I find the Three? She cast her mind out farther.

There was so much here, what with all the visitors leaving a little bit of themselves behind. She concentrated, looking for the stronger threats, and encountered some light lavender. Then she felt it: a sludge of muddy black, like thick oil. Something that made her cold to touch it.

Demon.

Riley homed in on the thing to her right. Pointing at a grove of trees, she said, "I think it's over there."

"You know that how?" Beck asked. At her frown, he added, "Not dissin' you, just askin'."

"Ah . . . just feels like a good place for it to be?" she said, knowing that sounded lame.

"Look, Riley, if you're using magic to locate a demon, I'm not going to complain," Jackson said. "Whatever gets the damned job done, you know?"

But she really wasn't using magic, nothing like what she and Mort were doing during her lessons. Instead, she was just "listening" to what was already there. Tapping into it.

"It's not magic. It's . . . I just sense stuff now."

"Ayden teach you that?" Beck asked.

Riley nodded. "She said everyone can do it, but we just don't bother."

"Sounds cool to me," Kurt said.

It wouldn't sound that way to some of the other trappers, but these guys didn't care, so Riley set off toward the copse of trees where the thread seemed strongest. Hopefully she wasn't making a fool of herself.

That, Beck hadn't expected. He knew Riley's abilities were changing, what with the lessons with the magical folks, but to have her "sense" where a demon was? That was spooky. And damned useful, if she could pull it off.

A quick glance at Jackson told Beck that his fellow trapper wasn't as weirded out by this as he was. Probably because Jackson didn't know how twitchy this would make the National Guild and the Vatican. If they found out about it.

Riley stopped suddenly. "I lost it," she grumbled. "I could feel it, and then it was gone."

"Well, just means we do it the old-fashioned way," Beck said, making sure not to sound critical.

"You sure you're up to trapping, Beck? I mean, with all that fancy book learning you've been doing?" Jackson said.

Beck would have taken offense at that if he hadn't heard the jesting tone. "I figure it'll all come back to me about the time a Three sizes me up for a meal."

"Amen to that," Jackson replied.

They had just entered the copse when Riley came to a halt. "Guys . . . " she said. "I can feel it. It's really close."

"I'm not seein' it," Beck said.

Then she looked up, into the trees. "Oh, crap."

He followed her gaze and saw the bright-red eyes. "It's above us. Back off real slow, people," he said quietly.

As they did, the demon leapt out of the tree and landed nimbly on the ground. Then it howled.

Damned if she wasn't right. This one was a mature Grade Three, with those double rows of teeth, all lean and muscled.

"They live in trees?" Kurt asked, eyes wide.

"Not usually, but since we've moved them out of the holes, they're learning new tactics," Riley explained. She looked at the apprentice. "You can do it. Just wait until the bait is thrown, okay?"

Kurt nodded weakly. "It's way bigger than I thought. Those claws are wicked."

He's starting to panic. "Its weakness is Holy Water, so you'll be fine."

"Blackthorne's daughter!" the thing bellowed, flailing its arms.

"I hate it when they do that," she said.

The instant Beck moved, the fiend's interest shifted. For a moment, he thought it was because of the chicken entrails he carried.

The Three hissed. "Trapperrr! Killer of Divines."

"Yup, that would be me. How's Lucifer these days? Still hatin' on you fiends?"

The demon growled at the mention of its master's name. "Chew yourrrr bones!" it shouted back.

"These guys really need a new script," Jackson said, stepping forward with a Holy Water sphere in hand.

"Here we go," Beck said.

He tossed the bag of chicken so it landed in front and to the left of the thing. The beast ignored it, which had to be a first. Its nostrils twitched and then it howled again.

Kurt's sphere came close, but fell short. When Jackson threw his, the fiend ducked and rolled out of the way.

"What is this thing, a damned acrobat?" the master asked.

Beck pulled out his steel pipe. "Then it's gonna be the hard way, demon. Trust me, I'm not in the mood for this kinda—"

Twin howls came from behind them. Beck whirled around. "We got two more. Close ranks, people. Riley, call for backup."

"It'll take them too long to get here."

"Yeah, but at least they'll find enough of us left to bury," Jackson said grimly.

"I . . . I . . . " Kurt began in a stammer. "I thought they didn't work together."

"They usually don't," Jackson said. "Except when they do. Like now."

"Stay in the middle of us. We'll keep them from gettin' too close," Beck said, knowing the guy had to be freaking out.

With a shaking hand, the apprentice extracted another sphere from his pack. "I'm good."

No, yer not, but at least you got guts.

"Welcome home, Beck," Jackson said sourly.

"Yeah, tell me about it."

Chapter Fifteen

Riley stared at the two new demons. Something about them wasn't right. Before she could determine exactly what was bothering her, the first fiend began its run toward them. Knowing Jackson would deal with it, she ignored it and kept an eye on the newcomers.

Just as the first demon closed in, the other two howled and headed her way. She threw a Holy Water sphere and it hit the closest fiend. But instead of breaking, the sphere went right through it and the demon promptly vanished.

What the . . .?

She heard a shout and then an "All right, Kurt!"

"Good throw!" Jackson called out. The apprentice's sphere must have taken down their Three.

"Riley!" Beck called out, and she turned in time to find a fiend launching itself at her. She swung at it with her steel pipe and hit nothing but air. When she dodged to the side to keep it from hooking her with its claws, it was gone, just like the other one.

"What the hell was that?" Beck said.

The only demon remaining was the one that Jackson and Kurt had secured in one of the steel mesh bags, still unconscious from the effects of the Holy Water.

An eerie silence fell around them.

Her breath coming in short pants, Riley closed her eyes.

There. It was the lavender thread, growing fainter by the second as its owner retreated from their location. Did that person have anything to do with the demons? Or was this disappearing act something new in Lucifer's arsenal?

Riley looked back at Kurt, who was high-fiving with Jackson, elated at capturing his first Gastro-Fiend. She remembered how that felt.

"Good job!" she said. "You kept your cool. Not easy to do."

The young man smiled. "Took three spheres, though."

"You'll get better, trust me," Jackson said. "Especially when you're the one paying for them."

The apprentice looked around. "What happened to the other fiends?"

"They vanished," she replied.

When Jackson's eyes met hers, she saw the concern, but it was Beck who asked the question.

"So tell me, when did demons learn how to disappear?"

~~*

Beck slept in, the jet lag and the overnight trapping punching his clock. He woke late, close to nine, which meant it was two in the afternoon, Scottish time. For a moment he was disoriented until Riley's soft breathing reassured him. She was tangled up against him, her hair spread across his bare chest.

Neither had spoken much as they drove home, too weirded out by what had gone down in the park. After showering, they'd climbed into bed, curled up in each other's arms, and fallen asleep, too exhausted to make love again.

Now, as he studied her, he again wondered what he had done to deserve her, deserve their future together. Stewart had once told him that true love could sneak up on you, hit you between the eyes before you even saw it coming. It'd been that way with Riley. Beck had always seen her as Paul's little girl, until suddenly, she'd become a young woman.

Now she's mine.

She mumbled under her breath and rolled onto her side, away from him. He resisted the urge to wake her so he could make love to her. If fate was kind, he'd have a lifetime of her curled up against him each morning.

Fifteen minutes later he poured ink-black coffee into a mug. As he turned toward the living room, he spied the calendar on the refrigerator and smiled at the big red heart that had been added to the date he'd been originally scheduled to return home.

His stomach demanded food—it was way past lunchtime by his internal clock—but instead he sat on the couch and studied the Christmas lights arranged carefully around the picture window. Then the sacks of Christmas ornaments Riley had bought at a thrift shop. The empty spot where the tree would stand.

He realized this wasn't his place anymore, and in some ways that was disconcerting. Riley was slowly changing it, putting her mark on his house. It troubled him that she didn't seem that eager to set the wedding date. Was it just cold feet? Or something else?

Maybe he could do something about that while he was home.

It felt strange to allow another person so close to him, into his life, under his skin. Beck closed his eyes and tried to picture what Christmas would be like if they had children, but he had no real frame of reference. He thought maybe there'd be the heavenly smells of roast turkey or ham, the excited shouts of little ones as they opened their presents, the love that would fill this house on that day. On every day.

It wasn't only about being able to love someone else, it was about the love that came back to you in full measure. God knew he was an empty well, but in her own way Riley was filling him up, bit by bit.

A movement near the sack of ornaments caught his attention. To his astonishment, a small black-clad body crawled over the side of the sack, toting a long strand of tinsel and a small black bag. A Klepto-Fiend.

What the hell?

The demon reached the floor, then carefully tucked its prize away in the bag. Once its treasure was safe, it clutched the bag, hugging it like it was the best thing in the entire world. Finally, it seemed to realize it was being watched. Its eyes popped open, then widened in shock.

"Mornin', demon," Beck said, keeping his voice low.

A single squeak of fright erupted from the fiend's mouth, and it fled in a blur of motion.

Before Beck could react, a soft padding of footsteps came from the hallway, then the sound of Riley extracting a coffee cup out of the cupboard.

"Did you know we have a demon in our house?" he asked quietly.

There was a clunk as the cup connected with the countertop. "Ah . . . maybe?"

"As a grand master, do you know how bad it looks if there's Hellspawn runnin' around my place?"

"Not good, huh?" When he didn't reply, she added, "Yeah, not good."

Riley joined him, but instead of snuggling up next to him, she sat at the other end of the couch. Her coffee mug was cradled in her hands and her hair tousled. She wore his Runrig T-shirt, a memento from one of the Scottish rock band's concerts. It nearly reached her knees. A baggy pair of his sweatpants and thick socks completed the outfit.

She looked over at him, puzzled. "When did you see him?"

"Just now. He was stealin' tinsel."

"Oh." Riley set her cup on the side table. "I was hoping he'd stay hidden."

"Why don't you ward the place, run him off?"

"Because . . . he was the one I trapped in the apartment building the night Dad died. You sold him and he came right back."

That didn't sound like all of it. "And?"

"He warned me when the Demon Hunters were after me and he told me how to free Ori so we could defeat Sartael."

Beck leaned back against the couch, trying to figure all that out in his head. "He works for our enemy."

"Well, duh," she said. "Wherever I go, he finds me. So I gave up."

"Riley . . . " He sighed. "This won't work."

"It's worked for almost a year, Beck. I found him sleeping

next to Rennie the other night, all snuggled into her fur. He's not evil. He's just obsessed with bling."

Then he cycled back through the conversation. "Was he at Stewart's place too?"

"Yes. Angus doesn't ward his house. Besides, I tried warding here and the little guy still found a way in. He knows not to spy on me when I'm in the bathroom or in the bedroom. Mostly, he just collects shiny stuff and spends hours counting it out in little piles."

Beck shook his head. Did Stewart know he'd had a wee fiend in his house? Of course he did, and apparently it hadn't bothered him. Which meant maybe it shouldn't bother Beck either.

"So . . . " Riley began, seemingly eager to change the subject. "Other than the little guy, you okay? You've been a lot quieter than normal."

"Sorry."

"No need to apologize. I'm just worried. Is everything okay with us?"

He hadn't intended her to fret. "It's not you or anythin'. It's all the changes."

"You don't like what I did to the house?" she asked, quieter now.

"No, no," he said, realizing he'd given her the wrong impression. "I like it all, I'm just not used to anyone goin' to this much trouble for me."

"It's what real families do, Den." Then she winced. "Sorry, that was kind of harsh."

"It's true, though. I never knew what I was missin' until now." He gestured toward the empty space in the corner. "Like a Christmas tree and all the decorations."

"From now on, you won't miss any of that. We'll celebrate birthdays and anniversaries and holidays like families should. You deserve that joy, Beck. God knows you've had your share of pain."

Just like that, she made him feel better.

Riley rose, laid a kiss on his cheek. "I'll make you some

breakfast. You have to be starved."

His stomach took that opportunity to tell her she was correct.

"Can we have pancakes?" he asked, looking up at her.

"Sure. Whatever you want."

Whatever I want.

He could get used to that, little demon and all.

Chapter Sixteen

For the second time in one week, Riley was at Stewart's house, telling the masters that things were wrong. This time it involved demons going *poof.*

Since it was nearly noon, they were in the kitchen. Stewart's housekeeper, Mrs. Ayers, had left them ham and cheese sandwiches, and thick slices of peach pie. Riley picked at her food, but Beck dove right in. When she didn't eat the second half of her sandwich, he devoured that as well. She'd forgotten just how much food he could pack away, and made a note to adjust her grocery budget while he was home.

"You saw the demons vanish too?" Harper asked Beck, as if Riley might have somehow been hallucinating.

"Yup, and so did Jackson. The apprentice didn't because he was too busy trying to pack up the Three he'd trapped."

"Kid do okay?" Harper asked.

"Kurt did well," Riley said. "He needs more practice, but he's on track. I think we should give both him and Richard more experience with the Threes before we move on to the Mezmers."

Harper nodded his approval.

"There is nothin' in the International Guild archives that talks about this kind of thing, Stewart said. "And especially not disappearin' Threes. They'd never leave a meal behind."

"I think . . . " Riley began, then sighed. Whatever she told Stewart could end up in a report to the Vatican. Dare she risk it?

"Lass?" he prompted.

After a quick look at Beck, she explained, "I think those demons were an illusion."

"Why would ya think that?"

"Mort's been teaching me how to determine if something is real, an illusion, or hidden by glamour. Those demons felt off. I know that's not a great explanation, but they just weren't right. And I felt . . . "

Here we go.

She told them about how she sensed the threads and detected a lavender one at the park.

"For once, I hope you're lying, Blackthorne," Harper said, pushing his empty plate away.

"No, sir, I'm not. Ayden taught me how to pick up that energy. I think there was someone else in the park with us, and they left just about the time the demons did."

"A summoner, maybe?" Stewart said.

"Or some other sort of magic user," Beck said. "I know I saw three demons, and only one was left when we were done."

"If someone is conjurin' these things up, that's a dangerous distraction," Stewart said, pensive. "Ya'd be splittin' yer forces, thinkin' ya've got more Hellspawn than ya do."

"But why? What's the point of fakin' a demon? Is it some sort of prank?" Beck asked.

None of them knew the answer.

"For right now, let's not share this with the rest of the Guild," Harper advised. "I'll talk to Jackson and ask him to keep it quiet. If someone else says this has happened to them, we can let the rest know." He looked over at Riley now. "Since you were involved, it's best we keep this under our hat."

"Because some will think I'm doing something to cause this?"

Harper nodded. "You have enough enemies as it is. No need to give them even more fuel."

"While I'm home, I'll try to be Riley's backup if I'm free," Beck said. "If I'm not with her, whoever she's trappin' with has to be someone she can trust."

Harper nodded. "Already done. Oh, and one other thing." He paused for only a moment. "Master Northrup of the National

Guild is flying in this afternoon."

"We'll try ta get an answer out of him about yer application for master status," Stewart said.

"What about the Vatican?" Riley asked, her voice quieter now. "Do they know I'm learning magic?"

Beck and the other grand master traded looks.

"They know what yer up ta," Stewart said. "They don't like it, but so far they've not made any moves that threaten yer freedom."

She couldn't help but notice that her fiancé was avoiding her eyes now.

"That's why you're home early, isn't it, Den?"

His eyes turned toward her, followed by a guilty expression.

"Yeah. Elias Salvatore came to the manor to let me know that Rome is gettin' skittish about yer studies."

"Just. Great. I asked you why you're home early, and you didn't say a word about the Vatican. You want to tell me why that is?"

Stewart cleared his throat. "I'm thinkin' this is a conversation best held in private. So off ya go, ya two."

He was right. Because this was likely to turn into a major argument, one they'd had before and one she'd thought resolved.

Riley thanked the masters, then clamped her mouth shut and was out the door, headed for Beck's truck, before either had a chance to reply.

"Riley."

She whirled around to find him close on her heels. "Why didn't you tell me? Is MacTavish having you spy on me so he can report back to Elias and Rosetti?"

Beck frowned. "It's not like that."

"The hell it isn't. Every time I sneeze, a report goes flying off to Rome. I'm sick of it. Do you understand?"

"I do, but there's no way out of it. You made a mistake with that damned Fallen angel and you'll be payin' for that the rest of yer life."

"You can't still be jealous of Ori."

"I'm not. Well, not much. But it's the truth. Yer either one of the most talented trappers the world has ever seen, or yer one helluva threat. Rome doesn't know which, and they're tryin' to figure it out."

"And you? What do you think?"

"Ah, Riley," he said, stepping closer. He touched her cheek. "You used yer boon from Lucifer to help Ori. You put yerself between me and Sartael, riskin' yer life against an Archangel to try to save me. You couldn't be evil if you tried. It's just not in you."

Her anger tamped down a bit. "How do I convince others of that?"

"Keep doin' what yer doin'. There's some reason you can sense these thread things. There's also some reason yer trainin' with both a necro and a witch. But don't be surprised that it's scarin' folks. That's just the way of it."

She looked away, still angry. "Next time, tell me what's going on. I don't like not knowing. Makes me feel stupid. It makes me feel like a kid."

"That wasn't my intention. I'll try to be more open from now on." He cocked his head. "But keepin' secrets goes both ways. Anythin' you need to tell me?"

She frowned. "No."

"How about a weddin' date? That'd be a good place to start."

Riley huffed and turned away from him. "There's no rush."

From the hurt expression on Beck's face, that wasn't the answer he wanted to hear.

Chapter Seventeen

That evening Riley found herself at the Summoners Society's headquarters, a three-story, gray stone building, lit up like some big party was in progress. Except tonight it was all about her being "inducted" into the society, provided that everyone played nice. Mort had already warned her that might not happen.

Beck studied the building as he leaned against the side of his truck. He was slightly more dressed up than usual, in nice slacks and a black sweater, even though he insisted he wasn't going inside for the ceremony. "Hasn't changed at all," he observed.

"Nothing much does with them."

"Are we okay?" he asked, looking over at her now.

Which explained why he'd been so quiet this afternoon—he was still brooding about her refusal to set a wedding date.

"We're good." She looked toward the building again, wanting to change the subject. "Remember the night my dad showed up in the middle of their meeting?"

"I'll never forget it."

Lord Ozymandias had stolen her reanimated father away from Mort's care, and then returned him to her at the summoners' meeting. Her father had been a mental mess, under a confusion spell, one that conveniently vanished right before the battle at the cemetery. Now, she knew it had all been part of Ozy's plan to defeat the rogue angel Sartael, but at the time, it had broken her heart.

"I don't know how long this is going to take," she admitted. "Could be a couple hours. You don't have to wait out here for me."

"That's okay. I brought a book. I've got a thermos of coffee and a blanket if I get chilly."

Her own smile caught her unawares. "Do you realize how amazing that sounds? You sitting in your truck with a book?"

Beck thought about that, then nodded. "I catch myself sometimes just readin' along like it's no big deal. I know how much of a blessin' that is. How much of my whole life is a blessin' now." He touched her cheek. "Sorry I acted like a jerk this afternoon. I don't like keepin' stuff from you."

Now she felt guilty because she sure hadn't told him about her chat with Lucifer in the cemetery.

When she didn't say anything, Beck continued, "You go mess around with the corpse stealers, and when it's all over, we'll get some barbecue. Okay?"

"Sounds good." Riley tipped up on her toes, gave him a kiss, and set off for the big stone mansion, the guilt still present.

"Lookin' fine," he called after her.

She wiggled her butt at him.

"No, I was wrong. Yer lookin' *mighty* fine, Princess."

She laughed and kept walking. *I love you so much.*

Just like the last time, Riley was met at the door by a dour butler. He had lost weight, but she didn't think it was right to mention it. Some folks could be touchy about that. Apparently this was also a holiday party, as he wore a Santa hat. It made him look silly, but again, she didn't mention that.

"Blackthorne, Riley," he said, checking her name off a list and taking her coat. "Summoner Alexander is already inside."

"Thank you," she said.

With a deep breath, Riley headed toward the ballroom. She'd made a point of wearing a dress, the green long-sleeved one she'd taken to Edinburgh in October. Along with the pretty earrings Beck had given her, knee-high black boots, and makeup, she looked good. Mortimer was putting his reputation on the line for her, so she'd repay that gesture with respect.

Though it was against Ayden's instructions, Riley had left the amulet in the truck. She knew better than to wear a witchy item in the midst of a bunch of summoners. They'd scent that magic like hounds after a hare, and the reaction would be about the same: lots of howling.

Nevertheless, she hadn't taken off her demon-claw necklace. In fact, she'd left it outside her dress, right there for all to see. She was a trapper first and foremost. If all went well tonight, she'd become a member of the Summoners Society so she could keep studying with Mort. If not, she'd just have to find another way to keep herself and Beck safe.

The room was as crowded as it had been the last time, approximately forty-five or fifty summoners present. The twin fireplaces—one at each end of the room—blazed away, and this time the string quartet was playing something by Vivaldi rather than Bach. The décor still channeled the Victorian era. Or in this case, the Civil War South.

Riley's eyes tracked immediately to Lord Ozymandias. He had a small crowd of summoners around him, but she noted they kept a respectful distance. Ozy was no one's friend. He was just too powerful for that.

A bar sat nearby, with necros lined up to buy a drink. There was even a table of hors d'oeuvres. It dawned on her that the Society would probably expect her to pay dues, just like the Guild, except she'd have no money coming in from any magical activities. She certainly wasn't going to reanimate corpses for a living, not after what happened to her dad.

Riley wove her way through the crowd, looking for Mort. A few summoners gave her a frown as she passed, but she kept moving. Since she was one of the rare few not wearing a robe, she stuck out.

After a slow trek around the room, including a brief chat with Lady Torin, one of the nicer summoners, she located Mort back where she'd started—standing next to Ozymandias, though the rest of the group had wandered off. Ozy was in his usual midnight-black robe. To her surprise, Mort's was black as well.

She walked up, nodded to the high lord, and pointed at Mort's robe. "When did this happen?"

"Last week," he replied. "I passed another magical level."

"A big one apparently." One he hadn't mentioned during their studies together. "Congratulations! That's awesome. Does this mean I have to call you Lord Mortimer now?"

"No. I'm not at *that* level yet."

"I have been urging him to take the test for some time, but he kept holding back," Ozymandias said. "Now that Mortimer has an apprentice, he has no real reason not to don the black robe. A lordship will be coming soon enough."

Mort seemed embarrassed by the praise, a faint blush creeping into his cheeks.

Ozymandias's strange eyes went to her pendant. "It was wise not to wear the witch's amulet tonight, but you do have a great deal of chutzpah to wear a demon claw to a summoners' meeting."

She smiled. "You guys display your level of magical ability by the color of your robes. This claw indicates my abilities as a trapper. Same thing."

To her surprise, Ozymandias's mouth tipped up into a matching smile. "Well said. Not all of us here will agree, but you have every right to claim that trapping. Especially since you almost died performing it."

"Exactly," she said, unnerved that he knew so much about the incident. Looking out at the room, she asked, "How does this go down?"

"General business first, then they'll call you and the other potential initiates to the front. The assembly will decide if you're worthy to join us," Mortimer explained.

"So I can get voted off the island, then?" she asked.

"You can. I doubt you will, though."

"Why?"

"Wait and see," Ozymandias said.

For the next quarter hour she and Mort circulated around the room, introducing her to the summoners and making small talk. All the while, she thought of Beck in the truck, reading his book. Hopefully he wasn't getting too cold, blanket or not. Knowing him, he wouldn't turn on the truck's heater.

When it came time for the meeting, uniformed waiters quickly set up the chairs, all facing a podium. Mort guided her to a seat in the front by two other summoners, each sitting next to a would-be apprentice. One was a young man, the other a woman in her thirties. They peered at Riley with open curiosity. Like her, the newbies weren't wearing robes.

"Do I have to sacrifice anything to join this group?" she whispered to Mort. "Kittens, puppies? Virgins?"

He shook his head, barely holding back a grin. "Just take a pledge that's remarkably similar to the one Ayden and her people use: *An ye harm none, do what ye will.*"

"That, I can handle." She hesitated, then added, "You and the witches have a lot in common. Why are you always at each other's throats?"

"Old prejudices. Silly, if you ask me, but then I've fought next to one and she kept me from becoming a demon's meal. That colors my thinking."

As it should.

What would it be like if the trappers, summoners, and witches all worked together? Was there any way to make that happen?

Not as long as they hate each other.

She suspected Lucifer would be happy if those prejudices never changed.

Chapter Eighteen

Under the able direction of the summoners' leader, Lord Barnes, the meeting went quickly. In many ways, it reminded Riley of the trappers' meetings, only with less swearing.

"First, we need to acknowledge a new black robe." Lord Barnes gestured toward Mort. "Please stand, Senior Summoner Alexander."

Mort did, but this time there was no embarrassment noticeable.

"I am honored to have reached this level. I thank Lord Ozymandias, in particular, for pushing me along."

Ozy dipped his head in acknowledgment from his position farther down the row. Mort returned to his seat, as Barnes shuffled papers on the podium.

"We have three new candidates for acceptance into the Society tonight. Let us begin with Summoner Gold."

Riley watched the process unfold. First Gold stepped forward, gave a brief bio on the newbie, who was an EMT in the real world. Only then did the applicant take his place in front of the assembly. Questions were posed, which the summoner, not the applicant, answered. The vote was taken and the EMT was in.

The next summoner and his applicant went through the same process, and the woman was voted in. Then it was Riley's turn. Mort took his place up front, but to her surprise, he gestured for her to join him. It appeared her vetting was going to be different.

"I have come before this body to propose membership for this talented young woman. For those of you who do not know her, Riley Blackthorne is a demon trapper, the daughter of Paul Blackthorne, who was a master trapper until his death earlier this year."

Murmurs began, as Riley knew they would. Her name carried a lot of baggage. While Mort talked, she made sure to keep her eyes off the crowd, firmly affixed on the exit sign at the other side of the room. When a piece of wood popped in one of the fireplaces, she barely managed not to jump.

"Riley has been studying with me since the first part of November. She wishes to learn magic, not for the purposes of summoning, but for protection," Mort continued. He sounded fully confident, though she suspected he was as nervous as she was.

Was the timing of his upgrade in robe color significant? Had he taken that magical test so that when he presented her application, they'd see a very senior summoner pleading her case? It sounded like something he'd do, especially if Ozy was guiding the process.

Mort laid out her other qualifications: a journeyman demon trapper who had killed two Archfiends, was studying Latin, etc.

When it came to the questions, Riley's mouth went dry. This was almost as bad as the night she'd first been presented to the local trappers' Guild, except that her dad had been there to guide her.

A thin, dark-haired summoner rose from his seat. "Is it not true that she summoned a demon in Oakland Cemetery earlier this year? If so, what keeps her from doing it again?"

Since that was a huge no-no in the Society now, it was a valid question.

Ozymandias rose. "With Summoner Mortimer's assistance, Ms. Blackthorne summoned that fiend at the behest of the Vatican and the Demon Hunters, in an attempt to break the spell that allowed Hellspawn to be on holy ground. A spell that I was forced to lay because of a Fallen angel. My arrogance threatened the lives of everyone in this city. Ms. Blackthorne and her father were instrumental in helping break the rogue angel's plan.

That is one of the reasons I am so vigilant against such a thing happening again."

The summoner who'd asked the question looked over at Riley. "Do you intend to summon demons if given the opportunity?"

She shook her head. "The last thing we need is any more of those things. Besides, if I try, I will have not only the Vatican and the grand masters after my head, but also Lord Ozymandias. No demon is worth that risk."

Ozymandias retook his seat, apparently pleased by her reply.

"What benefit does she bring to our society?" a female summoner asked.

"Riley will serve as an intermediary between us and the trappers," Mort said. "Given the dangers presented by Hellspawn in this city, and recent unfortunate events involving us summoners, it is vital we have a conduit to them."

"Is it true she is also in contact with the witches?" the woman asked, her eyes narrowing.

"Yes. She has been studying with one of them."

"Why?"

Mort looked over at Riley now, and she realized he expected her to answer.

Okay then . . . "Because witches and summoners conduct their spells differently. I want a firm grounding in both types of magic."

"What do you need to be protected from?" a man asked, rising. He wore a navy blue robe, which meant he was fairly senior in the organization.

"Go on, let them know what," Mort said. "All of it."

After clearing her throat, Riley told the group about Summoner Fayne and how she tried to call up a Fallen angel using Riley's blood in Edinburgh.

"Surely not. Sacrifice is anathema to us," the man replied.

"It is, except when one of you—or any magic user—goes off the rails. That's why I want to learn how to protect myself."

"Is this true?" the man asked, looking toward Ozymandias.

"Yes. Every word."

Silence now. It seemed the news that one of their own had very nearly conducted a human sacrifice to call up one of Lucifer's angels had struck home.

"Anyone else?" Barnes asked. More silence. "Then let us put it to a vote."

The results blew her away: Only eight summoners voted against her. The rest were good with her joining their group.

The necros had shown her more support than the trappers.

As she digested that surprise, she and the other two newbies were lined up in front of the members. Riley figured they would hand out the light gray robes and call it good. Instead, it was Ozymandias's turn. He walked up to the first new summoner and placed his index finger in the middle of the man's forehead. The fellow closed his eyes and twitched.

"Light gray," Ozymandias announced. Which meant the guy had little or no magical talent, as was expected. He was handed the robe, which he pulled on with great ceremony. Light applause filled the room.

The result was the same for the woman. Once the robe was on, more applause.

Gray is so not my color.

Then Ozy was in front of her, staring into her eyes. "Ms. Blackthorne."

"Lord Ozymandias."

His finger touched her forehead. It felt warm, comforting. Then a blast of magic blew through her like a summer storm. Her mind saw colors that didn't exist, heard music that had yet to be written and voices that were centuries old.

When she blinked open her eyes, she found Ozy watching her with a faint smile.

"Well, well," he said. He turned to the assembly. "Light blue."

There were gasps, which told Riley this wasn't the usual thing. A quick glance at Mort earned her a wink.

"My lord," a senior summoner said, rising. "Are you sure?"

Ozy's good humor vanished. "Yes, I am. Do you wish to test her?"

The man paled and shook his head. "No, it's just . . . "

"Unusual," the high lord replied.

"Very, Your Lordship."

"I should be light gray, right? Because I'm a newbie," Riley asked.

Ozymandias nodded. "We show our magical ability by robes that range from lighter to darker: gray, blue, brown, dark crimson, and finally black." His eyes sought out Lady Torin's. "Though some summoners prefer to wear the darkest crimson rather than black." She gave a nod in response.

Riley grew increasingly uncomfortable. "But I don't know that much."

Ozy tilted his head. "Your will to live, to protect others, was so strong that you blew apart Summoner Fayne's spell. You grounded her magic and destroyed her protective circle. That speaks volumes about what you are capable of."

"What level was Fayne?" someone called out from the back of the room.

"Dark brown."

More gasps. Whispers began among some of the attendees, making Riley even more apprehensive.

"I'd like to test her," a summoner called out.

Ozy gave him a perturbed frown. "Are you amenable to that, Ms. Blackthorne?"

"Sure." What else could she say?

The other summoner walked up and stared at her for a good ten seconds, as if he could somehow detect that she was a fraud. "Close your eyes."

She did, and felt the same rush of magic as when Ozy checked her out, except this time the level of intrusion was considerably lower.

"And?" Ozymandias asked.

"Ah," the man said as Riley opened her eyes. He appeared chagrined. "Light blue."

"It appears we have a consensus," Lord Barnes said.

Mort pressed a baby-blue robe into her hands and helped her pull it on. He had her raise the hood, as well. The fabric seemed to have a sheen all its own.

After Riley and the other new members recited the pledge, there was polite applause.

"Welcome to the Summoners Society, Riley," Mort said.

"Thank you." She looked over at Ozy. "You, as well, Your Lordship."

"Your father would be very proud of you at this moment," Ozymandias replied.

In her heart, she knew he was right.

Then there was more meeting and greeting. Now that she was one of them, the summoners were as nosy as little old ladies at a church picnic. They wanted to talk to her about trapping, about her father, about everything. Mort ran interference for her until he finally indicated that she could politely escape.

When she claimed her coat from the butler, she realized she didn't need it, not with the robe. She turned to find Mort beaming with pride.

"Did you know I'd test blue?"

"I had a suspicion."

Riley gave him a long hug. "Thanks, for what you did for me, for my dad. All of it."

"You thank me now. Wait until you see what I have in store for you at the next lesson."

"Levitation?"

He shook his head. "How to break a glamour spell. You're ready for it."

"Do I need to buy more aspirin for my headaches?"

"Get the giant economy size," he said.

Riley laughed, hugged him again, and stepped outside into the crisp night air, one of the newest summoners in Atlanta.

Beck hopped out of the truck as she approached. He took one look at the robe and raised an eyebrow. "Jumped a few hurdles right out of the gate, didn't you? You know, I'm not surprised."

"You promised me barbecue," Riley said, still weirded out by what had happened. Carefully removing the robe, she folded it and tucked it away in a special cloth carrying case they'd given her.

"Well, Summoner Blackthorne, do they have any clue what they're in for now that yer one of them?" he asked.

"Probably not. But what could go wrong?"

He cocked his head. "You really want me to answer that?"

"No. We'll find out soon enough."

And with my luck, it'll all go wrong.

Chapter Nineteen

Riley slept in, still wiped out from all the stress of the night before. When she finally dragged herself out of bed, Beck was already up—still on Scottish time. He was an early bird anyway, but now it was worse than that.

When she finally wandered into the kitchen, he wasn't there sipping coffee. Finally, the occasional *thump thump* registered. He was upstairs on the house's unfinished second floor, lifting weights.

That's not right. Not when she could barely lift a coffee cup.

As she munched on cereal at the table, her little demon buddy pattered his way across the counter.

"Dude, you do realize we have a grand master in this house, right?" she said, pointing upward as another *thump* rattled the ceiling.

The Magpie nodded, clutching his bag tight.

"Well, okay. Just don't annoy him, and he'll probably leave you alone. And please don't rip off any of his stuff."

The demon shrugged, as if Beck and all that he stood for weren't any big deal. He must have gotten over his initial shock. Then the fiend was gone, no doubt hunting another piece of jewelry.

By the time Riley had woken up enough to have a brain, Beck had come downstairs and hopped in the shower. After they both dressed, it was time to pick out a Christmas tree. That made Riley feel particularly happy, especially given the extra bonus of watching him flex his muscles as he chopped it down.

They'd just put on their coats and headed for the door when

Beck's cell phone rang. He took the call, frowned, and said they'd be there as soon as possible.

"What's up? I'm not on call."

"Apparently the jerk from National needs to see you. Now."

"But we're going to get our tree."

"Now," Beck repeated.

"Maybe they decided to make me a master and he wants to tell me in person," she said, though her gut told her that wasn't going to be the case.

"I wouldn't count on that."

"Why?" she asked, growing nervous.

"Because Harper said I should drive you over and he wants *me* at the meeting. He sounded damned angry."

"That's not good."

"No shit."

~~*

Unlike most of Stewart's visitors, the Guild's representative was not in the living room. Instead, he was in a room in the back of the house, a location that Stewart used for people he didn't like.

Clad in a nondescript shirt and slacks, Master Northrup sat in the corner in what had to be an uncomfortable chair, no doubt designed that way to ensure the visitor didn't feel the need to linger. The Scottish were known for their hospitality, unless they considered you the enemy.

A messenger bag rested at Northrup's feet. He looked to be in his mid-fifties or so, thick waisted, with bushy eyebrows that needed taming. He sported an expression that said he didn't like much of anything. Riley bet he kicked small children in his spare time.

Stewart and Harper looked like they'd love an excuse to rip this guy to pieces. That wasn't good news. They both held a dim view of the National Guild; the language they used to describe the masters on the board was scathing and, in Harper's case, often foul. Given some of National's stupid regulations and their love of useless paperwork, she could understand the loathing.

If he tells me they turned down my application . . .

Once they were settled in their chairs—Riley noted there was no offer of beverages, which was usually the gold standard in Stewart's household—the grand master gestured at the visitor. "Ya have the floor. Make it count."

Northrup shot him a glower, perhaps for being reminded that he was lower on the totem pole than Stewart. Nevertheless, he was and there was no getting around that.

"First of all, why is *he* here?" Northrup asked, pointing at Beck.

"He is here because he is a grand master and Riley's fiancé," Stewart replied.

"I know that," Northrup snapped. "He has no role in this business."

"Aye, but he does. Once Beck's fully initiated, he'll be takin' my place here in Atlanta. So he has every right ta be here."

"Yeah, I do," Beck said, crossing his arms over his chest. It was his you've-already-pissed-me-off look. "What happens to Riley affects me. So get on with it."

"I'll remember your lack of respect," Northrup replied.

"Good," Beck said. "Respect has to be earned. Yer not doin' it right."

Northrup huffed, then opened a file folder he'd retrieved from the messenger bag. He studied it, then looked up at Riley, as if comparing her with the photo attached to the top sheet.

"Your application for master is denied."

He hadn't even bothered to be civil, just delivered the news like a death sentence.

"Why?" Riley asked.

"You don't qualify," he said tersely.

"I killed an Archfiend and I passed the exam," she said. "Master Harper sent the results to you people. Surely you know that."

"We have concerns as to whether the exam was administered impartially."

"What?" Harper blurted. "That's bull. We had Master Delaney come down from Nashville to do the test, to make sure no one thought we were being partial."

"Delaney served as proctor?" Northrup asked, momentarily confused.

"If you'd looked at the results, you would have seen that right off," Harper replied.

"Well, it doesn't matter. She still doesn't qualify."

Riley's anger built. "The rules state that I have to, one, kill or capture an Archfiend and, two, pass the test. I've done both those things. In fact, I've killed two Archfiends, so I should be doubly good."

"There is no verification of that second kill."

"I saw the corpse myself," Beck said. "So did Grand Master MacTavish."

"The kill didn't occur in the U.S., so it's disqualified."

Which is complete B.S.

"But I killed one in Atlanta. The second one wasn't needed to qualify," she insisted.

"What's the real problem here?" Stewart asked, his accent growing increasingly pronounced. "Is it because Riley's a lass, or somethin' else?"

"She doesn't meet the qualifications. We have final say on the matter, and she isn't master material."

"How do you judge that?" she demanded.

Northrup took a deep breath and shuffled his papers. "We're done talking about this. We've got other things we're concerned about."

Riley clenched her fists.

"We've received word that you're involved in magic, working with necromancers and witches. Is that true?"

"Yes, it is." *I'm even a summoner now, but you don't need to know that.*

Northrup shook his head. "That isn't what the Guild stands for. Because of your behavior, you're on notice that if you continue to be involved with magic in *any* form, your license will be revoked."

Her jaw fell open. He couldn't be serious.

"Just how do ya suggest she do that?" Beck asked, his voice rougher now. Riley could feel the rage simmering beneath his words.

"No magic. That's the bottom line," Northrup said. "Frankly, it would just be simpler if you quit and saved everyone a lot of hassle, but we're giving you a chance to get back on the proper path. Trappers don't mess with magic. It's not our way."

The stupidity was so blatant, she didn't know how to respond.

Beck did. He bent over, scooped a shield sphere out of his pack and held it up. "And this would be?" he asked, his voice vibrating with fury.

"I don't understand the question," Northrup replied.

"Magic. That's what's inside this thing, ya know." He grabbed a grounding sphere, then a Babel sphere, holding them up one by one. "All of these have magic in them. Just how in the hell is she supposed to trap demons and not use this stuff?"

"That's her problem. No more magic. No more associating with necros and witches. That has to stop."

"For how long?" Riley asked, trying to judge the depth of this absurdity.

"For six months. Consider yourself on probation."

Six months? "So when a Three comes after me, how am I supposed to trap it? Or a Four?"

"That's for you to figure out. You started this by associating with those people. Consider this a detox period. If you think you can't cut it, then hand me your license. If you want to keep trapping and using magic, move out of the country. I'm sure the trappers in Europe are a lot more into that kind of thing. But here, we do it the right way."

Northrup wanted her to move out of the States?

Now was not the time to parse it out. Her only other choice was to follow the Guild's rules. But how could she tell Mort that she had to quit the Society when she'd barely joined it?

"God, you're a moron," she said.

"Keep it up and I'll pull your license here and now."

"Why are you doing this? You know that not all the magic users are bad. They've saved trappers' lives."

Northrup again ignored the question, slotting his papers back into his messenger bag. He looked over at Harper. "The National Guild is not pleased with the way things are going in Atlanta. Tonight's meeting will decide exactly what measures we'll need to take in the future."

"The hell you say," Harper said, his scar pulled so tight, Riley swore it would split open. "What sort of *measures* would those be?"

"Potential change of leadership," Northrup said curtly. "And it won't be one of your handpicked cronies, either."

Stewart muttered in his native language, shaking his head in disgust.

Northrup rose. "Meeting tonight at five. Tell everyone to be there. If they're not, they're out of the Guild."

Riley felt her fingers reaching for her pack, the urge to throw her license at the bastard so strong she didn't know if she could stop herself. Beck caught hold of her hand and squeezed it.

"No. Yer not givin' in," he whispered. "We'll fight this."

Northrup gave Riley the stink eye. "You have your warning, young lady. See that you abide by it."

Stewart didn't bother to show him out.

Once the front door banged shut, Beck growled. "Those bastards," he muttered as he let go of Riley's hand. "Who the hell do they think they are?"

"It's our fault, lad," Stewart said. "The International Guild has been too busy keepin' an eye on Europe, and not providin' enough oversight here. The National Guild has come ta see themselves as higher in the peckin' order than they are. They don't remember their history. They don't remember they exist *only* because of us."

"Then it's time to remind them of that fact."

"Aye, it is."

"I can't use magic," Riley said flatly. "All I can do is trap

Grade Ones and Twos. I can't make a living doing that."

"Clearly they want ya out of the business, which makes me wonder why." Stewart looked over at Harper. "Other cities are havin' issues with these folks, right?"

Harper nodded. "Every time I'm on the phone with one of the other masters, it's a nonstop bitch session."

Riley looked down at her hands, the shock setting in. The National Guild would keep finding bullshit reasons not to make her a master. Or they'd find a way to kick her out altogether. Everything she'd worked for hung in the balance.

"Riley?" Beck said.

When she didn't respond, he touched her arm lightly. She looked up at him, then rose. "I'm . . . going upstairs for a while. I need . . . "

Tears filled her eyes and she fled the room, not wanting the others to see them.

~~*

Beck groaned, knowing how badly she was hurting at this moment. He wanted to go after her, but he had to know the score first.

"What the hell is goin' on?" he demanded.

"It's not because of the magic," Harper replied. "The San Francisco Guild has been working directly with a coven of witches for the last three years, and National has never said a word."

"So the problem is Riley," Beck said.

"Maybe," Stewart replied, frowning. "Paul never cut the National fools any slack. He was on their case more than once about some of their asinine rules, and they didn't like it. I suspect they're gettin' even by takin' it out on his daughter."

"She gave them plenty of ammunition," Harper said.

"Yer blamin' her for all this?" Beck demanded.

"No, but she's anything but a run-of-the-mill trapper, and that makes people like Northrup nervous. You know how many of us have killed two Archfiends? Not that many."

"Do ya think they know about her visit to Hell?" Beck asked.

Stewart shook his head. "We made sure that didn't go any further than the Vatican, and those people know how ta keep a secret for centuries. National does know about Paul's deal with Lucifer. I also made sure they were aware that he's free of Hell now. Riley, as well."

"They know she sided with Ori in the battle against Sartael," Beck said.

"Aye, too many witnesses ta that, unfortunately."

"We got another potential problem. As of last night, Riley's part of the Summoners Society," Beck said. "It's only a matter of time before National finds out."

Stewart nodded. "She sent me a text. Mort warned me that he'd have ta do that ta keep trainin' her."

"Can't say I like her being a summoner, but it's no skin off my nose as long as it doesn't interfere with her job as a trapper," Harper said. "I think we need to give National enough rope to hang themselves. Because they will eventually."

"I agree," Stewart said. "Paul had some worries about these fellas, whether they were on the straight and narrow. Now's a good time ta take a closer look."

"Like maybe Northrup or one of the others is workin' for Hell?" Beck asked.

"Or . . . let's look at it from another perspective," Stewart said, shifting in his chair. "When I return ta Scotland, ya'll take over as master in this region. Now if Riley has ta move out of the country ta keep her job, what would ya do?"

"I don't know. Probably ask the Guild to relocate me."

"That's what I'd expect."

Beck blinked. "Why would it matter? MacTavish would just send another grand master in my place."

"Aye, but that grand master would not have been trained by Paul Blackthorne. Nor would his wife be someone who knows magic."

"And she stopped Armageddon," Beck said.

"Exactly. Lucifer has a stake in this city. He'll do anythin' he can ta get the pair of ya out of here. It's a matter of pride now."

"Meanwhile, Riley is gonna be trappin' without the spheres," Beck murmured, shaking his head. "It's dangerous enough for her as it is. When Hell finds out she's unprotected . . . "

"I'm thinkin' it's good yer home, lad. Just keep her safe while we'll work this out."

"And if we don't?"

"Then Paul's daughter will lose her chance ta follow in his footsteps," Stewart replied. "Lucifer will win this round."

Chapter Twenty

Beck tapped lightly on the door to Riley's room on the third floor. When she didn't respond, he entered. She wasn't in bed like he had figured she'd be, but sitting on the couch in the turret room, a thick comforter wrapped around her. Her eyes were red and she clutched a shredded wad of tissues.

Beck closed the door and joined her on the couch. What could he say? He knew how much becoming a master meant to her, knew it was her way of honoring her father. Now the Guild was trying to destroy everything she'd worked for.

Riley blew her nose, then looked over at him. "Ever since the first day my dad started teaching me how to be a trapper, I knew I was going to be a master. It didn't matter what McGuire or anyone else said, I'd be just like Paul Blackthorne. It's who I am, and now they're ruining it all."

Her shoulders shook as tears rained down. Beck pulled her into his arms, feeling those tears wet his shirt. It was his instinct to protect her, and not because she was weaker than him. In so many ways Riley was his equal and beyond. He'd eagerly face down a demon to keep her safe. But how could he combat a ruthless bureaucracy, one that threatened the life of the woman he loved?

"Ya've always wanted to be a master, but yer more than that. Ya can be anythin' ya want, Riley. *Anythin'*. I know this is breakin' yer heart, but it might be the beginnin' of somethin' new."

She frowned up at him. "You're saying I shouldn't fight these bastards?"

"No, not sayin' that at all. We'll fight them as hard as we can, but we might not win. But that's one battle, not the war. Yer not some wimpy little girl who's gonna give up. Yer gonna walk yer own path, set yer own rules." He kissed her forehead. "I'll be there for ya all the way."

She sniffled. "I don't know anything else but trapping."

"Right now ya don't, but yer learnin' magic, learnin' things that will make all the difference down the line. Don't let these people destroy yer spirit, ya hear me? If they do, then they've won."

She touched his cheek. "You're always there for me, aren't you?"

He nodded. "That's why no one should be messin' with us. We will kick their ass."

"All or nothing?" she said. "Like when we fought Sartael?"

"All or nothin'. That's the only way to go."

Because this war isn't over yet.

~~*

The church's meeting room was packed; word had spread that something major was going down tonight and that nonattendance would have serious consequences. Riley knew these guys wouldn't like that bullying tactic. Given the tension in the room, any little spark could cause an explosion.

Northrup sat in the front with Stewart and Harper. From the grumbles in the audience, the assembled trappers knew who he was, and he wasn't welcome. Somehow Riley didn't think Northrup noticed. Or maybe he didn't care.

Beck leaned over and whispered, "This isn't just about you. There's been bad blood between our Guild and National for the past few years. Yer just a way for them to get their foot in the door."

If he thought that would make her feel better, it didn't.

Jackson took his place behind the podium, looking pissed off. He called the meeting to order, then introduced Northrup.

The man made his way to the podium and addressed the group.

"As Master Jackson pointed out, I'm from the National Guild. We've been getting complaints about certain issues in this Guild, and we felt it was time for us to take a closer look." He flipped a piece of paper. "The number of Hellspawn in this city has risen over last year's totals. You've had major demon assaults and an issue with fake Holy Water. To be honest, we wonder exactly what kind of leadership is allowing this to happen."

"What the hell does that mean?" one of the trappers called out. "The Holy Water thing wasn't our fault."

Northrup ignored him. "First order of business: Journeyman Remmers, your application for master trapper has been approved."

There were shouts of congratulations. Riley smiled, even as her heart broke. Remmers beamed, then gave her a worried look.

She answered him with a thumbs-up. "Go you!"

He smiled back. "Your turn's coming."

No, it's not.

Once the noise died down, Northrup continued. "Journeyman Blackthorne has been notified that her application for master has been denied."

"What? Why?" someone called out.

"She does not qualify because we've learned she has been associating with witches and necromancers."

"Since when is that a crime?" Barton asked.

Northrup speared him with a glare. "Because of this behavior, Blackthorne has been ordered to no longer have contact with any of the magic users in this city."

"About damned time," McGuire said.

That comment didn't surprise her.

"She is on a six-month probation and is forbidden to use any form of magic during that period of time, or she will immediately forfeit her license."

Silence fell as that last part soaked in.

"How is she supposed to trap if she can't use the spheres?" Remmers asked. "That's just not possible, unless she wants to be a corpse."

Northrup shot him a look. "She should have thought of that before hanging around with the corpse peddlers and the hags."

Hags? It was good none of the witches had heard that.

Remmers stood now. "Why do you guys care how we trap demons?"

"This is a National Guild matter, and anyone who isn't comfortable with this decision can hand me their license right now."

"My God," someone said. "Did he just say that?"

"The question stands," Jackson said. "Why do you care? As long as the demons are caught and the city is safe, how we accomplish this job is our business."

"I would expect more from a master, but then, we know this city's leadership isn't what it should be." He looked down at Riley now. "So? What's it going to be? Are you going to abide by the probation?"

"Sorry, Princess," Beck mumbled.

Riley rose, but she wasn't shaking. She was far too angry for that.

"If I follow your rules, no one will want to trap with me since I can't provide proper backup. If I trap on my own, I'll be chewed up or dead. But if I use one of the spheres, *like any other trapper,* I'm out on my butt. This is a Catch-22."

The man didn't deny it.

"You're painting a bull's-eye on my back. Every demon who wants payback will be after me, knowing I have no way to defend myself. Same for any necromancer."

Again, the man didn't deny it.

"You're deliberately trying to get me killed."

"Then save all the hassle and hand in your license now."

"No way. I may not be able to trap like anyone else, but I am *not* giving up my license."

"Your decision. Stick to the rules and you'll be fine in six months."

"What keeps you from changing those rules down the line?"

Beck called out.

Northrup smiled. "Nothing. If any of you see this trapper violating the terms of her probation, contact me and I'll deal with it." He motioned to her. "Hand me your trapping spheres."

Instead of giving them to Northrup, she walked up to Harper and delivered them to him, one by one. That action spoke reams to the other trappers, and murmurs of approval came from some of them.

"This isn't over yet," Harper said quietly.

"No, it's not," she replied.

He nodded his approval at her attitude. "Watch your back."

"You watch yours, too."

"Hell, if that isn't the truth."

"Anything you want to say, Trapper Blackthorne?" Northrup asked. "Because if not, it's time for you to leave the meeting. You'll only be disruptive from this point on."

He had that right, but his comment angered some of the trappers, who began grumbling among themselves.

On the way out, Riley picked up her backpack, then touched Beck's arm. "Can I take your truck? I need some time alone."

He nodded his understanding, eyes sad. "I'll find another way home. Go somewhere safe and let me know where you are. If you need me, call."

"I will." She placed a kiss on his cheek and headed for the rear door. In the last row, her three apprentices stared at her, eyes wide.

She needed to reassure them that their world wasn't ending.

"Master Harper will help you finish your training. Don't give up, no matter what."

"But—" Kurt began.

"It'll be okay." *Even when it won't be.*

When Riley reached the door, she knew all eyes were on her. She turned. "Master Northrup?"

"Yes?" he said, looking up from his notes. Apparently, he'd thought she'd already vanished off the face of the planet.

"So you know, Blackthornes have been trapping demons

for centuries. We don't give up. So play all your dumbass head games, but I'm here to stay."

"Amen!" someone called out.

A few claps began, and then more filled the room as Riley crossed into the hallway. She kept her back straight and her eyes forward, refusing to show any weakness. That little stunt might have cost her license, but she didn't care.

Once she reached the parking lot, she sent Beck's truck toward downtown and refuge, knuckling away the tears as they fell.

Chapter Twenty-One

Riley retreated to the Grounds Zero. More than once, this place had offered her asylum, but tonight the hot chocolate tasted like boiled gym socks laced with mothballs. She knew it wasn't the drink's fault.

The life she had fought for, bled for, and nearly died for was being pulled out of her hands, like a toy she'd been allowed to play with until someone changed their mind.

Her way of honoring her father's sacrifice, his love, the sacrifices her mother had made, was vanishing because some pencil pushing bureaucrats didn't like what she stood for, the choices she'd made. In many cases, the choices she'd been forced to make.

She was past the swearing stage, past the crying stage. Now she was just numb, like when she'd buried each of her parents.

She could fight on or tell National to cram it and work on her own. But that was dangerous. Beck had told her about some of the freelance trappers, their prison records and how they'd cut your throat just to make a dime. With Beck returning to Scotland, she'd be on her own. No way he would go for that.

After an hour at Grounds Zero, she still wasn't ready to go home. Beck hadn't returned her text when she'd told him where she was, which meant things were still going strong at the meeting. She suspected none of it was good. After bussing her table, she headed for her other refuge: Oakland Cemetery.

This time she drove right up to the Blackthorne mausoleum, not keen to wander around in the dark. Her sense of security, her I-can-handle-most-anything mantra was fragile right now, with her backpack strangely light, empty of all her spheres. At least here, on sanctified ground, she was safe from demons.

Riley chose to sit on the cold earth in front of her parents' graves, the snow finally having melted away. It seemed only right that she be here, as so much of her life was wrapped around this one piece of earth.

Her father's voice floated through her mind, like it often did. *It'll be okay. All things happen for a reason.*

"Sorry, Dad, but I'm not buying that right now."

She bowed her head and let a few more tears slip down her cheeks, then wiped them away. Time passed. The night grew darker and still, Riley didn't move. It was as if she'd become a statue. *Can't stay here forever. Den will worry.*

In fact, she was surprised he hadn't called her yet.

The sound of footsteps on the asphalt brought her around. If Lucifer was back to harass her . . .

But it wasn't the Prince.

"Simon?" *What are you doing here?*

Her ex-boyfriend closed the distance, stepping off the road and onto the ground surrounding the mausoleum. His hands were jammed into his jeans' pockets, his expression angry and troubled. Now that she looked at him closer, she could see his thread, a warm teal.

"I'm glad I found you," he said. "I got to the meeting late. Beck told me what happened. He said you'd probably be here if you weren't at Grounds Zero."

The man she loved knew her so well. "I was at the coffee shop earlier."

"Can I join you?"

Riley almost said no, then changed her mind. Simon was worried about her, that much was evident.

"Have a seat," she said, "as long as you know I suck at being good company right now. There might be a lot of swearing and calling certain people buttheads. Just warning you."

"You probably won't be the only one swearing," Simon said, as he took a seat on the ground next to her. It reminded her of the night they'd sat vigil for her dad. The night they'd shared their first kiss.

"I'm sorry, I don't have any strawberry Pop-Tarts tonight," she said.

He thought for a second, then smiled. "God, it's been a long time, hasn't it? Or at least it feels like it."

"Yeah. Lots has happened since then."

"What the hell is National thinking?" he blurted.

The old Simon hadn't gotten angry that often, and it confused her when the new one did. Still, this was him now, and she'd have to adjust. Lord knew he'd done that for her.

"They just want me out of the Guild, for whatever reason. I can go freelance, but Beck would throw a fit. But I need to earn my own money. I won't sponge off him, even if we're going to be married someday." She sighed. "Maybe I could go work at a restaurant or something. Fewer hassles."

Simon shook his head. "No, that's not what you're trained for."

"What can I do?" Riley spread her hands. "No magic, and I'm hosed. Harper can appeal the decision but—"

"Actually, he can't. He's no longer in charge of the Atlanta Guild. Northrup is. He took over right after you left the meeting."

Her jaw dropped open. "What? That's insane. The trappers let him do it?"

"So far they have, but Beck said a lot of people are very angry. This isn't going to go the way National thinks it will. They've overstepped their authority."

Simon looked off into the distance for a moment, then back at her. "There is another option. You can work with me."

You? "Doing what?"

"Exorcisms. Until they assign me to a new location, Rome wants me to handle any demonic possessions here. I need backup. There aren't enough lay exorcists to form two-person teams. You'd be a great partner. You know demons and you know how to kill them if they come after me."

In that second Riley heard Lucifer's voice in her head, telling her how she had a new opportunity coming her way and how much he hoped she'd take it.

"Ah . . . no, that's not a good idea."

"Why not?" Simon replied.

She hesitated, wondering if it was wise to mention what the Prince had told her. Not with Simon so plugged into the Vatican. It was better if Rome thought she was completely off the chief Fallen's radar.

"If you don't want to, I understand," Simon continued, sounding disappointed. "I just figured you might want to keep doing what you do best, and you'd get paid too. I receive a fee for each exorcism, and I'm willing to share half of that money. I'm living at home, so my expenses are pretty minimal."

Riley cocked her head. "It's really nice of you to offer, but why are you doing this after everything that happened between us?"

If anything, Simon grew more solemn. He took a very long breath and let it out slowly, as if carefully formulating his reply.

"Even when it all went bad between us and I knew you hated me, you watched my back. Not everyone is like that."

She'd learned that lesson big-time earlier that week.

"What I do is pretty white-knuckle and it's way scary," he continued. "But you know what that's like. I need someone who won't fold when a demon whispers in their head. I need someone who knows how they play their mind games, and can give it right back. That's you."

He'd caught her interest now. "What are these possession demons like?"

"It's not always like in the movies," Simon admitted. "Some are Mezmers who have the ability to physically inhabit a body or an inanimate object. Others are Hellspawn you've never heard of. That kind of knowledge is master level or higher."

That clicked. "My dad said something about there being other demons than the ones trappers capture."

"There are, and I learned about some of those during my training. I suspect the grand masters know about even more than that."

Riley issued a low whistle. As if five grades of fiends wasn't bad enough.

"Come on, help me out here," Simon pressed, clearly eager for her to join him.

If I turn him down, Lucifer won't get to mess with my life. Or at least not this way. But if I say yes, I could keep Simon from getting hurt. Maybe even dying.

She hedged. "The Vatican is okay with this?"

"I called them right after I talked to Beck. Father Rosetti gave his personal approval."

What? It would have been after midnight in Rome, and yet he'd reached Rosetti and received an okay, all in one call? It seemed her ex-boyfriend rated pretty high with the Vatican types.

"Why would Rosetti give his okay? I mean, come on Simon, I sold my soul to Hell."

He winced. "But you got it back. That counts, Riley. Rosetti believes you'd do a good job."

It was more than that, and they both knew it.

"Ah, let me think about this. I need to talk to Beck. It's not just about me anymore."

Simon nodded his understanding. "Call me in the morning. I'm really hoping to work with you again. It'd be cool."

"If I don't sign on, maybe you can get one of the other trappers to help you."

He shook his head. "There are some I trust, but the Vatican only approved me working with you."

"We're talking about the same guys who put me through Inquisition Lite last spring?"

"Believe it or not, you've made some friends in Rome. Me? I just want someone I can trust watching my back, and that's you."

Wow. "I'll . . . call you. No matter what, thanks for thinking of me."

He rose. "Don't let National break you. You're better than those jerks. Always have been."

As Simon walked away, her mind reeled at what had just happened. How so much had changed since the last time she'd sat with him in this cemetery.

What have I got myself into?

Whatever it was, the Prince of Hell had to be loving it.

~~*

Beck heard his truck pull into the drive and the engine turn off, but no sound of a slamming door. He drummed his fingers on a knee. Should he wait her out or not?

Too anxious for patience, he grabbed up his coat, set the alarm, and exited the house. Riley sat in the truck, staring at nothing. He walked up to the door and waited until she rolled down the window.

"Someone keeps promisin' me a tree. We still have time to get one?"

She blinked at him as if he were speaking Martian. "Ah . . . yeah, I guess. The tree place is open until ten."

"You want me to drive?"

"No. Better not. You still got your head in the Highlands."

He joined her in the truck and secured his seat belt, but she still didn't move.

"I missed you," he said simply.

Riley looked over at him, then nodded. "I missed you too."

Her silence made him nervous; he didn't know how to deal with it. A mad Riley, a crying Riley, he understood. A quiet one wasn't good.

"Simon find you?"

"Yeah. He told me about Harper."

Beck swore. "I still don't believe they did that. He nearly died trying to clean up the local Guild all those years ago, and now they say he's doin' a shitty job. I thought Stewart was goin' to rip Northrup's head off."

"So everyone's screwed, then."

"Pretty much."

"Simon offered me a job."

He jerked his eyes toward her. "Doing what?"

"Serving as backup during his exorcisms."

"Well, damn. He didn't say a word about that to me."

"I think he came up with the idea after you guys talked. He even called the Vatican to get their approval, and they were all for it. Or at least Rosetti was."

They were? "You know why they're doin' this, don't you?"

She nodded. "Two reasons: I can keep Simon alive, and it gives the Vatican another way to keep an eye on me, on top of those reports Stewart sends in every month."

"Yeah. Rome saw an opportunity and jumped on it. They're not usually that fast about stuff, so this must be important to them."

"There's an issue," she said. "One I haven't told anyone about."

Beck listened as she told him about meeting with Ayden in the cemetery, then about Morgaine interfering, and encountering the Prince of Hell. His eyebrows rose as she gave him Lucifer's prediction, and how the Fallen had thought it would be a great idea if she took this new "opportunity."

Beck decided now was not the time to chew her out about keeping secrets. He wasn't exactly a model citizen when it came to that himself.

"What is that old bastard up to?" he asked.

"I don't know. I didn't tell Simon because he'd have to tell Father Rosetti, but I don't like it that the Prince is involved."

"That makes two of us."

"If he wants me to do this, that's a bad thing, right?"

"Or, because he is the Prince of Lies, he's telling you that to keep you away from the Vatican's business."

"Oh man, I hadn't thought of that. Which is it?"

He shrugged. "Let's go buy a tree. That much makes sense."

Beck finally received a smile from her, and it lit up his heart.

~~*

As Riley drove them to the Christmas tree farm outside the city, Beck's phone pinged. He checked it and shook his head. Riley couldn't help but notice that it didn't take as long for him to read the messages now. He might not realize it, but he had come a very long way.

"Well I'll be damned," he muttered.

"Lucifer sending you dirty texts?" she asked.

"No, it's Justine."

Justine Armando, a.k.a. the Red-Haired Stick Chick, was probably the only woman on the planet who could fire up Riley's jealousy beast. Even now, it popped open its eyes and began rending the bottom of its cage with its claws, eager to pounce on the reporter and cut her into sushi.

"What does she want?" Riley asked through clenched teeth.

"She wants to know what's goin' down between the local Guild and National."

"How did she even hear about it?"

"Probably Stewart's doin'. He's kept in touch with her since last spring."

"Why?" Riley demanded. "He knows what she's like."

"He also knows that if we need someone to get the message out to the everyday folks, it's Justine. Like her or not, she's good at what she does."

Unfortunately he was correct; Justine, with all her perfectionism and single-minded devotion to her job, was good at uncovering secrets. She dug into stories until they bled, often at the cost of people's personal lives.

Like Beck's.

"So what are you going to do?" she asked.

"Not sure. I'll talk to Stewart and Harper, see what we want to feed to her. Is there some reason yer stranglin' the steerin' wheel?"

Her knuckles *were* white, but she shot him a glower anyway.

"You know why."

He laughed. "Still jealous? Well, there's a way to fix that. We just pop down to the courthouse, pick up a marriage license, and get hitched. Done and done."

He wasn't joking. Not in the least.

"Beck . . ."

He looked over at her now, his good humor gone. "Some reason yer not ready to get married?"

"It's been kinda busy, you know?"

"I get that. I also get that both of us are doin' stuff that could get us killed. Waitin' is not a good idea. You should know that, Riley."

She did, on some basic level. Still, marriage was a huge step, even to a guy she loved more than anything.

"I'll work on it."

"That's all I ask." He leaned over and placed a kiss on her cheek. "Oh, and Justine? Her text said she got married a month ago. Just got back from her honeymoon."

Riley blinked. "Really? The She-Barracuda actually settled for one guy?"

"Yup. Thought you might like to know that, in case you were jealous or anythin'."

"Me? No way."

He chuckled. "You just keep tellin' yerself that."

~~*

Once they had picked out the perfect tree, Riley paid for it as Beck lined up the truck lights so he could see the victim properly. Then he borrowed an axe and went to work.

She leaned on the bumper, arms crossed to stay warm, letting this moment burn itself into her memory. Their first tree. Their first Christmas together as a couple. If she agreed, it could be their first holiday as husband and wife.

Not yet. She wanted it to be perfect. The second time Beck had proposed to her had been that way. She wanted the same for the actual wedding, which meant they needed to wait a few months.

He's not going to like that. He was much like her. Once the decision was made, the task got done. Stalling wasn't normal for her.

Part of it was her age. She was just eighteen. That wasn't considered young when her mom had married, but nowadays it was. Didn't mean the marriage wouldn't survive, just that her life would change again. She knew it was what she wanted, but it was still a gigantic step.

Wood chips flew and finally the tree toppled over. Beck straightened up, a sheen of sweat on his forehead. He'd ditched his coat partway through, so his T-shirt clung to his muscles now.

She clapped, appreciating the view.

"That was work," he said. "Some reason we couldn't have just bought one already cut?"

Riley pushed off the bumper. "And miss my Backwoods Boy going all hunky woodsman with an axe? No way."

Beck smirked, then flexed, which caused her to laugh.

"Not the response I was hopin' for," he said.

"Gotta keep you humble."

Riley dropped a kiss onto his sweaty cheek and helped him load their tree into the back of the truck.

~~*

It was close to ten-thirty by the time the tree had been positioned in the stand. Riley heated up a pizza while Beck swept up all the needles.

Then he paused and looked at the tree. It was a Scots pine, like the one at the manor, but shorter, just a bit over six feet tall. He took a deep breath, savoring the rich scent. He knew that was one reason Riley liked a fresh tree.

Her folks used to do that. At least, before Miriam died and it got too expensive for Paul and his daughter to buy a real tree. Instead they'd had a dinky fake one sitting on the kitchen counter.

Which was more than I had.

Now he and his pretty lady had one of their own, and he was

damned proud of it. Even if it was just a tree.

When the oven dinged, he put away the cleaning supplies, washed his hands of the tree sap, and joined her at the table.

"So what should I do about Simon?" she asked, pouring herself a soda.

Beck had wrestled with that all evening, veering from "Sure, go for it" to "No way, no how."

"I'm . . . not comfortable with the idea," he said, picking up a piece of pizza. It was packed with meat, just the way he liked it.

"What are your objections?" she asked.

In the past she would have gotten in his face, demanding to know why he felt he could dictate her life. Now she asked his opinion and then asked him to justify it. In some ways, this was worse.

"First thing—it spooks the hell out of me. I've read about some of the demons you'd be dealin' with, and they are seriously hardcore."

"Hardcore how?"

"Like, they can tunnel into yer mind like whirlin' razor blades, and you'll be lucky to be able to drool when they're done."

"Wow."

"Yeah. They don't just mess with yer head. If they become physical, meanin' they hop out of whoever they've possessed, they can jump into you, tearin' you apart from the inside."

"So, like Olympic-grade Mezmers, then."

Beck pondered that as he added hot sauce to his slice of pizza. "Yeah, just like that. It isn't always Fours, either. Sometimes a Fallen gets bored and comes callin'."

"Ewww. I hate those things. So you're saying you don't want me to work with Simon?"

He set down the half-eaten slice and sighed. "You gotta understand, if I could, I'd lock you away in your family's mausoleum so no demon could ever come near you again. The thought of you out there trappin' those things scares the livin' hell out of me."

"Same on this side. I worry about you all the time, even though I know you can handle almost anything that comes your way."

"Just like you," he said. "That means I have to suck it up and accept that the woman I love, the woman I will marry someday, has a life of her own, and that life sometimes puts her in serious danger. I really hate it, but there it is."

Riley put her hand on his and gave it a squeeze. "Then I'm going to try one of these exorcism things with Simon, just to get an idea of what it's like."

"What about the Prince?"

She shrugged. "He's going to keep messing with me no matter what. At least I'll be doing what I love and screwing him over at the same time."

"That's not how it sounded to me."

"Maybe I am playing into his hands. We'll find out soon enough."

Beck went back to eating, but she must have sensed he was troubled.

"I'll be careful," she said.

"You have to be. I can't do my job safely if I'm worryin' about you all the time."

"Understood. So, do we decorate the tree tonight or tomorrow?"

He thought about that. "Tonight." He wiped his hands on a paper towel. "You know why."

"Because it's only going to get weirder the next few days?"

He nodded, rising from his chair. "No other way it can be, not with both the Prince and the National Guild's dumbass in town."

Chapter Twenty-Two

When she called Simon and gave him the news the next morning, he told her he already had a job for them. An hour later, he picked her up in a sedan that was probably his parents'. As he drove them north of the city, his stereo played a Christian pop song by Unspoken, one about starting a fire in your heart. His taste in music clearly hadn't changed.

"Getting my head in the right place," he explained, when she asked about the title and artist. He hesitated, then asked, "Did your faith change after you were in Hell?"

That question caught her off guard. "How did you know I went there?"

"Father Rosetti told me."

Of course he did. After all, Stewart had no choice but to keep the Vatican informed about everything she did, even when it involved an excursion to the fiery pits.

Her silence seemed to make Simon uncomfortable. "I'm sorry, that was kind of a direct question."

"I just didn't expect it." Riley gnawed on her lip. "I don't know if my faith changed, but my perception of the situation did. When I talked to Lucifer in the cemetery, he was a charming trickster. In Hell, he was a total bloodthirsty warlord. He warned Ori that if he tried to overthrow him, both Ori and I would suffer eternal torment. Judging from what Lucifer did to Sartael, he wasn't lying."

"I can't imagine what it'd be like."

"Best you don't. I'll do everything I can never to see that place again."

"Even if it means sacrificing someone else's life?"

It must be the day for deep questions.

She sighed. "I'd like to think I'd do the right thing, but . . . " Riley shook her head. "Look, if you're having second thoughts about me helping you—"

"I'm not. You answered exactly how I would have. You never know how you'll react to a situation until you're in it. That was the problem with me, at least before I almost died. I was too sure of things. Now I know not to be."

"I never would have thought I'd sell my soul just to overthrow Sartael. In the end, it was Beck who killed him, not Ori."

"Is it true that grand masters go to Hell if they're wounded when they try to kill a Fallen?"

Simon had been doing his research. "Yes, but I can't say much more than that."

"I figured that would be the case."

"Did you get to meet the pope?"

Simon smiled now. "I did. We had a special Mass and he blessed us when we graduated. I really like him. He's kind."

"Better be. He's the leader of how many zillion of you guys?"

He chuckled. "What's it like to be engaged to a grand master?"

"Strange," she said before she could stop herself. "Cool and strange. Beck is so much stronger now. He knows stuff he can't tell me about, but he's doing exactly what he should be."

"Bet the Prince loves all these secrets we keep. Helps him in the long run."

She looked at her companion. "You know, I was thinking the same thing."

~~*

A few minutes later, they pulled into a drive demarcated by a "Sold" sign. The driveway led to a large, two-story brick house set back from the road. The yard was well landscaped, and there was a three-car garage.

"Nice. So what's the story here?" she asked as he parked the car.

"Demonic structure-possession," he said. "Buyers found out about it the day they took ownership. They could have had the sale voided because that contingency was covered in the contract, but they love the house."

"So you're here to kick the demon to the curb?"

"That's it. Ah, here's the real estate agent," he said as another car pulled in beside them.

The agent was an older woman, with silver hair styled as though her life would end if it wasn't perfect. Maybe in the world of house sellers, it would.

Simon introduced himself, handing over some official-looking identification card. The agent studied it and handed it back.

"Are you sure you're old enough to do this?" the woman said, eyeing him like he was ten.

Riley barely contained a snort. Usually, that question came *her* way.

"I'm certified by the Vatican to deal with the problem," Simon replied evenly. He gestured. "This is Riley Blackthorne. She's a journeyman demon trapper and is going to provide support during the exorcism."

The agent's attention moved to Riley.

Don't you dare call me a kid.

After a curt inspection, the woman nodded, and they followed her and her vapor trail of perfume to the porch. She unlocked the door and reset the alarm.

"I really don't think this is for real," the woman said. "The new owners are a bit flighty, you know? Why would a demon inhabit a house in Buckhead? Now, down in some parts of Atlanta, I could see it, but not up here. This is a respectable neighborhood."

As if demons only targeted the poor.

Simon politely didn't reply, waiting quietly for something to happen. Riley tuned in to the vibes and got nothing, just an empty house. Then something shifted—something cold and dark and evil.

"It's here," Riley said. "I can feel it."

Simon raised an eyebrow, but didn't contradict her.

The real estate lady gave her a skeptical look. "How do I know this isn't a scam?"

A howl cut through the air like a knife through fine silk. It began low, then escalated, rattling the windows. Upstairs, something shattered and rained down onto a wooden floor. A window or a mirror, perhaps.

Abruptly, the howl cut off, replaced by a truly chilling cackle that raised the hairs on Riley's neck and made her wish Beck were here.

The agent's face went as pale as her coiffure, and she backed away from the door. "Was that—?"

"Yes," Simon replied. "Let's get the paperwork signed, then we'll take care of it."

"Sure. Fine. Whatever you want," the woman said, hustling away from the house on her high heels.

"That sounds like a nasty one," Riley said, trying to curb her nerves.

"Not as bad as some of them," he said gravely.

Ten minutes later, the real estate agent was gone. She'd been so eager to leave that Riley swore she'd probably have given them her ATM card and PIN just to escape.

"So how does this go?" she asked.

"We'll start by anointing ourselves with Holy Water before we enter the house. I usually do a brief prayer, get my head in the right place, because once we're in there it's the demon's reality, not ours."

"Serious mind games?"

He nodded. "You know how that goes."

That was the truth. They'd both been played like pawns by Fallen angels. At least Ori had tried to save her life in his own convoluted way. Sartael had ripped Simon's faith into shreds. Fortunately, he'd not destroyed it. In fact, it looked to have become stronger than ever, if Simon was facing Hellspawn again.

He popped open the trunk of his car and pulled out a black suitcase. Inside were a large metal cross, three bottles of Holy Water, and an aspergillum, the device priests used to sprinkle the sacred liquid.

"That's it? No super-secret Vatican weaponry or anything?"

"The weapon is in my faith and the power of God."

He checked the label on one of the bottles, then handed it to her.

"Pour a *very* small amount into my hand," he said.

Riley did as instructed, watching as he intoned a prayer in Latin, then used the Holy Water to draw a cross on his forehead with one finger, his eyes closed.

She held her silence as he murmured to himself. Once he was done, he opened his eyes and smiled at her. "Your turn."

Riley gave him the bottle and he dropped a bit of the liquid into her left palm. The instant it touched Heaven's mark, it tingled. She stared down as the crown seemed to pulse with white light.

"That's amazing," he said.

Riley hesitated. She wasn't Catholic, but she had her own particular sort of faith. It was impossible not to believe, after encountering angels, both good and evil.

She dipped her finger into the liquid and carried it up to her forehead. A cross? No, she already had Heaven's mark on her. Instead she drew a heart, for love, because she had found that to be as strong as any weapon a demon could wield.

Closing her eyes, Riley whispered a prayer for success and protection.

The tingling in her palm ended and she opened her eyes to find Simon studying her.

"Father Rosetti said you had your own way of doing things. That was a heart, wasn't it?"

"Yes. For love. It felt right."

"That's exactly what you need then." He screwed the lid onto the bottle, replaced it, and closed the suitcase. "You ready?"

She nodded. *Here we go . . .*

Simon pulled the suitcase and his trapping bag out of the trunk, handing her the latter. She knew it'd contain Holy Water, spheres, and a steel pipe.

"Can't use the spheres," she reminded him.

"But I can if we need them. Or you can, and we just don't tell anyone."

"That would be cheating," she said.

"Yes, it would," he said, winking.

"You know, I like the new you."

"So do I. The old Simon was a stuck-up jerk."

She blinked at his candor. "You said it, not me."

"My family agrees. I could be a real self-righteous ass." He looked at the house now. "First rule for exorcists: Know thine own self. The demons will tear you apart if you don't."

The final item that came out of the trunk was a plain metal box, about ten inches square. The lid had clamps on the outside and was engraved with crosses and Latin phrases.

"If we can get the demon free of the building, it'll go corporeal and we need to trap it in this container," Simon explained.

"A bit fancier than the bait boxes we use for the Fours."

"The Vatican has more cash than trappers."

"*Way* more. Why do I think this isn't going to be easy?"

"Because it never is," he replied. "Just be ready for anything."

Riley followed behind him, carrying the trapping bag and the weird metal box, her heart pounding. When she trapped, she knew what to expect. This was totally new and totally scary.

"How many times does an exorcism go bad?"

"Ah, about two or three times in ten," he said matter-of-factly.

Which was actually about the same odds as trapping a Three or a Five. That, she could handle.

They stepped inside the house.

"It's really quiet. Sometimes they're like that, hoping I'll go away. Other times they rain hell on me the moment I get inside the door."

"Which is worse?" she asked.

"The quiet ones. They've usually got more power and they know it."

"Oh goodie."

Riley felt that cold wave roll through her again. Her gaze instinctively rose to the ceiling. "It's upstairs."

"I knew you'd be good at this. How can you tell?"

"Ori taught me some things." *So did Ayden.*

He studied her. "Ironic, isn't it? One of Lucifer's angels helping us trap one of their own."

Something like that.

Simon set off toward the stairway without hesitation, Riley following right behind. Once they were upstairs, the cold seemed concentrated at the end of the hall. He led the way, murmuring what sounded like a prayer.

He paused at the door, then, after a quick look at her, stepped inside. The instant Riley crossed into the room, the temperature plunged at least twenty degrees. Her mind screamed for her to flee, a primal reaction to a predator.

Blackthornes don't run. But that didn't keep her from being scared.

The room was painted a light green and had a dark hardwood floor and a bank of mullioned windows that overlooked the backyard. Empty white bookshelves lined the walls, and a stacked-stone fireplace sat at one end.

A library. "I can see why the new owners don't want to lose this place."

Simon nodded. "It's telling that the Hellspawn has set up residence in this room. Fiends hate knowledge."

"Fiends hate everything."

Her companion paused, then picked a spot and set his suitcase on the floor. From it, he extracted two bottles of Holy Water, not the papal version, but the kind Riley usually bought, along with the cross, and the aspergillum. He handed the bottles to her.

"Make a consecrated circle around us, about ten feet in

diameter, but leave one spot open for now in case the fiend comes at us before we finish all our preparations."

As Riley did the scut work, he laid out his supplies, including various spheres. Once the circle was complete, she walked it, checking that there were no gaps except the one he'd requested.

"Now what?"

"We seal the exits."

Following his direction, they applied Holy Water to each potential escape route, including the fireplace and the windows. Even the heating duct and cold-air return. Simon was nothing if not thorough.

Meanwhile, there'd been not one bit of noise.

Maybe it's taken off. And maybe tomorrow its master would just wave a white flag, admit he was wrong, and give up the fight against Heaven. *Not happening.*

"Okay, close the circle," he said.

She laid the last bit of Holy Water in place and stepped back. Simon recited the Lord's Prayer in Latin, just like he had the night they sat vigil for her father, except this time there were no candles denoting the circle. To her surprise, the Holy Water glowed white like it was lit from within.

He looked over at her. "You ready?"

Riley nodded in response, not allowing her knees to knock. She was a trapper. This was just another job. She squared her shoulders and murmured a quiet prayer that she'd be alive tonight to tell Beck the exorcism had been no big deal.

Her companion took a deep breath.

"Demon! I am Simon Michael David Adler. I am a child of God, seeker of the Light, believer in the Risen Lord."

The power of his words sent shivers down her spine. This was still Simon, but not the boy she remembered. Not at all.

"You are trespassing here, foul fiend. Leave now, or perish!"

The stone fireplace began to bleed.

Chapter Twenty-Three

A loud buzzing came, like a swarm of irritated bees dumped out of a hive. It seemed to come out of the walls, the ceiling, the floor. The Holy Water flared brighter in response to the threat.

"I know of you, Simon the Betrayer," a voice said, oily and deep, raising goose bumps on Riley's skin. "Your heart is not as pure as you claim." Each word was elongated, full of cunning.

"You are an abomination unto the Lord and shall be driven from this place," Simon replied.

"Why do you care? This is not your dwelling. Do you think to remove the stink of your rotten soul by fair deeds? If so, you will fail. Your soul will be ours soon enough."

"God is my shield and sword. The Enemy will have no power over me and those who stand by me this day."

The blood rolling down the fireplace dried and cracked. A fire burst forth in the hearth now, and inside it Riley saw Hell. The flickering souls that lighted purgatory's walls, the moans and cries of the damned. The stench of demons and brimstone. In that instant, she was once again standing in front of the Prince, hundreds of demons behind her, all calling for her blood.

Lucifer sat on his throne, clad in armor, his sword lying across his knees. His voice boomed throughout the chamber. "Seek my enemies and destroy them. Side with them and your punishment will be eternal. This is your last warning. Now begone!"

Shocked, Simon asked, "Is that—?"

"Hell? Yes. Or at least how I saw it. It's different for everyone."

"That will be your eternal home," the demon continued.

"Your pretty words do not frighten me, Simon the Betrayer. I rule in this place. This is my domain."

Riley's mouth took off before she could stop herself. "Really? An empty library? That's your domain? Boy, you must really suck at being a demon if that's the best you can do."

Oops.

Curiously, Simon did not shush her like she'd expected. Instead he nodded his approval, indicating that he wanted her to get in the fiend's face. That, she could do easily.

Riley obligingly ramped up her attitude.

"Hey, demon!" she said, taking a step forward, mindful of the circle of Holy Water that protected them. "You know what Lucifer told me about you guys? You remember him? The Dark Prince who holds your leash? He hates all of you; he'd kill every one of you if he could, just because you're so stupid."

The fiend began hissing again.

"You know, he's right. Look at you! Living in someone else's empty house like a squatter. I bet a Klepto-Fiend has more brains than you."

A roar of anger pushed her back.

"Blackthorne's daughter! Foul child! Killer of the higher fiends!"

"Yup, that would be me. So what are you going to do about that, little boy?"

The instant the challenge was issued, the demon materialized in the wall, a creature no more than two feet tall. It was a Mezmer, a Grade Four Hellspawn, but different than the ones she'd trapped before. Its claws were much longer and its eyes reflected Hellfire like those of the bigger fiends. It demonstrated the power of those claws by swiping them against the expensive wood paneling, ripping it into thick splinters, which hurtled through the air toward them. Riley instinctively ducked as the spears slammed against the protective circle and bounced away.

Simon did not duck, and his voice grew stronger as he swung the aspergillum in the air, releasing the Holy Water. "The power of God is eternal. None shall stand against His mighty will. You are Lucifer's spawn and an abomination to all things. I cast you down and into bondage, in His holy name!"

Fire roared out of the hearth like a tornado, swirling around them with claws and teeth made of flames. The floor underneath them shook as if there were an earthquake, and the bank of windows shattered, sending shards of glass throughout the room. The circle bloomed around them, shielding them from the debris.

Petrified, Riley held herself still, knowing that to break the holy barrier was to die.

"Lord, purge this pitiful Hellspawn from this place, wash this house clean of the fiend's stench," Simon intoned. "Break the Enemy's spirit and cast him down in your unbreakable prison."

He switched to Latin now, reciting phrase after phrase that rolled off his tongue with no hesitation, as if they were sacred weapons. Riley could understand most of it, but it was the demon's reaction that most fascinated her.

Once powerful, the fiend cowered under the power of the ancient words. Twisting in agony, it gave a final tormented shout that shook the foundation of the house.

Then it vanished.

Riley jumped in surprise as the metal box rattled at her feet.

"Holy crap," she murmured, stunned. Simon had managed to imprison the thing *inside the circle*. She had no idea what kind of power that required, but she knew it was major.

"All glory be to God," Simon said, "for he is Master of all who dwell in Heaven, on Earth, and in Hell. *In nomine Patris et Filii et Spiritus Sancti,*" he said, crossing himself.

"Amen," she added, and meant it.

The box continued to vibrate, muted howls coming from within.

Simon didn't reply, but remained silent for another minute or two, as if slowly disengaging himself from the fight. Riley took that opportunity to look up toward the ceiling and give a heartfelt nod of thanks. That had been far too scary.

Finally he turned toward her and smiled. "Congratulations.

You've just exorcised your first demon."

"Ah, no, I just watched. You did all the heavy lifting."

"One of the most difficult things is to get the demon to lose control. You have a natural talent for it."

"Pissing off Hellspawn?" she said, smiling as well. "Yeah, that's my thing all right. Works on Guild officers and everyone else, too."

"Just so you know, this wasn't one of the really bad ones."

She looked over at the open space where the windows used to be, at the piles of glass and debris on the floor. A cold breeze blew into the room, ruffling her hair. "Really?"

"No, not at all. This one was a minor annoyance."

"If you say so." *Hope the homeowners have good insurance.*

The time felt right, so she dug in her pack and offered Simon a symbol of his tortured past. He stared at the charred wooden cross, the one he'd worn the night the Tabernacle was destroyed. The night he'd nearly died.

"You still kept it all these months," he said softly.

"You asked me to. If you're not ready for it yet, I'll hold onto it until you are."

"You didn't wash it."

The charring rubbed off on her fingers. "No. It seemed right somehow, you know?"

He nodded and took the holy object from her. "Like my faith. Charred, but not destroyed." He kissed the cross and tucked it away in his suitcase. When his eyes met hers, they were misty. "You are a blessing, you know that?"

"So are you, Simon Michael David Adler."

The box at her feet bumped again. She stared down at it. "Jack's gonna love this thing."

Simon didn't answer, but broke the holy circle, collected his various articles of faith, and repacked them. He trod carefully across the broken glass toward the door.

"We are going to Jack with this, aren't we?" she asked.

He looked back over his shoulder at her. "No. The Vatican isn't like the trappers."

"Which means?"

"You'll see soon enough."

~~*

The monastery was an hour south of the city, nestled in a quiet country setting with pines and gardens and walkways. Riley hadn't even known it was here. She made a mental note to come back in the late spring, maybe pack a picnic lunch and have some quiet time with Beck.

Simon pulled up to the main building and asked her to remain in the car until he introduced himself and produced the necessary paperwork. While she waited, the metal box at her feet kept quivering. She could hear the demon's voice in her mind, and it was loud enough to give her a headache. Clearly, the ones that possessed houses and people were much stronger than the fiends she usually trapped.

She'd sent Beck a text earlier, letting him know all had gone well. He only now responded.

TELL ME ABOUT IT TONIGHT. GOT STEAK FOR SUPPER.

She grinned. Her guy was definitely a carnivore.

Simon returned with a young monk at his side who was clad in blue jeans and a black T-shirt. To Riley's surprise, he hopped into the backseat. He was tanned and looked like he worked outdoors.

"Hi, I'm Friar Michael," he said.

"Hi. I'm Riley," she replied. "This is my first time here. It's very pretty."

"It is. We seek God's beauty in all ways."

Clearly they were doing it right.

Simon slid into the driver's seat and sent the car down a side road into the woods, where he finally pulled up close to a windowless metal shed. Once Friar Michael had unlocked the door, Riley followed Simon inside, carrying the metal box. The friar clicked on some lights and closed the heavy sliding door behind them.

Riley could only stare. Each of the four walls was adorned with a large, ornate cross. Around each cross were Latin inscriptions. Even the ceiling had a cross in the very center, as did the floor.

When she ventured deeper into the room, she felt something brush against her skin. Some might claim it was magic, but she knew better—it was the power of faith itself.

In the very center of the space was a marble dais, resting directly on top of the floor's large cross. On top of it sat a sturdy cage, large enough to hold a person as long as they remained on their knees. It was constructed of fine metal and had to have cost a lot of money. When Riley moved closer, she could see religious symbols engraved into every inch of the metal.

"Is this like a demonic holding tank or something?"

"Only for a short duration," the friar replied.

He swung open the gate, took the box from Riley, and set it inside. The gate swung shut and clicked.

"So how does this work?"

"This building sits on holy ground," he said.

"But the demon isn't actually touching it."

"The power of this place will reach through its prison and destroy it."

"Really?"

As if in response, a shriek came from the box as the container thrashed around inside the cage. Riley gritted her teeth until the screams died, along with the demon.

"*Deo sit omnis gloria,*" the friar intoned.

"Amen," Simon murmured.

Friar Michael opened the cage, removed the metal box, and took it outside, where he dumped the demon's ashes on the ground. They glowed brilliant red for a moment and then turned silvery gray. During the next rain they'd be absorbed into the soil.

Rome: 1. Hell: 0.

"I always thought you guys were all about praying over the fiends, not killing them. Well, except for your Demon Hunters."

"These particular demons, if they gain their freedom, will promptly return to the location where they were captured," the monk said. "Often with tragic results."

Simon nodded. "They've been known to take revenge on those they find in the building, or the person they originally possessed."

"Oh." That explained everything. "Better dead, then."

"That's the way we view it," Friar Michael said.

~~*

After a visit to the monastery's gift shop, Riley and Simon headed toward home. She waited a while, then asked the question she'd been thinking about since the exorcism.

"I'm confused. I thought once a trafficker sold a demon to the Vatican, the monks prayed over the fiends and they vanished. Now you're saying Rome kills them?" Simon nodded in response. "Even the little ones?"

"They're still Hellspawn."

She winced at the thought of her little burglar getting snuffed.

"There's more to it than just that, isn't there?"

Now her companion looked uncomfortable. "If you really want answers, ask Beck," he replied, which told her Simon knew more than he was telling her.

"More secrets, right?"

"More like hidden truths. Ask him. Maybe he can tell you."

"I will."

I bet he won't give me a straight answer either.

Chapter Twenty-Four

Beck found his fiancée sitting on the couch, staring at nothing. She looked up at him, nodded, and went back to staring. He locked the door behind him, placed his trapping bag in the front closet, and then plopped down on the couch next to her.

"You aren't all chewed up or anythin'. That's a good sign. Better than trappin, then."

"Yeah."

"So what was it like?"

She stirred from her mental holiday. "It was off-the-charts creepy. You know, I'm used to demons snarling and clawing and trying to get into my head, but seeing one come out of a wall is a whole new thing."

"It does freak you out."

She blinked in surprise. "You've seen an exorcism?"

"Yeah, in Glasgow. It's part of the grand master training. This priest summoned a Four out of a little old lady. Like you said, it was creepy."

"Simon kicked butt. He was rock solid. This is exactly what he's supposed to be doing."

"Then it all worked out for the best," Beck observed.

"I think it did. We took the thing to a monastery south of town. They put the demon on holy ground and killed it." She looked over at him. "Then I bought some fruitcake from the monastery's gift shop."

"Dessert after our steak tonight?" he asked.

"No. It's going to Stewart's place for Christmas Eve dinner."

"You are a cruel woman."

She ignored that. "Why do trappers sell the demons, rather than kill them like the Vatican does. Why go to all the hassle?"

Beck sighed. He'd known this would eventually arise, but not quite so soon.

"It has to do with the balance between the Light and Dark. I can't tell you much more than that. You'll find out if you become a master."

"If? What happened to your 'we'll fight them and win' speech?"

He wisely kept his mouth shut, knowing she'd growl at him no matter what he said.

"Where do the grand masters fall on this scale of Light and Dark?"

"In the exact middle. Or at least, that's where we should be. It doesn't always work out that way."

"You can't explain it any better than that?"

He shook his head. Riley's frown returned again, and that meant there was more.

"What else is buggin' you?" he asked.

"Besides all the stuff you can't tell me?"

"Besides that."

He watched as her anger diminished. "I'm worried about Ayden. It's scaring me that she's been so quiet."

"What's this Morgaine lady like?"

"Arrogant, pushy, with a serious case of ego."

That meant he might have something to work with there. Instead of letting Riley know what he had in mind, Beck switched topics. "How's about I grill the steak and then we each open a present?"

Riley blinked at the abrupt subject change. "It's not Christmas yet."

"It's Christmas somewhere, right?"

"Ah, no, not really," she said, smiling. "Well, maybe one little present. What can it hurt?"

He hugged her. "Yer so easy."

"In your dreams, Backwoods Boy. Only in your dreams."

~~*

Beck found the Terminus Market adorned with Christmas lights and crowded with holiday shoppers, all hustling around buying gifts: a new skillet, a woven basket, a handcrafted rocking chair. Despite the festive atmosphere, as he wandered among the market tents he found himself remembering the day the demons rampaged through here, killing and maiming. There was no sign of the carnage now, other than a permanent shrine to the dead located at one of the market's entrances.

He had told Riley he had some things to do, but hadn't bothered to mention where he was headed, or that the things were witch related. Although she'd given him a skeptical look, she hadn't challenged him on his half-truth, as if somehow knowing it was best not to ask.

The witches' midnight-blue tent was easy to find; all you had to look for were the silver and gold stars. There were two witches present, one of whom was Ayden. That hadn't been by chance; Beck had texted her to find out her schedule, and whether Morgaine was working tonight. The answers had both been in the affirmative.

"Beck," she said, her face breaking into a smile. "Goddess, look at you." She came out from behind the table of goods, and they hugged.

"Riley sends her best," he murmured.

Ayden's smile dimmed. "I miss her." She shot a quick look behind her to the witch at the far end of the table, who had her hands crossed over her chest, frowning.

"That's Morgaine?" he whispered.

"Uh-huh," Ayden replied, her voice tight.

"She's the reason yer not able to teach Riley now?"

"Yes. The other witches are undecided, but she raised a huge stink."

He scratched an ear thoughtfully. "Got a big ego?"

"Oh, Goddess, yes."

"Let's see what I can do with that."

Beck moved over to the table, looking at it like he was eager to buy something.

"What do you suggest for a young woman who's learnin' spells and such?" he asked, addressing Morgaine directly.

She gave Ayden a look, then returned her attention to him. "What kind?"

"Summoner magic. She was just accepted into their society."

Morgaine huffed. "That's not real magic."

Beck met her gaze. "Well, it's the best she could get. Seems you people didn't want her to learn *yer* kind, so she went somewhere else."

Morgaine blinked. "I don't understand." Then it dawned. "Are you talking about the Blackthorne girl?"

"Yup. The summoners were really happy to have her. Didn't even start with the light-gray robe, either."

Morgaine frowned. "What did they assign her?"

"Blue. Seems she's got some talent." He poked at an amethyst crystal on the table. "What about this? Think she'd like it?"

Morgaine's mouth had dropped open. "Blue? But . . . "

"I told you she had talent," Ayden said. She switched her attention to Beck. "For Riley, I'd recommend the bloodstone. It's the dark-green stone with the red spots. It increases energy and strength and also grounds and centers. She needs all of that."

"Definitely on the groundin' and centerin'," Beck replied. "She's a whirlwind on two feet."

He looked over at Morgaine, who had finally regained her composure. Was she going to get on the team, or continue to be a pain in the ass?

"I agree," Morgaine said. "She seemed a bit . . . agitated the last time I saw her."

He picked up the stone, examining it. "Probably because you left her glued to the pavement in Oakland Cemetery. That'd piss anyone off."

Morgaine's frown was back again. "She needs to learn respect."

Ayden laughed. "You don't get it. She's not a follower,

Morgaine. She's a trailblazer. Like her fiancé here."

The other witch studied him closer now. "Just who are you?"

"Denver Beck," he said. "I'm a demon trapper and a grand master in the International Trappers Guild." He wasn't quite there yet, not until he went through the official ceremony. Still, the other masters called him that, so he'd decided to own it.

The woman's face actually paled. "I . . . didn't know."

"Now you do." He offered the bloodstone to Ayden. "I'll take this for Riley. She'll like it. She's been puttin' things in the bag you gave her."

"Good. She needs all the protection she can get." Ayden rang up the purchase. "Of course, now that she's with the summoners, that won't be as much of a problem. I'm just sorry we couldn't have taught her our kind of magic."

"So is she."

As Ayden handed him the stone, all wrapped in tissue paper and inside a small plastic bag, Morgaine spoke up. "Um, I didn't realize she was that . . . interested."

When Ayden tensed, he hoped she would hold her tongue.

"Maybe we should rethink this situation," Morgaine added. "I mean, it wouldn't be right if she only learned magic from *them*, would it?"

"That'd be Riley's decision, not mine," Beck said. He nodded to Ayden. "Thanks. You have a blessed Yule, now, you hear?"

"Merry Christmas to you," she replied, winking.

Then Beck walked away, leaving behind the fertile seed he'd planted.

Stewart and MacTavish had taught him that a person's insecurities are often their weakest link. If he was lucky, his conversation would bear fruit. It certainly wouldn't be an apology, at least not from Morgaine, but if it got Riley back with her friend and the opportunity to learn witchy magic, then his evening had been well spent. He'd even scored her another Christmas present to boot.

Win-win.

Chapter Twenty-Five

Riley's first day of trapping without using magic sucked. Big time. She got stuck with the little fiends, the Magpies and the Biblios, while her three apprentices went trapping Threes with Master Harper.

By the afternoon, she was one big angry mess, ready to explode. Beck, she'd noticed, had kept a respectful distance as she'd trapped, but he'd been watching her back. Which pissed her off even more. He was a grand master, for God's sake, not a freaking babysitter.

They had just sold some fiends to one of the demon traffickers. Her grand total for the day: three Ones. It was pathetic. Even the trafficker had remarked on that.

"Anyone you want me to catch so you can kick the crap out of them?" Beck asked, sensing her mood as they left the shop.

"Yeah, I got a few people," she shot back. "Starting with Northrup. What's Jerkface up to now that he's usurped Harper?"

"Nothin' that we can tell."

"Huh. Are you sure the National Guild is okay with what he's doing?"

Beck paused at his truck, keys in hand. "You know, that's a damned good question. Might be time to find out."

Before she could reply, his phone buzzed. "Beck. Hey, Jackson. Yeah, we can do that. Get a beer later? Good. See you then."

He ended the call and smiled over at her. "How's about we go trap a Four?"

"You know I can't—"

"I know what you can do, and what you can't. You can still be backup while I catch the thing."

"All right, but this pisses me off."

"Really? I hadn't noticed," he said, then chuckled. "Not. At. All."

She snarled at him, and that made him laugh.

Keep it up, dude. Just keep it up.

~~*

They'd just finished supper, tired from the successful capture of the Four at the convention center, when Riley's phone rang.

"Hey, Simon. How's it going?"

"Not good. I need your help. Beck's too, if he's free."

She looked over at her guy. "An exorcism?"

"Yes. It's going to be a rough one. It's a little girl. She's five and won't live to see the new year if we don't get this thing out of her soon."

Oh, my God.

"Hold on." Riley covered the phone and explained the situation.

"I'm in. Just tell me when and where," Beck replied, his voice hardening to steel. Mention that a kid was in trouble and he was all over it.

Riley returned to the call. "We're both in. Where do you need us?" She took down the address Simon provided on a piece of paper from the kitchen.

"If you have a cross, or some other religious item, wear it. This is one of the bad boys. Usually Father Hicks would handle this, but he's conducting an exorcism in Athens at the moment and we can't wait any longer."

The tension vibrating through his voice made her shiver.

"Got it. We'll be there." She ended the call, thinking through all that Simon had told her.

"Bad?" Beck said, already restocking his trapping bag.

"Yeah. He's scared. I could hear it in his voice."

"Then it's good that it's the three of us."

As he packed, she headed for the bedroom and her jewelry box. Inside she found her mother's cross. When she returned to the living room, she offered it to him.

"Simon wants us fully protected. It was my mom's."

"But what about you?" he asked, tucking it into his pocket.

She held up her left hand, the one with the crown embedded in the palm. "I'm good."

Beck bent closer, kissed her, and whispered, "Yes, you are."

~~*

The house was big, somewhere between McMansion and a castle. Maybe demons preferred the fancier places. Why try to steal a soul in a run-down house with a leaky roof and bad plumbing?

Simon was already there, fidgeting with the gear in his trunk. Unlike at the last exorcism, his movements telegraphed his worry.

"You have any idea how many exorcisms the Vatican makes these guys do before they're on their own?" Riley asked as Beck turned off the truck's engine.

"I'm guessin' it's quite a few. Looks bad if one of them dies, and the Vatican doesn't like bad press."

"He's way spooked," she said. "He wasn't this way the last time."

"Then whatever's in there is big trouble."

Once they were out of the vehicle, Beck slipped his backpack over his shoulder. To Riley, it appeared heavier than usual. As they approached Simon, he turned toward them. He wore his charred cross, and she smiled at that.

When he saw her looking at it, Simon touched it reverently. "I thought that I might need this today. That if I could survive the Tabernacle . . . "

He could survive whatever was waiting for them in the house.

Okay, now I'm really freaked out.

The McMansion appeared normal—no Hellfire flaring out the windows, no swarms of demons crawling on the roof, nothing to show that evil resided inside. Still, Riley felt the cold even here on the lawn, rolling out in waves toward her. She closed her eyes and tried to follow the thread, and then felt herself breaking out in a sweat, her heart pounding erratically.

Her concentration wavered when a black BMW pulled into the driveway and parked.

"This should be the little girl's parents," Simon explained.

As they climbed out of the vehicle, it was easy to see that the couple had been through nearly as much hell as their daughter. They were both listless, exhausted, with bluish-black smudges under their eyes that spoke of little sleep. Their clothes were wrinkled, their lives in tatters, a suburban dream turned into a hellish nightmare.

Simon stepped up to them. "I'm Simon Adler. You're Mr. and Mrs. Gill?"

The man nodded. He looked over at Riley, then at Beck. "I was told there would only be two of you."

"I decided it was best to have a third person in on this. Beck is a grand master with the International Demon Trappers Guild."

"You came all the way to Georgia to help us?" the wife asked, her eyes widening.

"No, ma'am. I live here in Atlanta. I was home for the holidays."

"Oh, I see."

"Riley is a journeyman demon trapper. They both have considerable experience with Hellspawn," Simon continued.

"Carrina's only five. Why would this happen to her?" the woman sobbed, tears trickling down her face. Mr. Gill put a reassuring arm around his wife's waist.

"It just does," Simon replied. "It's nothing you did wrong. Hell will target just about anyone."

"But what kind of god lets that happen?" the mother asked.

"The kind that has sent us to help you," Simon replied softly.

"Don't worry, we'll get your little girl out of there," Beck said.

He sounded so confident. His words, and the way he delivered them, gave the parents hope, and Simon a needed dose of courage. If Riley was honest, she needed that courage as well.

Another car pulled up, and this time a portly man in a clerical collar joined them.

"I'm Father Vonn, the Gills' priest," he said, offering his hand.

Simon shook it and made the introductions.

"You're Paul Blackthorne's daughter?" the man asked.

"Yes, I am."

"Father Harrison spoke of him with great fondness. I'm sorry for your loss."

"Thank you."

Simon shifted weight on his feet, then beckoned them away from the couple.

He addressed the priest. "Keep them out here, *no matter what happens*. It's far too dangerous for any of you to come inside the house. You understand?"

"It won't be easy, but I'll try. It was hard asking them to stay away from their daughter today, but they were too close to the breaking point." Vonn paused. "We'll pray for your success."

"Thank you," Simon said, then looked up at the building. "We're going to need it."

The trek to the front door seemed to last forever. The cold continued to grow, then suddenly switched to heat, then back to cold.

Now that's just eerie. A quick glance at Beck told Riley he was feeling the same thing.

Simon set his suitcase on a cedar bench on the porch, opened it, and handed Riley the Holy Water. She poured a small amount into his hand and he anointed himself. She drew the heart on her forehead and also put some of the sacred liquid on her left palm. When she turned toward Beck, she wondered what he'd do.

"What did you put on your forehead?" he asked.

"A heart. Because love is stronger than evil."

A caring smile came her way. "I'll do the same, then."

He performed the anointing, and they were ready to go inside.

Knowing the Gills couldn't hear her, Riley asked, "Was the house haunted before?"

"The parents say it wasn't, but sometimes there might be an entity present that they don't know about. They just moved in over Thanksgiving. The girl began to act odd a week ago. At first they thought she was sick, until things started flying around the room."

"So the demon could have been here all along," Beck said.

"Possible. It took several months for the house to sell," Simon said.

"Don't worry, we can do this," Riley said. "We've all faced worse than this thing."

"May God grant us victory," Simon replied.

The interior of the house was as nice as the outside. A stone-tiled foyer led to a large living room with a bank of tall windows overlooking a manicured backyard. At the far end of the room was a huge Christmas tree, beneath which were countless presents. Three embroidered stockings were tacked to the mantel: Mom, Dad, and Carrina.

"What a hell of a Christmas," Beck said.

"The little girl is upstairs in her bedroom," Simon said. "We have to get the demon out of Carrina without harming her. She's too young to grant it her soul, so the fiend won't care if she dies."

"Then why would it mess with her in the first place?" Riley asked.

"Leverage," Beck replied. "The parents' souls are its target."

"What mom or dad wouldn't want to save their kid?" Simon said. "Father Vonn has been keeping them from taking that final step, but if we fail, one or both of them are going to become this demon's possession." He took a deep breath. "Then, when Carrina's old enough, the fiend will probably guilt her into giving up her own soul because of her parents' sacrifice. It's happened before."

Riley glowered up the stairs, furious. "Then let's get this damned thing out of here."

"Her bedroom is at the end of the hall," Simon said, leading them up the stairs.

It was like every horror movie Beck had ever watched as a kid. What else was he supposed to do when his mother was out drinking all night? The movies had scared him, but he'd still watched them because sometimes the things on television were less frightening than real life.

He'd learned some vital lessons from those movies—never wander off on your own, never turn your back on an open door, and never forget that you're the prey.

Not this time around.

"Hold up a minute," he said. As the others waited, he extracted the one weapon he hoped he wouldn't have to use. The Glock was in a paddle holster, and he attached it to his belt.

"Holy Water bullets?" Simon asked.

"Yeah, Elias sent me some after I tangled with the Archangel. Sort of a 'congrats, yer still alive' gift. Haven't had a call to use them yet."

"As long as the fiend is still inside her, it's safe and it knows it."

"Yeah, that's the problem."

After pulling out a steel pipe, he handed Riley his pack. They both knew there'd be spheres in there that she wasn't supposed to use.

"Don't argue with me on this," he warned.

"Not going to," she said, shouldering it.

The hallway was strewn with refuse. Pieces of cracked wallboard, light switches hanging loose on the walls. Stinking garbage. Like Demon Central, but with a much better address.

"Makes Hell look good," Riley said, shaking her head. "The demon did all this?"

"Just trying to ramp up the terror. You take over a small

child's mind, then go crazy. The parents won't harm their daughter, so the fiend can do anything it wants," Simon replied.

They shuffled through the trash.

"It's too quiet," Riley said.

"I was thinkin' the same thing," Beck replied.

They were about ten feet from the girl's bedroom when a glow formed around the edges of the door. It was bright red, and for a second, Beck swore he could see flames. The door rattled, then began to bulge. He remembered this from one of the movies, and instinct took over.

"Get down!" He grabbed Riley and shoved her to the floor, covering her with his body as the portal exploded toward them in a shower of lethal wood. The shards impaled themselves into the walls like spears.

Once the missiles had ended, he called out. "You okay, Simon?"

"Yeah, I'm good. Filthy, but good."

As Beck regained his feet, he saw the fire in Riley's eyes.

"You didn't have to throw yourself on top of me. I'm not stupid. You tell me to take cover and I'll do it."

"Sorry, I had no choice." He looked over at Simon, who was dusting off his clothes. "It's part of the man code."

"It is," Simon replied. "Doesn't mean you can't handle yourself. Just means he doesn't want you hurt."

Riley frowned, first at her ex-boyfriend, then at Beck, but it didn't make any difference.

"Next time I might do the same to you," she said.

"Fine by me," Beck replied, which was the diplomatic answer, rather than the truth.

Riley was still muttering under her breath about macho pigheaded males as Simon led the way into the little girl's room. It must have been pretty before the demon came to call, but no longer. The white walls had scorch marks on them, as did the tattered pink-and-white polka-dot curtains. The bed frame was in pieces, each piece an excellent weapon. Sections of the ceiling were now underfoot, as was broken glass and who knew what else.

"It looks like a damned war zone," Beck said.

"In more ways than one," Simon replied. "It'll be impossible to put down the Holy Water with this mess. That was probably its plan."

"Guys . . . " Riley said, pointing.

In a corner, Carrina nested in a circle of dolls. The little girl was pretty—her hair falling in golden ringlets, her cheeks rosy, her eyes a deep blue. Her dress had ponies on it, and her shoes were pink with little sparkly bows.

Her smile revealed the one thing the demon didn't bother to hide: twin rows of razor-sharp teeth.

Beck's flesh crawled over his bones.

Chapter Twenty-Six

"Give it up, demon. We know what you're doing," Simon said. "That's not what she looks like, not with you inside of her."

The little girl rose from the sea of dolls, cocking her head, studying them.

Then her blue eyes slitted like a goat's.

"Simon the Betrayer!" she said, though the voice was anything but childlike. More like something from your blackest nightmare, the scrape of ten thousand demon claws against the inside of your skull.

"I hate it when they do that," Simon said, shaking his head.

"Blackthorne's daughter!"

"Good. I was feeling left out," Riley said.

"Angel Killer! Destroyer of Demons! Hated Enemy of Hell!" the thing shouted at Beck.

"Hey, no fair, you got three names," she said, grinning over at him.

"I earned 'em," he replied, winking back. "How's this goin' down, Simon?"

The exorcist-in-chief took a worried look around them. "We can't set a protective circle, so we're just going to have to wing it. If you two could watch my back, that would be good. I'm going to be totally occupied trying to cast the demon out of the child." He looked over at Riley now. "Once she's free, get her out of the building."

"What about you guys?"

"We'll be okay. Do yer thing, we'll do ours," Beck replied.

"Got it."

Riley took a position behind and to the left of Simon. Beck was in a similar position to the right. Simon pulled out his gear, held up a large wooden cross, and announced himself to the demon.

"Hear me, spawn of Hell. I am Simon Michael David Adler, child of God, seeker of the Light, believer in the Risen Lord. I know of your evil and I call you forth in God's holy name!"

In response to his challenge, the little girl shifted in appearance, her hair turning straggly and unwashed, hanging in greasy strands, her pretty dress filthy and torn. There were dried tears on her puffy and bruised face.

For a brief second Riley could see the fear, the desperate pleading in her eyes, and then they changed from the deep blue to a fiery red, the child subsumed by the demon.

The debris began to shift around their feet, moving as if inhabited by snakes. The instant she thought that, a slithering sound began, following by hissing.

"It's feeding off our thoughts," Riley cautioned.

Beck nodded and began to hum to himself, no doubt one of Carrie Underwood's songs.

Riley devoted her mind to reviewing her last Latin assignment. *Present tense, fourth conjugation. Remove re from infinitive, add amus to the stem.*

The noise in the room settled down, as did the movement at their feet. Simon continued on, Latin pouring forth, still holding up the cross, his arm shaking from the exertion. The demon rocked back and forth on its feet, as if searching for a weakness. Then it stared at Beck and grinned.

The back wall of the bedroom vanished, replaced by a scene she didn't recognize: a long corridor with things embedded in the walls. Gradually a single figure appeared in the hallway, shuffling away with his back to them.

Even Simon grew silent, caught by the scene playing out in front of them.

"Oh, sweet Jesus," Beck said. "Not that."

"Is that you in Hell, after you killed Sartael?" Riley asked.

He nodded, swallowing hard. Sweat had popped out on his forehead, and he shivered now. Riley watched, riveted, as he slowly dragged his gravely injured body down the corridor. Once, he stumbled too close to a wall, stared at it, then shied away in horror.

"There were faces in the walls," he said. "They wanted me to set them free. I knew if I did . . . I'd be there with them forever."

Her time in Hell had been full of demons. His had been stark loneliness. Or maybe not, as now Lucifer appeared in the scene. She couldn't hear what was being said between them, but she knew what the Prince was offering.

Beck shook his head, then waved the Fallen angel away with an angry gesture. The Prince disappeared, and the man she loved continued down the corridor, dying with each step. She remembered sitting by his bed, holding his hand, praying that he'd come back to her. And he had.

The scene froze, as if it were playing off a disc. Riley knew exactly why it had ended there—the demon did not want Beck to see his mother saving him from eternal torment.

It was time to break the fiend's hold.

"Hey, Beck? You survived that. This is nothing but a bad rerun."

He acted as if he hadn't heard her.

"Den! Remember that heart on your forehead? That's what your mother did for you, at the very last. She didn't have to, but she loved you in her own way. That's our best weapon against these things."

The demon didn't like that and growled at her. "Love is a lie," it hissed.

"No, it's not. It's what you can never feel. So give it up. The girl is ours, and we're not leaving without her."

The dolls at the feet of the fiend began to stir, standing up like an army. From the tiniest of them to the biggest, their mouths sprouted teeth and their eyes became as fiery red as the demon's.

"Beck?" Simon called out. "We need you to be with us *now*."

The urgency in their companion's voice must have reached him. He shook himself, then blinked as if awakening from a nightmare.

"Yeah, I'm here." He glowered at the fiend. "Lucifer didn't get my soul then, and yer not gettin' it now."

Simon began intoning in Latin again, this time with more strength and insistence.

"Bring it, demon," Beck said, beckoning.

The dolls went mobile, springing into the air, claws and teeth extended as they dive-bombed Riley and the others.

She stepped closer to Simon, bashing the flying bodies with her pipe. Beck was doing the same, trying to keep the dolls away from their friend. One clamped onto her arm, biting through her jacket. She tore it off and threw it against the wall.

How could they stop this thing without hurting the little girl?

For a moment, Riley was free of the aerial menaces, and she stepped back to regain her breath. Simon might eventually break the Hellspawn's hold, but right now they weren't winning this battle.

Beck shot a glance in her direction, pulling another doll off his chest and stomping it with a boot. "Any ideas?"

She shook her head. "It's not backing off."

Out of the corner of her eye, she saw something shift in the debris near the bed. Whatever it was rose slowly above the ruined mattress and hovered in the air. It was diaphanous, the walls of the room visible through it. In some ways it appeared angelic, but the serrated claws and long, sharp canines put an end to that comparison.

"Heads up, we got a second Hellspawn in the air," she said.

Simon hesitated for a fraction of a second, then carried on, his focus solely on the fiend in front of him. Beck shot a quick glance her way, then turned back toward Simon.

"Can you handle it?" he asked.

"Got no other choice," she replied.

Riley dug out a Holy Water sphere. The Guild might find out, but right now, that didn't matter. Getting dead just wasn't an option.

As Simon's voice rose in a punch of Latin and he swung the aspergillum in an arc, the air demon shrieked and dove right at her. Desperate to time it right, she waited until the last moment, then threw the sphere straight at its face. It veered but the glass shattered against its shoulder. Wounded, the fiend went into a spin, sweeping Riley off her feet and into the trash on the floor.

She rolled away from the claws, regained her feet, and bashed the thing across its head with her steel pipe. Her blow hit true, and the fiend shrieked in agony and fell, stunned. Riley pulled another sphere out of Beck's pack and slam-dunked it into the demon's face. Its eyes blazed with pain, then it melted into the floorboards, a gray sludge that made her stomach churn and nearly empty.

Her chest heaving and her heart pounding, Riley readied herself for the next assault.

"You okay?" Beck called out.

"I'm good."

Simon took a deep breath. "Foul spirit, hated by all angels in Heaven, I cast you out of this child in the name of the Father, the Son, and the Holy Spirit!" he cried. "Be gone, dweller of the pit, spawn of Lucifer! I command you in God's holy name!"

Something shifted in the air, like a pressure change before a massive storm. Riley's ears popped and her head spun. The demon roared in fury, though it still looked like the little girl.

"She's free!" Simon called. "Get her out of here!"

"Where the hell is she?" Beck said.

"Carrina?" Riley cried. "Honey, where are you?"

A faint whimper came from the mound of covers that had once graced the bed, now piled in the corner. Riley dove at the pile and unearthed a small, pallid face with two dull-blue eyes, surrounded by a tangled mop of blond hair.

"Carrina?" she asked. *Are you real, or another demon?*

The girl raised her head, tears flowing freely. "I want my momma!" she cried. Her thread was weak, a mix of slimy gray and pink. It didn't feel like an illusion to Riley, but what if she was wrong?

Trust your gut, her father's voice echoed in her head.

"I've got her!" she shouted.

A furious bellow filled the room as the demon shed its glamour, growing to some seven feet in height, its skin purest black and its eyes filled with billowing Hellfire. Nude, it was impossible to ignore that it was male.

Ohmigod. She'd never seen a fiend like this before.

"Blackthorne's daughter!" it bellowed. "Give me the child!"

"Get screwed, demon," Riley shouted, taking a cautious step backward. "No way you get this girl again."

The walls quaked around them. "Give me the child, Ori's whore. Give me the child or I shall rend the flesh from your bones. I shall cleave my body into yours and—"

"We're done," Beck snarled. The gun barked twice as he put one bullet in the fiend's head, followed by one in the chest.

The demon shuddered, stunned, its eyes widening. When it hit the floor, the room shook. A cloud of choking brimstone rose as it died in writhing agony.

Riley shielded the little body in her arms, feeling the child shiver in terror. Making the sign of the cross, Simon slowly turned toward them, his face ashen. As his shock lessened, he reached for his phone and sent a text, no doubt letting Father Vonn know the child was safe.

Still glowering, Beck walked to a window and shoved it open, taking deep breaths.

The fresh breeze reached her and Riley inhaled deeply.

"How did you know she wasn't another demon?" Simon asked. "Was it because of Heaven's mark?"

"No. I just trusted my instincts." *Thanks, Dad.*

Once the air cleared, Riley realized the child in her arms was very stinky, and though she doubted Carrina's parents would care, she knew what she had to do.

"Guys? You need me for anything?"

They both shook their heads.

"Carrina needs a quick shower. She smells too much like

that thing, and I don't want her parents seeing her like this."

"I'll go on down, tell them everything's okay. That'll buy you some time," Simon replied.

"I'll wait up here for you," Beck said.

Always the protector.

Riley walked out into the hallway, making soothing noises. The child kept whimpering, shooting anxious glances as if she expected the demons to return and claim her.

"Carrina? I'm Riley. You're safe now, honey. Both the demons are gone now. They can't hurt you anymore."

"Bad . . . hurt . . . burn . . . "

"I know. Let's get you cleaned up, okay? Then we can go see your mommy and daddy."

The little girl seemed too shocked to understand what was happening. It took some wandering, but Riley found the master bedroom. As she entered the room, Carrina finally stirred to life.

"Not 'posed to be here."

"I'm sure your mommy and daddy won't mind."

In the huge bathroom, Riley stripped off the child's filthy clothes and threw them in the trash. Then she swore under her breath. The kid was a patchwork of bruises.

"Hurts," Carrina said, rubbing at one of them.

"The big demon did that to you?"

She nodded. "When I cried."

Which would make her cry more, generating an endless round of torment.

Riley helped the child into the shower, and the instant the water hit her skin, she began to cry again. They shampooed her hair, which was short, hacked, like someone had gone at it with scissors.

"Did the demon make you cut your hair?"

The little girl nodded. "It hurt Hector."

"Hector?"

"My kitty."

By "hurt," Riley suspected the kid meant the cat was dead.

Burn forever, demon.

"I'm so sorry, honey. Did I tell you about Max?" As she finished washing the girl, Riley launched into some of her funnier Max-the-neighbor-cat tales, carefully avoiding the ones that involved anything demonic.

"He's big and fluffy. *Really* big," Riley explained, drying off her own arms. She was nearly as wet as the little girl.

Carrina looked up into her eyes. "You don't have a kitty?"

Riley shook her head. "No. Maybe someday."

"Maybe me too," she replied.

The shower seemed to have helped. They always had for Riley, getting the demonic stink off her. Now it would be up to the kid's parents to help her heal from the trauma. It certainly was going to take a lot of time and love.

"That's better," she said, pushing the girl's wet hair out of her face. Two sad blue eyes looked back up at her, and Riley's heart cracked. The tears came without notice.

Carrina held out her arms and Riley pulled her closer, hugging her tightly.

"You'll be okay. It'll be scary for a while, but soon you'll forget all about those nasty demons."

The little girl shook her head. "No. Never." She pulled herself out of Riley's arms. "Why did you come to my house?"

"Because of you. This is what I do. I help little girls get away from bad things."

"Can I do that when I'm big?"

It was such a solemn question that Riley answered it honestly.

"Yes, you can. Someday, if you want, you can fight the bad things too."

The girl gave a single determined nod as if that reply had decided her future. If the look in this child's traumatized eyes meant anything, Lucifer had just made a lifelong enemy.

A few minutes later they exited the bedroom, Carrina dressed in a white, adult-sized bathrobe and a pair of her mom's panties, knotted on the sides to keep them in place. It was the best they could do, as her clothes were in her room and no way would Riley subject the kid to that scene.

Beck met them in the hallway. "The parents are gettin' worried. Luckily they didn't hear the gunshots."

"Noisy demons have a purpose in life," Riley replied.

Carrina took one look at him and shied back.

"He's okay. This is Beck. He killed the demon." The child blinked at him, then at Riley. "He's a good guy. I swear it."

"Do you have a kitty?" the girl asked, all serious.

"No," he said. "But I have a rabbit."

Carrina blinked. "Bunny?"

"Yeah. Her name is Rennie and she's way cool." Beck quickly pulled out his phone and showed her a picture of his rabbit. "See?"

A tentative smile teased the corners of Carrina's lips. Then she held out her arms, wanting to be held. For a moment, Beck hesitated. Riley gave him a look that said he better not back away, not with this little one.

So he picked her up and settled her in his arms, smiling down at her. "You're the bravest little girl I've ever seen."

Carrina gazed up at him. "I was . . . ssscared."

"So was I, but it's okay to be scared. When I have a little girl, I hope she's as brave as you."

And in that hopscotch way of thinking that small children possess, she asked, "What does the bunny eat? Carrots?"

As Beck told her all about his rabbit, Riley trailed along beside them, marveling at how he'd put the kid at ease. He was a natural. When there was a pause as Carrina thought up another question, Beck angled his head toward the child in his arms.

"Someday?" he asked.

She smiled back. "Someday."

You are going to be an awesome father.

The instant they exited the house, there was a cry from Carrina's mother and Beck was besieged by weeping parents. Once the girl dove into her mom's arms, her father put his arms around both of them.

"My baby! Oh my God, my baby!" Mrs. Gill sobbed.

Riley teared up at the reunion. Then she noticed someone

standing next to the priest and Simon. Someone very familiar.

Justine Armando. Her personal nemesis.

"Did you know she was going to be here?" Riley asked as Beck rejoined her.

"Nope."

"If she hits on you, I swear to God I will rip her to pieces," she said under her breath.

"Not likely, since she's married. But still, I'd like to see that. It'd be a tough fight. I bet those heels of hers could be lethal weapons." He grinned over at Riley. "But I'd put my money on you every time."

"Why does she always show up when I look like crap? It's like the universe sends her a text message or something."

Beck laughed and ran his arm around her waist. "I love you, even when yer lookin' all jealous."

With a smile, Justine broke away from the priest and walked over to join them.

"Beck, Riley, good to see you again."

Just like we're old friends.

They did owe Justine. Her own brand of tenacious come-hell-or-high-water journalism had helped clear Beck of two murders in his hometown.

"Justine. How goes it?" he asked, his voice warmer than she'd expected.

"It goes well. I'm doing a series of articles on the increasing need for exorcisms in the U.S. I talked to Father Rosetti and he suggested a couple of cities, one of which was Atlanta. When I called the diocese, they said there was an exorcism scheduled today. I had no idea it involved you and Riley."

"Well, yer timin' is good, as always."

Justine hesitated. "I hear you two are engaged. Congratulations."

"Yeah, we are. Hopin' to set a date soon," he said, giving Riley the side-eye.

Just guilt me in front of your ex-girlfriend.

"Thanks," Riley replied. "It'll probably be sometime in the

spring. It's been kinda busy lately."

Justine nodded. "I heard from a source that the National Guild is being draconian with the local Guild, that Master Harper is no longer in charge." She zeroed in on Riley. "Is it true that you've been ordered not to use any magic?"

Once a reporter, always nosy.

"Yes. Which limits how I can handle trapping demons."

Justine frowned. "Why in Heaven's name would they do that?"

"I have no idea," Riley replied.

"Care to answer a few questions about the exorcism?"

"Officially, we're not here," Beck replied. "Unofficially, that was one badass demon. Two actually."

"And the little girl? Will she be okay?"

Riley answered, looking over at Carrina and her parents. "I think so. She's tough."

"Like you then," Justine replied, nodding.

Riley studied her former rival anew.

"Congratulations on your marriage, by the way," Beck said.

"Thank you," Justine said.

A quick glance revealed a plain gold band instead of some honking huge diamond. Riley had expected the latter.

"So who's the lucky fella?" Beck asked.

"Philippe is a journalist with Reuters. We met covering a story. He scooped me, and then asked for a date."

"Smart man," Beck replied. He looked over at Simon. "I got a couple things I need to talk over with our exorcist. I'll be right back," he said, leaving them alone.

Silence fell between them. Riley scuffed a toe in the dirt.

"Well, this is awkward," Justine said.

That was for sure. Beck might call Riley his woman, but she always felt like a little girl next to this lady. As if her eighteen years somehow just didn't measure up.

"How do you look so good all the time?" Riley blurted. "I'm always a mess and . . . " She shook her head. "I know, it doesn't matter, but it sorta does."

Justine laughed. "You think I look like this every second of the day?"

"You have every time I've seen you."

"Oh no. That's not how it works." Justine pulled out her phone, flipped through some photos. "Here, this is what I looked like after I got caught up in a riot in Karachi."

Riley looked at the photo and gasped. Justine was covered in mud, her hair a mess and her shirt ripped. Behind her, a cloud of tear gas rolled across the street.

The reporter scrolled to another picture. "Here's the riot in Morocco." More scrolling. "Here's me in New Delhi after the bomb blast. I can be just as grunged up as anyone."

"You've just ruined my image of you as a designer airhead."

One of Justine's perfectly plucked eyebrows quirked upward. "And you're clearly not some stupid kid."

They grinned at the same time.

"You are jealous of me because of Beck," Justine said. "Because he and I were once lovers."

Riley nodded. "That's part of it."

"He's a good man, but he wouldn't have been happy with me," the woman added. "And though I like him very much, he is not like Philippe."

"So we both found love."

Justine nodded. "We are very fortunate women." She hesitated. "I would not have been able to handle a husband who is a grand master. Too many secrets. The reporter in me would have had to know all of them."

Riley laughed. Beck looked over at them, puzzled, then went back to talking to Simon and the priest.

"So, off the record, what exactly is going on with the National Guild?" Justine asked.

Riley groaned. "You are smooth."

"In this case, I'm concerned. Demanding that a trapper work without magical spheres is tantamount to forcing the person to commit suicide. That makes me very curious about what is really going on."

Riley looked over at Beck and Simon. "Off the record?"

"You have my word."

Which, Riley had learned, was pretty golden.

"It all began when I was in Edinburgh . . . "

Chapter Twenty-Seven

Justine left shortly after Riley ended her tale. She could tell she'd given the reporter something to think about. After blessing the family, Father Vonn left as well.

Before the Gills departed, Simon warned the parents not to reenter the house until the demon carcass had been removed—there was someone special the Vatican hired to do that task—and the place had been thoroughly blessed by Father Vonn.

As their car pulled out of the drive, Riley waved at Carrina. For a moment the girl didn't respond, then she raised her hand shyly, tears streaking down her cheeks.

"Make a note, guys: That little girl is going to be one of the Vatican's Demon Hunters someday," she said. "It might be an all-boys club now, but that's going to change."

Simon gave her a strange look as the family drove away. "You may be right. Carrina's been forged in fire," he said. "The pope says that experiences like hers make the most committed warriors against the darkness."

"Like you, then," Beck said.

"Like all of us," Simon replied.

Silence fell for a time.

"So, what are you doin' tonight, Simon?" Beck asked.

It was an unexpected question.

"Nothing, after the team clears the house. My folks are at some church event and the sibs are scattered wherever. Why?"

"Well, I've found that after a big thing like this, it's best to get some food and chill down. Ease back into real life."

"Oh, I see." Which told Riley he'd probably never done that

before.

"You like barbecue?" Beck asked. Simon nodded. "Ever had Mama Z's?"

"No. Is it good?"

"You've never had Mama Z's?" Beck exclaimed. "Good Lord, man, you've been missin' out. It's what barbecue would be like in Heaven, if they had that kinda thing."

"It's really good. He's not blowing smoke here," Riley added.

"How about we pick up some, and you come over to our place to eat," Beck offered. "We can see the house, hang, talk about whatever. No pressure."

Simon gave the idea serious consideration. "I have to stay to release the corpse. The clean-up crew should be here in about thirty minutes or so."

"Fine. How's about I stay here with you?" He looked over at Riley at this point. "Can you pick up the supper, and we'll slip back home when we're done here?"

"Sure." Because she always loved walking into a restaurant looking like the Wrath of God and smelling worse.

"That work for you?" Beck asked their companion.

"Yeah, sounds good," Simon said, smiling. "I'll go back up and start cleaning. See you soon, Riley."

As he walked into the house, she shot Beck a look. "I'm happy that you invited him. But why did you?"

"I know he's been trained to handle this kind of thing, but he's gonna be too much in his own head right now. He needs to be around other folks who understand. And besides, I like him."

"At one point, you couldn't stand him."

"Only because he was dating my girl. Now? I think he's a good dude." Beck bopped the end of her nose with a finger. "And I just love seein' you all green-eyed jealous every time you and Justine get together."

"You are a dog, Denver Beck."

He grabbed her up, planted a kiss on her lips that made her body sing, then let her go. "Get lots of food. I'm starved."

Then he was off toward the house, whistling a tune.

One of a kind. That's what her father had said about the poor boy from South Georgia. *Got that right.*

~~*

Riley hurried home, took a fast shower, then went to Mama Z's. She returned home only a few minutes before Simon and Beck pulled up. The guys were joking back and forth, laughing. Simon had always been so serious, and now he was razzing Beck about some song they'd listened to on the radio. He carried a duffle bag, probably containing a change of clothes. All the trappers had them in their cars.

Once the guys had taken their showers and changed, they joined Riley at the table, where she had laid out pork, chicken, and beef barbecue with all the trimmings. Simon said grace, then they fell on the food like they hadn't eaten in a week. By the time the guys started to slow down, Riley was done.

"This was great. Please let me kick in some cash for the meal," Simon said.

"Thanks, but it's our treat. Our way of thankin' you for keepin' Riley workin' while National gets its head out of its ass," Beck said, wiping a smear of sauce off his lips.

Riley rose from her chair. "There's brownies and ice cream for dessert, so leave a bit of room."

"Too late," Simon replied. "I haven't had this good a meal since I was in Rome. And for God's sake, don't tell my mother that or she'll kill me."

They all laughed.

Beck finished eating a short time later, so Riley scooted them into the living room. Simon claimed a chair while the other two sprawled on the couch.

"So what was the most memorable thing while you were on sabbatical?" she asked, her feet curled up under her as she leaned against Beck. His arm went around her shoulders and pulled her close.

Simon thought for a moment, then said, "Masada."

"The fortress?"

"Yeah. It overlooks the Dead Sea." He paused. "I met a rabbinical student. His name was Yair. We talked about God and destiny and what was wrong in the world."

"On top of that mountain?" Beck asked.

"To start with, then he invited me to join him in Jerusalem. He walked me through some of the older sections, took me to the Wailing Wall." Simon pointed at the T-shirt he wore, one with small sparks flying upward on the front of it. "Yair gave me this. He said it was our job to find the sparks of light, nurture them, and slowly heal the world."

"Heal the world," Riley murmured. "I like that."

"So do I. My last night in Israel we had dinner with Hasim, a friend of his named. He's Muslim."

"One from each of the three big religions," Beck said.

Simon nodded. "We talked about everything. About God, about our lives, about war and death and Hell," he said, quieter now. "I learned a lot that night."

"So we're all sparks, then?" Riley asked.

"Me? I think I'm the guy who keeps the sparks safe from the darkness, so they can multiply and light the way," he replied.

Riley liked that just as well. "So how did you connect up with the Vatican?"

"Father Rosetti texted my parents, asked how I was doing. Mom told him I was headed to Rome next, so he invited me to lunch."

"That had to be a surprise."

Simon smiled. "Oh, it was. Rosetti asked how I was doing, where I'd been, what countries I'd visited. All sorts of questions."

"He was feelin' you out?" Beck asked.

"Definitely. He wanted to know where I was in my spiritual journey, had I turned away from God entirely or was I at least still 'in the tent,' as he put it. I told him I'd found some peace in some very strange places."

"Like?"

"I went to Nepal, spent time with the monks. Did some

hiking and a lot of thinking and praying." He smiled over at Riley now. "I listened to your advice and spoke to an imam and a rabbi. I spent an entire day with an Indian holy man. I even sat in one of those stone circles Ayden likes so much."

Nodding, Riley thought of how much she missed her friend.

"In the end," Simon continued, "I realized that I'd been tested and failed big time. My faith had been too rigid. Instead of a strength, it was a straitjacket."

"Good analogy," she replied, marveling at how far Simon had come since last spring.

"Hell didn't break you," Beck said quietly.

"No, but they came really close. Once I knew that, I could deal with some of the guilt." Simon looked over at Riley now. "The fact that you forgave me for what I did to you meant a lot. I owe you."

"As you forgave me. It had to be hard for you to see me at Ori's side before that battle downtown."

"It frightened me, because I knew that meant your soul was his. But I also knew you wouldn't have given it up unless it was for a just cause."

"Ori taught me how to kill demons, and that kept me and others alive. That's all he wanted, for me to survive. In the end, he got his wish."

Beck nodded. "In the end, Hell didn't get any of us. I'd say that's somethin' good to remember, no matter how bad it gets."

"Amen," Simon said.

His phone rang at that point and he took the call. As he listened he began to smile. "That's very good news. Thank you so much for letting us know. It means a lot."

When the call ended, the smile came their direction. "Carrina's parents had her checked out by a doctor—she's got a lot of bruises and lost some weight, but nothing else is wrong."

"Thank you, God," Riley murmured.

A while later Simon left, genuinely happy, as though he'd had the best night of his life. Maybe he had. As he pulled out of the driveway, he waved. Riley and Beck returned it.

"Good guy," she said. "He's way lonely, though. I hope he finds someone someday. He deserves happiness."

"I used to be that way, but not anymore. Not since you."

Riley turned toward her guy, feeling the warmth of his love. "There's a couple more brownies left. We could split them with the rest of the ice cream."

Beck shut the door, locked it, and pulled her close. "I have a much better idea."

As he kissed her, all thoughts of brownies and ice cream vanished.

~~*

The next day brought a ton of paperwork at Harper's place—somehow His Snootiness Master Northrup hadn't bothered to take all that on. The usually grouchy Harper was even worse, his conversation liberally seeded with swear words, most of them overlapping each other.

Northrup was conspicuously absent; rumor had it he was meeting with the local archdiocese for some reason. That made Riley nervous. Was he spreading lies about her to the Church, in hopes of keeping her away from Simon and the exorcisms? For that matter, did he even know about them?

There you go again, borrowing trouble. Ayden always warned her about that.

When the offer of a trapping run arose, Riley eagerly snapped it up, keen to get her apprentices out of Harper's way. Since she couldn't serve as a full backup, Beck agreed to step in—mostly because she'd texted him and said that Harper was one swear word away from a full meltdown.

The Gastro-Fiend they needed to trap had decided to chomp its way through some restaurant dumpsters in Virginia-Highland, a trendy neighborhood near Piedmont Park. It was easy to track the thing, since it had tipped the trash containers over and spread debris everywhere. It was like following a stinky road map.

Beck was in teaching mode, so she stepped back and let him handle Richard and Kurt. It reminded her of what it'd been like when she'd been the apprentice and he'd taken her trapping. While he coached Richard on how to capture the gluttonous Three, who'd found nirvana in the dumpster behind a noodle place, Riley kept an eye out for trouble.

She couldn't escape the feeling that they were being watched. As she concentrated, a faint green thread appeared in her mind and slowly grew stronger. A movement at the end of the alley brought her around to find Jackson walking toward them.

What's he doing here? It was his day off.

Beck shot him a quick look and called out, "Good timin'. Richard is about to take this thing down."

The man didn't reply, just kept moving closer. As he did, the thread shifted, growing muddier. Darker.

"Beck?"

"Yeah?"

"I don't think this is Jackson. We might have another demon."

"Real or an illusion?"

She focused on it, feeling the immediate headache kick in. "I don't think it's real. But if it is and we ignore it . . . "

"Understood. You and Kurt deal with it. Richard and I will get this one. Just be careful."

So calm. Not a hint of "what the hell is happening here?"

Kurt took a stand about eight or nine feet away from her, a Babel sphere in one hand and a Holy Water sphere in the other.

"Good move," she said, nodding. "We have no idea what this thing is. One thing for sure, if this is an Archfiend, you and Richard are running for it. Got it?"

He gave her a frown.

"Got it?" she repeated, more forcefully now.

Kurt nodded unhappily.

"If this is a Four, its strength is getting into your mind and molding it like Play-Doh."

Jackson's image vanished, replaced by that of a Three.

"Hey, that's good, right?" Kurt asked.

"No, it's not. Higher-level fiends can mimic lower-level fiends. This could still be a Four."

"Then what do we do?"

"You nail it with the Holy Water sphere and see what happens."

Kurt nodded, his jaw tensed and shoulders tight.

Rather than let the demon get closer to the others, Riley walked out to meet it, Kurt next to her.

"Lucifer!" she shouted.

The fiend cocked its head but kept coming.

So it was either a very high-level fiend, or . . .

Its thread began to pulse in her mind now, shifting through colors like a rainbow.

"Nail it," she said.

Kurt's toss was perfect, hitting it mid-chest. If there'd been an actual chest to hit. Instead, the sphere sailed through the demon and smashed on the pavement.

"It's not real," he said, furious. "And I just wasted a sphere."

"You good?" Beck called out, right after a snarling howl cut through the air.

"Fine. You?"

"It's down and going in the bag. Richard did you proud."

She smiled at that news. "I'll be right back."

Riley broke into a sprint down the alley, following the thread, which had now morphed into pure lavender. When it grew thinner and finally vanished, she began muttering a couple of the expletives Harper had used that morning.

This time, the thread had been strong enough that she'd felt something else.

Witch magic.

By the time Riley rejoined the others, Richard was all smiles at his latest trapping, while Kurt remained pensive. As the two apprentices hauled the bagged demon to the truck, she dropped back to talk to Beck in private.

"Illusion?" he asked.

"Yeah. I felt witchy magic."

He blinked over at her. "Why would one of them do that?"

"No clue. I can't ask them or I'll lose my license."

~~*

Once the snarling fiend was delivered to Fireman Jack, Beck took off on her. Apparently he needed to talk to Stewart, though he didn't say about what. Riley polled her apprentices, and burgers were the odds-on favorite choice for an early supper. She took them to her favorite burger joint, and they indulged in an orgy of carbs, salt, and fat.

Richard was still boisterous, in a great mood; Kurt less so. When Riley asked him what was up, all he said was, "Girlfriend problems."

"As in . . . ?"

"As in when I asked if we could get back together again, she said we couldn't date if I was a trapper. It's . . . " He struggled for a word.

"Complicated?" Riley supplied. He nodded. "Probably always will be. Where does she work?"

"At one of those New Age shops. She's a witch."

That was interesting. "Her people aren't happy you're dating?"

"So. Not. Happy. Eslee's family is giving her all kinds of grief, saying I'm not the kind of guy she should be hanging with. I think she's way cool. She's like a bright spring day. They tell her the only thing worse than dating a trapper is dating a necromancer."

Riley groaned. "Sorry. That happens more often than we'd all like."

"It's not like we're enemies. It seems more territorial than anything," he observed.

Which was right. The prejudices were deep and inexplicable and really needed changing. But how?

As if the universe, or at least the witches, had been listening to her thoughts, a text message arrived on her phone. As she popped the last of her fries into her mouth, she gave it a quick read.

WE WISH TO SPEAK TO YOU ABOUT MAGIC & YOUR ROLE WITH

THE SUMMONERS. BELL, BOOK & BROOMSTICK. TONIGHT. 7 P.M.
AYDEN WILL BE THERE.

It was from someone named Rada. Ayden had mentioned the
woman before; she was a very senior witch who only involved
herself in things when they needed an arbitrator. No matter who
she was, if Riley attended she would be in direct violation of
Northrup's edict.

Carrina's lost little voice surfaced in her mind at that moment,
asking questions, wanting answers. Why was it possible for a
child to seek knowledge and not her? When had she given over
control to someone else, allowed them to dictate her actions?

"Wow, look. A sure career breaker in one simple text." She
held up the phone so her apprentices, in particular Kurt, could
read the message.

"You going?" Richard asked. They all knew what was on
the line.

"I don't know yet. I'm not sure why they want to talk to me
now, when before I was total pond scum."

"It could be a trap. Something Northrup set up," Kurt replied.

"Possibly."

The meeting location sounded kosher: Bell, Book, and
Broomstick in Little Five Points. Whoever had sent the text
knew one of her weaknesses—she'd get to see Ayden again.

If, down the line, Riley finally regained permission to deal
with the magical folks, and she'd blown off the witches' invite,
that'd just make it harder. If she accepted it and someone found
out, she'd be booted from the Guild.

Her stubbornness reared its head. Knowing she'd probably
regret it, she sent a quick text accepting the invite, then a message
to Beck that she had a special errand tonight, she might be late,
and he shouldn't wait up for her. That she'd be fine.

Riley had just sent her apprentices on their way and was
exiting the restaurant when her phone rang.

"Let me guess," Beck began. "Yer off doin' somethin' I
won't like, right?"

"Pretty much something National wouldn't like, but it

doesn't involve demons."

"That's a start. Anythin' you can tell me?"

"No. It's one of those plausible deniability things."

"Let me know when yer done doin' whatever National wouldn't approve of."

"I will."

"By the way, when Remmers was trappin' with yer apprentices the other day, they had another phantom demon."

Which neither of her newbies had mentioned. Maybe it was becoming routine for them.

"Any of the other trappers have a problem?"

"Nope."

"Since I wasn't there, this might not be about me."

"Hate to break it to you, but it's not always about you, Princess," he jested.

She rolled her eyes. "Bite me, Backwoods Boy."

"Lookin' forward to it. Later, Riley."

Chapter Twenty-Eight

There were a number of ways to get into the heart of Little Five Points. Riley opted for the one most folks wouldn't expect. She climbed over a low wall at the end of a side street, then worked her way back to the Bell, Book, and Broomstick. If this was a setup by Northrup's crew, she wanted to know that before she bumbled into a trap.

If she'd been any good at illusion spells, she'd have cast one, Guild be damned. Although with her luck, and her lack of skill in that department, she would probably end up looking like a giant walking orange. Still, she wore Ayden's amulet, hidden away under her clothes. No reason to tempt fate.

As Riley trudged past Mort's house, she ignored the urge to stop in. She missed him, missed his lessons. He'd taken the news of her no-magic thing fairly well, but had warned her that she had to show progress in the next month or so, or the Society would take notice.

It was more than just the magic. Not having any contact with Mort or Ayden had reinforced how much she cared for those two, how much they were part of her life now. To Northrup and his cronies, it was just about the magic. For her, it was about the friendships that had sustained her during some of the worst times of her life.

One way or another, she was going to get this settled with the National Guild. But first, there were the witches.

The shop was closed, so she rapped on the door and waited. It was quickly answered by a girl about her age, with long, wavy blond hair in a braid that reached her waist.

"I'm here for the meeting," Riley said.

The girl nodded, beckoned her in, and locked the door behind them. As she led her through the darkened shop, Riley remembered the first time she'd come here. Funny how smells could trigger memories.

Something nudged at her senses, but she couldn't quite decipher it. Too many magical items around. She and the witch went out the back door into the garden behind the shop. It was only then, under the security light, that Riley could see a quartz crystal woven into the plait of the girl's hair. She wore a long teal skirt and a plain white T-shirt with no tattoos visible. Since she appeared overly nervous, whatever was going down tonight might not be good.

The yard behind the shop wasn't like most green spaces inside the city—this one had a solid wall enclosing it, and in the center, a genuine stone circle. Candles had been lit, but no bonfire. A brazier served just as well, sending flames and ashes into the air.

Since the last time Riley had been here, the murals on the wall had increased in size, now stretching almost halfway around the enclosure: forest scenes with various fairies, the occasional unicorn, and vast valleys filled with trees—Tolkienesque in some ways, Arthurian in others.

Though she noted all that, her eyes weren't riveted on the scenery, or on anything else but the barren spot just behind the stone circle. It was too easy to imagine a twenty-foot-tall dragon surging out of that ground, all fire and anger, just like it had the night Ayden had summoned her father's spirit. Paul Blackthorne had come, but so had the being that had pulled him from his grave.

Lucifer. Prince of Hell and CEO of All Things Infernal.

Riley shivered in the night air and the young witch noticed.

"The circle has a lot of power. That's probably what you're feeling."

No. In this case, the power of memories was stronger than that of the old magic.

As Riley approached the group of witches, her mind tracked off in safer directions. The collective noun for witches was coven; however in this case, given the piercing glowers she received, perhaps a *storm of witches* was more appropriate.

There were eight of them, two of whom she knew: Ayden and Morgaine. Her friend wore a frown, but somehow Riley didn't think it was aimed at her. Morgaine seemed put out, which told Riley that this meeting wasn't her idea. They were both in long skirts and cloaks. Seemed it was a fancy-dress evening and Riley hadn't gotten the memo, as usual.

"Demon trapper," Morgaine said evenly.

"Witch," Riley replied in the same flat tone.

Ayden smirked, a flare of amusement in her eyes now.

"Why is she here?" asked one of the others, an older woman with fiery red hair—a color that had to have come out of a box. Mother Nature had better taste than that.

"Riley was invited," Ayden replied.

"You dared to—" the woman began.

"She didn't. I did," a familiar voice said.

Riley turned in shock as an elderly woman walked toward them, clutching an oversized purse. "Mrs. Litinsky?" she blurted.

"Hello, Riley dear," the woman replied.

Her former next-door neighbor—the diminutive silver-haired matron who had taken care of Riley after her father's death, and after her own near death at the hands of a Three—was a witch. And Riley hadn't known it.

Or had she?

The woman had always offered her special teas to help her sleep, given her much-needed advice, acted like a loving grandmother would. Or in this case, a crone, which Ayden had patiently explained was not an insult.

"So you're Rada?" Riley asked. The woman nodded. "I never suspected. I mean, you don't have anything in your apartment that says you're a witch."

"My altar is in my bedroom. Some of my family are Russian Orthodox, so I don't overdo it. The older you get, the more you realize the faith is in here," she said, tapping her chest, "rather than in all the trappings."

"Is Max your familiar?"

She shook her head. "Just a cat. As if that isn't enough."

Riley laughed. "Well, thank you. For everything."

The old woman nodded. "Now, let's get this circle set and do some business."

As they followed her into the ring of stones, Riley leaned over to Ayden and whispered, "Why didn't you tell me?"

"She asked me not to. It was just fate that you ended up living next to her. She told me she was watching out for you."

"She did. She was one of the people who were there for me the night Dad died."

Ayden touched her elbow. "Rada is the oldest witch in Atlanta. She holds a lot of power, at least in terms of political savvy. She doesn't do much magic, but then, she doesn't have to. Work with her, not against her. Okay?"

"It all depends on what she's after," Riley replied. Loyalty to the old woman or not, she had to deal with her own conscience.

Ayden nodded, then broke off to join the other witches.

Did my dad know she was a witch? Probably. There was so much he hadn't told her.

It was the young witch who called the corners and invoked the circle. Riley found herself studying the girl. Again, she had a faint taste of something familiar, but it was muted by all the power around her. Once the circle was in place, the other witches opened their lawn chairs and parked themselves in a semicircle. Of course, that left Riley the only person still standing.

How special.

"Thank you for coming to us tonight," Rada said, settled in her own chair. "I am aware of the difficulties this must pose with your superiors."

How had she heard about Riley's no-magic ultimatum?

"I am surprised you dared to come here at all," Morgaine said.

"In the past," Riley said, emphasizing those words, "I've had a good relationship with the witches in this city. We've fought side by side. I saw no reason not to accept your invitation."

"Even if you lose your demon trapper's license?" Rada asked.

"Yes, even then." Riley wanted to say more but held her tongue. No matter how furious she was at the National Guild, that fight wasn't these ladies' business.

Rada nodded as if divining Riley's thoughts. "I asked you to join us because we have a problem, and we need your help."

Morgaine began to mutter under her breath.

"I am willing to help you," Riley replied, "but you know I'm on a short leash."

"We are aware of that leash, but a few of us believe you are in the best position to keep us safe."

"From what?"

"The trappers do not yet realize that the National Guild intends to outlaw the use of *any* magic during the trapping process."

"What? I thought they were just playing games with me."

Rada shook her head. "No. We witches have supplied that magic to the trappers for a number of reasons. First, it is the right thing to do. No one wants a world overrun by Hellspawn. The second is that it works well in conjunction with the Holy Water. And there is a third reason."

Riley remembered back to the first time she'd met Ayden, and what the witch had said as she'd taught her about the spheres the trappers used.

"The third is that you can't be accused of working for Hell when you're helping us keep folks safe."

Rada tipped her head to indicate Riley was correct. "If the National Guild disallows the use of our magic, we no longer have the thinnest of protections against those who claim we are evil. They'll blame us when their children are hurt, when their pets go missing, or when they're fired from a job. There is a fine line between a friend and an enemy."

"This is stupid! Holy Water works great, but it's the magic that grounds the Fives, makes the Fours lose their ability to charm, and stuns the Threes long enough for us to get them restrained. It keeps Hellspawn out of peoples' houses and businesses. No magic? We'll have lots of dead trappers and civilians."

Rada nodded. "Which leads me to wonder why the National Guild is being so willfully ignorant. Is it because they truly hate magic, or is there some other reason?"

"How am I going to get them to change their minds?" Riley asked. "Because they're not listening to me right now."

"You are a remarkable young woman. You have authority beyond what you realize. You may think that no one really knows about you, about your father, about what nearly happened in Atlanta last spring. You would be wrong," the old woman insisted. "The word has spread, and the name Blackthorne carries a power beyond that of any other trapper. Well, except for, perhaps, the young man you are marrying."

Because he killed an Archangel.

"Unfortunately," Rada continued, "we cannot be seen to aid you in this task. We are walking a tightrope as it is. Are you willing to do this for us?"

"Keep the National idiots from changing their policies?" Rada nodded. "Oh man. I can try, but I don't know if I'll be any good. Their representative hates me."

"Ask yourself why that is," Ayden said softly. "Maybe that will help you find a way to prevent this."

Riley studied her friend, knowing what was at stake here.

"Okay, I'll do what I can." Somehow her mouth didn't stop there. "But I want something in return."

Every one of the witches' eyes was on her now. Most were not friendly, and she began to feel like a small frog in a pond full of hungry fish.

"You dare to ask something of us?" Morgaine demanded. "You? A trapper?'

"If I'm going to pull your butts out of the fire, then yes, I do. Because we all have something to lose. Even you."

"That's not acceptable," Morgaine replied. "You have no

power over us."

"Take it or leave it. Because that's my line in the sand."

Riley felt magic slither around her feet, like the thick coils of a serpent. It took her only a moment to detect the source, and, of course, it was Morgaine. "Call it back, witch. Call it back now."

"Or?" the woman taunted.

With a look of apology to Ayden, Riley slid the steel pipe out of her pack.

"Or you're about to find out why Hell's fiends know my name."

Chapter Twenty-Nine

"Morgaine, remove the spell," Rada said in a tone of voice that brooked no argument.

The spell vanished instantly.

"Thank you." Riley slotted the pipe back into place inside her pack, surprised that her hands weren't shaking. Even Beck would have thought twice about what she'd just done.

"What is it that you want from us?" her former neighbor asked.

"First, if I can get the necromancers onboard, I want you to send a representative to sit down with them, at least monthly. It doesn't have to be anything formal; you just need to talk. This pissing match is totally Stone Age."

Anxious looks flew between some of the witches. It was as if she'd just suggested they jump into an erupting volcano.

"We have nothing we need to speak to them about," Morgaine insisted. "They're arrogant jerks."

Pot. Kettle. Witch.

"And *there's* the problem. You're so . . . " She hunted for a word that wouldn't get her turned into something small and furry with buckteeth. "You're so caught up doing your own thing, you don't realize there's common ground. Both of you use magic. Both groups will lose big if people begin to believe magic is bad. If you at least talk once in a while, share information, you might be able to keep the locals from lighting up the torches and sharpening their pitchforks."

"They have nothing to contribute," one of the witches complained. "They never listen to us anyway."

"I know they're arrogant." *No more than some of you.* "But it doesn't matter if you're a demon trapper, a witch, or a summoner—we're all fighting on the same side. Because believe me, the Prince of Hell loves this kind of crap. The more we squabble and try to harm each other, the stronger he gets."

"That's—" Morgaine began.

"An idea we will seriously consider," Rada cut in. "What else?"

"I need a promise that none of your witches will ever put a spell on me again without my permission," she said, glaring at Morgaine. "Like the one you did in the cemetery, or the one you tried here."

"You were not harmed," the woman retorted.

"Would you have done that immobility spell to me anywhere else in the city?"

"Of course. Why would it matter?"

"Because if I hadn't been on holy ground, I would have been at the mercy of any demon who wandered by," Riley replied. "You put my life at risk, and I won't have it."

Morgaine appeared taken aback. Clearly that hadn't occurred to her.

"No spells. None," Riley said again.

"We can do that," Rada agreed. "Anything else?"

"I want to continue training with Ayden. I don't want to learn just summoner magic."

A heated discussion began among the witches, which Riley tuned out.

She felt another tug on her mind, one too hard to ignore. It happened again, stronger now. As she looked from witch to witch, she could see the color of each one's life energy. It was like being inside a rainbow.

Then, there was the lavender, the thread she'd encountered when she'd been trapping. When her eyes landed on the young witch who'd brought her to the circle, Riley paused. "What's your name?"

"Ah . . . "

"Name," she demanded.

"Eslee."

Everything fell into place with amazing simplicity. Well, at least most of it. What Riley had been feeling was the thread of this girl's life force, the same lavender energy she'd encountered in Piedmont Park when the illusionary demons came after them, and again when Beck had been trapping with her and the apprentices.

"You're Kurt's girlfriend, aren't you?"

The girl's eyes widened, then she cast around a wary glance at the others. "I was. How did you know?"

"I felt you in Piedmont Park a few days ago and in Virginia-Highland earlier today." The girl went rigid. "You've been casting illusion spells, making it seem as if there were more demons than there were."

"Ah . . . " the young witch began, then she clamped her mouth shut.

"Eslee? What did you do?" Rada demanded.

Instead of answering her superior, the girl glared over at Morgaine. "You wouldn't let me date him. You said Kurt was beneath us because he was just a trapper. But I really like him and so I . . ."

"What kind of spell was it?" Ayden asked.

"We were trapping a Grade Three demon in the park," Riley explained. "She created two other imaginary demons, but at first we had no idea if they were real or not."

"No one got hurt," the girl protested.

"But we could have. Until I figured out they were illusions, we thought they were for real, and that made us believe we were surrounded. One of us could have been injured. Or died."

The girl's eyes began to moisten. "I didn't mean for you to get hurt."

"I know. Why would you put your boyfriend in danger?"

"I wanted him to think trapping was too dangerous and quit. Then we could date and no one would be all pissy about it," she said, glaring at Morgaine again. These two seemed to be related in some way.

"So if Kurt said, 'I want you to quit being a witch and then we can date,' would you do it?" Riley asked.

"No! Of course not!" the girl replied, indignant.

"But that is exactly what you expected him to do," Rada said solemnly. "It's not right to manipulate people like that."

Eslee hung her head in shame, tears falling. "I didn't mean to hurt anyone," she murmured. Then she looked up, worried. "You won't tell him, will you?"

"No, because you're going to," Riley answered. "Then, if he still thinks you're worth all the hassle, you guys have a chance." Glaring at Morgaine, she added, "For that to work, the rest of us have to stay out of their faces. Is that clear?"

"You have no right to tell us what to do," the witch began.

"In this case, I agree with Riley," Rada said sternly. "Our closed-mindedness isn't Stone Age, but it is medieval, and we all know how well that era treated us."

Riley turned back to the girl. "About a week ago, did you conjure up a fake necromancer in Demon Central, then have him call up a demon?"

"No. I wouldn't know how to do that."

"Well, someone did," she grumbled. She studied Morgaine for a moment, but the woman shook her head.

"I have no issues with you resuming your studies with Ayden," Rada said. "Clearly you have talent, if you could determine the source of the illusion spell."

Riley gave a nod, understanding that was an apology of sorts. "Is there anything else you wanted to talk to me about?"

"No." Rada smiled like she'd just pulled a perfect angel food cake out of the oven. "You are free to go. Please come see me soon. Max misses you. And bring that handsome young man of yours. I'll bake your favorite cookies."

"We'll be there." After shooting Morgaine a sour look, Riley smiled at Ayden and crossed out of the sacred circle. To her surprise, Eslee was right behind her.

When they reached the front of the shop, the girl unlocked

the entry door but didn't open it. She took a very large breath, like she was working up the courage to speak.

"Do you think Kurt will hate me when I tell him what I did?"

"I don't know, but you have no future together if you try to make him give up what he really wants to do in life. That's wrong."

"Even if he could get hurt or killed?"

"Even then. It's his choice. Do you think I like the idea of my fiancé out battling Hellspawn, a walking target for every fiend who wants to butter up Lucifer? It makes me sick sometimes, but that's what Beck is all about. If I insist he stop doing what he loves, we're through. He knows it goes both ways."

The girl nodded numbly. "I won't do anything like that again."

"Then this evening hasn't been a waste." As the door opened, Riley couldn't resist. "Why does Morgaine hate demon trappers?"

"My aunt used to be married to one when she lived in New York. They divorced, so now she doesn't like any of them."

"Of course. It couldn't be anything the least bit rational. Thanks."

Riley stepped outside and the door closed behind her. She blew a stream of air through her lips. The witches wanted her to stop the National Guild from instituting a truly suicidal policy, but despite what Rada claimed, Riley had no real power. She and all the other trappers were totally screwed.

As she drew closer to Mort's doorway, it opened and his nephew stepped out. It should have startled her, but nothing regarding the necro surprised her anymore. He just seemed to know things.

"Hey, Alex. How's it going?"

He shrugged. "It goes. My uncle wants to talk to you. He said you were headed back this way after the witches' meeting."

"How did he know that?"

"He just does. He knows everything."

"So what's going on with you? Usually you're in a pretty

good mood."

"Ah, nothing."

She entered the house. "Come on, we know each other fairly well. You can spill."

Alex shut the door behind her, groaning as he did. "You know how I was going to major in physics and all?"

She nodded.

"My head's just not there anymore."

"Girl?"

He shook his head. "Magic. I want to study with my uncle. That's creating some major hassles with my parents, who do not see 'corpse collector' as a viable profession."

"Even though Mort is doing really well?"

He nodded. "Mom is sorta sympathetic because Mort's her brother, but my dad isn't talking to me. He says I have to stop believing in fantasy."

"I suppose pointing out that sometimes you'll actually be using that magic to stop demons won't make them any happier."

"No, definitely not. Uncle Mort said your father didn't want you to become a trapper. How did you convince him?"

"I wore my dad down. I kept researching everything I could find about trapping, and I told him what I'd read. I made sure that what I said was wrong in some way, and he kept correcting me because he was a born teacher. Finally he just gave up, and we applied for my apprentice license."

"Huh . . . Don't think that will work for my dad. He's a brain surgeon. He wanted me to be one too, but he was okay with the physics-major thing because it sounded cool."

"Unlike necromancer."

"Yeah. Well, thanks. Maybe I'll figure something out." Alex pointed toward the rear of the house. "Uncle's in the back room, chilling out."

What Alex did not say was that Mort wasn't alone. Oh no, not alone at all. Sitting in a chair near the fireplace was the High Lord of All Things Necromantic, Lord Ozymandias. He wasn't wearing his usual wormhole-black robe. In fact, he was in slacks and a navy turtleneck, which made that odd glowing sigil in the middle of his forehead even odder.

"Riley," Mort said, waving her in. "That didn't take long."

"Bad news never does," she said. "Lord Ozymandias."

She usually wasn't that polite to this dude, but she was a member of the Summoners Society now and someday she'd be studying with him. No reason to piss him off too soon. No doubt her mouth would get that job done eventually.

"Ms. Blackthorne. I realized that I've failed to congratulate you on your engagement to that young man who killed my Hellish tormentor. So, congratulations. If Beck can handle a raving-mad Archangel, he'll do fine with you."

Which sounded like a compliment, but . . .

She grinned. "Thanks. I'll let him know you said that. Somehow I don't think he'd disagree."

"No doubt."

Riley chose an overstuffed chair and sank into it, surprised at how tired she was. "What's up, guys?"

"I gather Rada told you about what the National Guild is planning?" Ozy said.

Rada? He was on a first-name basis with the oldest witch in the city?

"Yes. It wasn't hard to figure out that it's a totally dumbass move, either."

"Indeed. Makes me wonder why they're even considering it."

"Some trappers just can't deal with magic," she said.

"And some trappers are wise enough to know they need it anyway," Ozy shot back. "Like you. I understand your superiors have warned you away from us. Clearly you are ignoring that order."

"I don't obey stupid people."

Ozy actually smiled. "Good for you. The problem is, if they refuse to use magic, that is just the opening gambit. What's next? Will there be a backlash against those of us who do? Will there be laws passed requiring that no magic be used on the Sabbath, for example? Or that it be regulated by the state or local authorities? We have enough of that when we're summoning the dead."

"You think this is a war against magic?"

"Yes, and I think this is just the opening salvo."

"So what are you guys going to do about this?" Riley asked.

Mort shrugged. "Not much we can do. It would only backfire on us if we were seen to be meddling with trapper policies, no matter how ignorant those policies may be."

"You're absolutely correct," Ozy said, looking back at her now. "Which means . . ."

"Let me guess," Riley said. "It's all on my shoulders, right?"

"How thoughtful of you to volunteer," he replied smoothly.

"I'm not volunteering, and you know it. I'm stuck in the middle again, and that means it sucks to be me."

"And that is different . . . how?" Ozy said, a hint of uncharacteristic humor in his voice.

She opened her mouth and closed it again. Then began to grin. "Yeah, situation normal, all screwed up."

"That being said, you do have leverage, and I'm sure that Rada has already pointed that out."

"I got jack, Ozy; come on, you know that."

Mort twitched at her shortening of his superior's name, but His Lordship didn't seem to mind. In fact, she thought he kind of liked it.

"On the contrary, you have some powerful allies. The witches, us, a number of trappers, the grand masters. You just need to learn how to use all of that to your best advantage."

"Yeah, well, it looks like I don't have a choice. But if I can make National back off and not do this stupid thing, you'll owe me a favor as head of the necromancers."

"Such as?"

"One of you and one of the witches will need to actually talk every now and then. Compare notes, that sorta thing. Build a bond. Stop being enemies."

"Did you demand the same of Rada?" Ozymandias asked.

Riley nodded. "She agreed to my terms."

"Then I shall as well."

Riley had to fight to keep the astonishment off her face. That had gone far too easily, which meant Ozy had some sort of ulterior motive for playing nice.

She rose, really wanting to get home to Beck and away from all the stupid politics.

"Any luck figuring out who summoned the Five?" Mort asked.

"No. Stewart thinks it might have been a higher-level demon, which is not good news." *I'd rather it be some lovesick witch.*

"Have you been practicing the techniques I taught you?" Mort asked.

"Yes, I have." *In between all the drama.*

"Good. It may be the only way to keep yourself safe. If a demon can walk right up to you, and you have no idea it's not what it appears to be, then you have no chance at all."

Tell me about it.

Chapter Thirty

It wasn't until Riley was snuggled in bed next to Beck that she confessed where she'd been and what had gone down.

He didn't seem surprised. "Anyone see you?"

"I'm at the point where I don't care anymore. They pull my license or they don't. Like you said, I'm more than just a demon trapper."

He kissed her on the forehead. "So why were those folks so eager to talk to you?"

First she let him know about Mrs. Litinsky, and was pleased to learn that Beck had been as clueless as she'd been.

"I'll be damned. I just thought she was some sweet little old lady."

"She is, but she rules those witches with an iron fist. Now, for the bad news." Riley let the bomb drop about Northrup's plan to ban magic.

Beck abruptly sat up in bed. "Are they fuckin' crazy?" he demanded. He rarely swore like that, but in this case it was justified.

"Maybe. I'm not sure yet. I might have an idea of how to handle them."

"Such as?" he asked, staring down at her with such a deep frown, she wondered if he'd ever smile again.

"I think they're trying to use me as their 'here's why magic is bad' poster child. That's why they're setting me up to fail."

"And?"

"I also think if National's plan is revealed before they're ready, it'll explode in Northrup's face. The other board members won't want to take all the heat and they'll back off. Especially if the everyday folks find out exactly how much magic they use without realizing it."

"How will you pull this off though? It's not going to be easy."

Riley had to agree. "I have an awesome weapon, one that is tenacious and in-your-face and can't be bought off, even if she does have a clothes budget that would bankrupt a small country."

Beck caught on immediately. "Justine? You go there, and there might not be any way back into the Guild for you. They'll see you as a traitor."

"Better a traitor than allow those morons to get more trappers killed."

"It's still a dangerous move."

"I know. That's why I'll do it, not you or any of the others. Northrup and whoever's supporting him already hate me. Might as well go for the gold."

He whistled under his breath. "We need to let the masters know."

"You warn them; just keep your distance so if it does explode, none of the crap hits you."

Beck's lengthy sigh told her he wasn't happy about her falling on this particular metaphorical grenade. He pulled himself free and slipped out of the bedroom, headed toward the front of the house. Riley heard him rooting around in the supply cupboard, the one where they stored their trapping supplies. When he returned to the bedroom, he was carrying a short sword in a scabbard. He set it on the nightstand.

She leaned up on her elbows. "I promise I'll stop stealing the covers. Honest. No need to arm yourself."

He didn't laugh. "That's for you. You know how to use a sword—the angel taught you. I want you to carry this with you from now on. The demons aren't your only enemies."

"Ohhkay . . . " Riley knew it was better not to argue with him when he was in protector mode.

She waited until he was back in bed, then tugged on his arm, pulling him close. "I'll be careful."

Beck touched her cheek, then kissed her.

"You are anythin' but careful, Riley," he whispered. "And I love you more than I can ever say."

"That's exactly why I won't let these fools win."

~~*

Riley met her former nemesis at the cemetery early the next morning. It was the kind of place where if anyone was following her, they'd stand out; and she wouldn't have to worry about demons here. Given what had gone down with the witches last night, Riley felt pretty safe from them as well. That left the National Guild and a certain Prince.

Justine exited her rental sports car wearing jeans, a short leather coat, and an Atlanta Braves T-shirt. No matter how much she dressed down, she'd always look like a fashion model. Just good bone structure, maybe.

She slept with Beck. Judging from the bad-boy smile that used to creep onto his face nearly every time she was mentioned, back before he and Riley became a couple, his time with Justine must have been off the charts.

Riley sighed. There was no way that history would go away, so she just had to deal. Now she knew exactly how her guy felt every time she mentioned Ori.

"Good morning," the woman said, joining her on the steps of her family mausoleum.

"Thanks for coming to talk to me. I think what I have to tell you will be of interest."

"Can I record the interview?"

Riley shook her head. "No. Not because I'm worried about me, but there are other people involved."

Justine nodded and put the recorder away. "Is this about the National Guild?" she asked.

"Yes. You've heard things?"

"I've heard some rumors that I find really outlandish. So what can you tell me?"

Riley laid it all out, what she'd heard from the witches, how their source had an inside track to what was happening at the National level.

Justine didn't seem surprised. "That's the rumor I heard. You sure it's legitimate?"

"Yes. The witches are spooked, and so are the necromancers."

"Why the latter?"

"Lord Ozymandias wonders if this is just an opening play to add greater restrictions on the use of any kind of magic."

Justine tapped her chin with her gold pen. "That is a possibility. There is a new group of 'concerned citizens' who want all magic banned, even something as simple as wearing a talisman or carrying a rose quartz. They're still very small, but gaining influence."

"I'm willing to bet a year's worth of hot chocolate that a certain Hellish Prince is behind this. It's just his style."

"I'll defer to your knowledge on that," Justine replied. Her meticulously plucked brows furrowed in thought. "I'll make some phone calls, see what I can scare up." She hesitated. "What will you do if you no longer have a trapper's license?"

"Not sure. I could go freelance, but those guys are rough and it'd be even more dangerous. I could help Simon out until the Vatican assigns him his next location."

"I've heard the Vatican is thinking of allowing women to join the Demon Hunters somewhere down the line, though not soon enough to solve your problem."

Riley stared at her. "Really?" Justine nodded. "Well, I'm not Catholic so that won't be much help."

"At the speed Rome moves, it could be a decade or more before any changes occur. Nothing goes fast with those people."

But it would be fast enough for Carrina.

"*Demonland* finally get to them, did it?" Hollywood's idea of the Demon Hunters drove the Vatican batty, but then, it did Riley as well.

Justine smiled. "Partly. But I think it's more than that. You have made ripples in Rome."

"Not always in a good way, either."

"You might be surprised," Justine said. Since the captain of the Demon Hunters was an ex-boyfriend, she might not be exaggerating.

Justine rose and dusted off her jeans. "I'll let you know what I find out. If this is what the National Guild is planning, you're up against some very powerful people."

"I'm not worried."

"You should be. For the record, I see why Beck loves you."

"And for the record, you have to know I hated you like crazy."

"*Hated* as in past tense?"

"You're growing on me, Justine," Riley said, grinning.

"The ring on my finger helped, didn't it?"

"A little. It's more that I found out you can get just as dirty as me."

The reporter laughed and headed for her car. "I'll be in touch. Be careful."

"Same to you. If they'll try to stop me, they'll do the same to you."

"They can try," the woman replied.

Chapter Thirty-One

When Northrup entered Harper's office, Riley was head-down in Guild paperwork, rocking away to the tunes coming from her earbuds.

"Where's Harper?"

"Good morning to you too," she said.

Her boss stepped out of the kitchen, coffee cup in hand. "I'm here. What do you want?"

"I've been told this trapper was in the company of a necromancer last night."

Crap.

"When?" Harper asked.

"The time doesn't matter, it's the—"

"It does to me."

Northrup fluffed up. "At about seven."

Which was a total lie, since she'd been with the witches at that point.

Harper raised an eyebrow at her. "Blackthorne?"

"Seven? Nope. Where was this meeting supposed to have happened?"

"In what you call Demon Central."

"I wasn't down there last night. I wasn't on call."

"Then where were you?"

"Anything else you need?" Harper cut in.

Northrup scowled. Had he been enough of an idiot to think her master would just believe his lie? Apparently so.

"I got called by a reporter named Armando this morning, and she asked all sorts of questions that told me someone's been blabbing about what's going on in our meetings. Would you know anything about that?"

Harper sat at his desk, placing his coffee near a stack of papers. "I know the woman. She reported on the demon battles we had last spring."

"So you've been talking to her?"

"Not since last spring."

That was cagey; Stewart had been chatting with her, but Harper didn't bother to mention that.

Northrup's eyes narrowed. "I spoke to the archbishop about you," he said, pointing at Riley.

"Okay." There wasn't much else she could say.

"If the Church has a problem with Blackthorne, they need to come to me," Harper said.

Northrup ground his teeth, which indicated that maybe his time with the archbishop hadn't been as successful as he'd hoped. "I'm calling a Guild meeting tonight at eight. Make sure all your people are there. Every one of them. There are going to be some changes made."

"I'll let them know," Harper said, acting bored.

The National Guild's representative left, purposely allowing the door to slam behind him.

"So who *were* you talking to at seven last night?" her master asked.

"The witches, so I didn't lie to that fool."

Harper guffawed, a sound so rare she suspected Lucifer had just completed a triple Axel on his new skating rink in Hell.

"Why did he call a meeting?" she asked.

"Stewart thinks this asshole's next move will be to disband the local Guild."

"What? He wouldn't!"

"He most likely will. Let's just hope that reporter lady can crack this mess wide open, so we can demand a recall election."

"And if not?"

"Then the Atlanta Guild may well go freelance."

"The entire Guild?" she said, astounded. That was radical

even by Harper's standards.

"It's the worst option, but I sure as hell am not sending anyone out to trap demons unless they've got magic in their bags. I *will not* bury any more of my people. This shit has to end."

Spoken like a badass master who was willing to do anything to keep his people safe. Riley's respect for the man nudged up another notch.

"Amen," she murmured, then stuffed her earbuds back in and returned to reconciling the run reports. All Hell might break loose tonight, but the paperwork always had to be done.

~~*

Riley pulled into the church parking lot early, her gut churning in worry about exactly what would happen during the trappers' meeting. She'd talked to Justine and they'd made their plans, but as she saw it, there were only a few scenarios, none of them good. The more she thought about it, the more she agreed with Stewart—Master Northrup would strip the city's Guild of its official status.

Northrup had the right to do just that, but only in extreme cases, where the master was completely ineffective or compromised by Hell. Neither of which applied to this situation.

What did he and the other National Guild officers gain by pissing off the local trappers? Why did they want to separate Atlanta from the herd?

Before she could work through potential answers, her phone lit up. "Hey, Den. So where are you?"

"Runnin' a bit late. I'll be there in about ten minutes. The masters and me were plannin' some strategy. You talk to Justine?"

"Yeah, we're set."

Riley pulled herself out of her car, more tired than she had a right to be. As she hiked across the parking lot, she heard a noise behind her and turned. It was Kurt. She waved at him, but he didn't respond. She didn't see his car, so he must have walked to the meeting.

"Well, gotta go," Beck said. "You keep an eye out for trouble."

"I will. Love you."

"Love you too."

She ended the call and waited for her apprentice to catch up to her.

"Have you had a chance to talk to Eslee yet?" she called out.

No reply.

A profound sense of wrongness embraced her. Her apprentice was usually in a good mood, and even when he'd broken up with his girlfriend, he'd talked about it.

The wrongness continued to grow as Kurt came nearer. On her chest, Ayden's amulet began to grow warm as Riley sensed darkness, the kind Hell fosters. Careful to get every word correct, she slowly wove the spell Mort had taught her, the one that stripped away a glamour.

Kurt's form wavered, then slowly peeled away like a skin from a rotten apple. What remained wasn't her apprentice, and wasn't a necromancer or a witch. Those last two, she had a chance with. This thing was much worse.

Archfiend.

Riley swung her backpack off her shoulder, pulled out the sword, and let the scabbard fall at her feet. There wasn't time to call for backup, but if she could stall for a few minutes, other trappers would be arriving. Beck, Jackson; any of the masters would be great. At this point, she wasn't fussy.

Riley took a step back, then another. Holy ground lay behind her, at the entrance to the church, because no one bothered to ward a parking lot. A car pulled in, one that she recognized. Doors opened and all three of her apprentices exited.

No!

"Why are you doing this?" Riley asked, trying to draw the demon's attention her way.

"Because you took what was mine," the fiend replied flatly.

The last vestiges of the glamour fell away, revealing something unusual. It was certainly an Archfiend, with that domed head, the multiple eyes, the bat wings with claws that could rip out your guts before you even felt the slice. This one was clothed in not only a loincloth, but in black chest armor, armor that molded across breasts. *A female?* She'd never seen an Archfiend like this before.

With a leap, the she-fiend was airborne, shooting straight up with astonishing speed, a fiery curved sword in her hand. The demon pivoted mid-air and sent her gaze toward the three newcomers.

"Get back in the car!" Riley cried. "Go!"

The trio stood rooted in place, stunned by the monstrosity hovering in the air.

There was no way she could reach them in time. "Get out of here!"

They sprinted for the vehicle and had just flung themselves inside when the she-demon landed on the hood, its fiery sword poised to carve a hole in the roof. Kurt threw the car into reverse, dislodging the fiend, then turned and spun gravel out of the parking lot.

Which left her alone to face this thing.

As long as they're safe, it doesn't matter.

The demon flew back toward her.

"Yeah, that's right. You want me, not anyone else."

"Tonight you will die."

"What, no 'give me your soul' offer?'"

"Not for you, Blackthorne's daughter."

Whatever was driving this thing, it was personal.

"What did I ever do to you?"

"You took everything from me," the fiend said as she winged closer.

"You were at the college, weren't you? You were the one who put that message on the computers."

"Yes. You deserve torment."

Riley knew better than to run. The thing would just swoop down and grab her with its claws, or cut her in half with that blazing sword. The only way she'd defeated Archfiends in the past was by outsmarting them, because they were faster and stronger than she'd ever be.

Instead Riley slowly backed up, step by step, trying to get closer to holy ground. That was what had saved her in Edinburgh—that and a statue of Abe Lincoln.

"Were you in Hell when I was down there?" she asked, buying time.

"I saw you in front of my master. I tasted your fear."

A few steps back. "I felt yours too." Which wasn't a lie.

The fiend snarled. "We all fear in Hell. It is the way of things."

Her voice was smoky, dark, and full of hate.

"What if all you guys stopped doing your master's bidding?" It was a silly question, but it bought her a few more steps toward survival.

"He would only kill us and make more."

"So you're slaves?"

That made the fiend snarl louder. Maybe antagonizing this thing wasn't the smartest tactic.

"Look, I'm sorry for whatever I did to you, but killing me is not going to be a good move. I know of at least two grand masters who would hunt you down and make sure you die slowly."

"Death does not matter," the fiend said, moving nearer now, her wings causing the dust to swirl beneath them. "It only matters that you die."

"You have a real one-track mind, you know that?"

A quick glance over Riley's shoulder revealed that she was at least forty feet short of her goal. Still, she kept taking one cautious backward step at a time. The fiend's armor was going to make killing it nearly impossible.

Buy more time. That was the only real defense she had. "Did you call up that Five in Demon Central?"

The fiend grinned as its wings fanned the air in front of her. "Yes. It was easy to appear like a summoner. But you did not die."

"Sorry I didn't cooperate."

"Now I know I want to kill you myself."

"Why? After brownie points with Lucifer or something?"

Thirty-five feet now.

"No! I hate our Prince," the Hellspawn replied, wings beating faster in agitation.

"So why do you want me dead?"

All of the fiend's eyes narrowed in hatred. "I will kill you, I will scatter pieces of you all over this accursed town. Then I will devour that grand master of yours. I will take *everything* from you as you did from me."

Beck. At least this thing had come after her first.

"What did I do to you?" she demanded.

Far too short of her goal, Riley's time ran out. With a cry, the Archfiend flew straight at her, its sword slashing through the air. On instinct, Riley dove and rolled out of the way, feeling the heat of the blade as it sliced into the ground where she'd been standing. Dirt flew into the air. She jumped back onto her feet and ran for the steps, knowing she had only one chance.

The beat of the wings drew closer, and she ducked as the blade swung in what would have been a decapitating blow. Riley stabbed upward as the fiend passed overhead, slicing into a foot. The demon howled as black blood sprayed into the air.

Riley's fingers were nearly numb; she was grasping the sword too tightly. On her chest, Ayden's amulet had grown so hot, she feared it would burn her.

The demon was on the ground now, limping toward her, its armor glistening in the night. The many eyes glowed red, the fangs dripped saliva. This thing was going to rip her apart and leave her dismembered corpse for her fellow trappers to find. One of whom would be the man she loved.

"No way," Riley said, shaking her head. "I've got too much to live for."

The fiend laughed, a sound that made her heart triple-beat. "As once did I," the she-demon replied.

This particular Archfiend would be difficult to kill, as the armor reached from her neck to her groin. But unlike human

armor, it couldn't wrap around the body, as it had to accommo-
date the wings. Which meant the sides and back of the creature
were vulnerable, if Riley could get close enough without being
clawed to shreds.

Without warning, the demon pounced at her, just like a cat
would at a mouse. All Riley saw were wings and fangs as it
closed in on her. Ori's relentless training kicked in, and she
shifted to the left at the last possible moment, striking at the
fiend with her sword. It scraped along the armor, then nicked one
of the wings. The fiend cried out and raked her with its claws,
flinging her across the parking lot.

Riley struggled to regain her feet, then reclaimed her blade,
which had landed nearby. Her left shoulder screamed in agony,
and she forced back the tears. Then it hit her. She was going at
this like a trapper, but she was much more than that, just as Beck
had said.

Mort's glamour spell filled her mind. As blood ran down her
chest and arm, Riley stammered through the incantation and felt
it fail.

"You are weak," the fiend said, as it pressed a clawed hand
to its wing. "I do not know how you killed him."

Riley repeated the spell, and this time she felt it take hold.
Her sword began to change, glow, catch fire just like the one
Ori had "loaned" her during their training. Now if she could just
keep the spell in place long enough . . .

The fiend reared back, shocked. It knew angel fire when it
saw it. Or at least, the illusion of it.

"How can you do this? Your demi-lord is dead."

"Maybe he's not," Riley said. At least not in her heart.

"No. The Archangel Sartael killed him."

"Not before Lucifer's executioner taught me how to kill
you."

With a shout, Riley charged, knowing it was probably
suicidal. The fiend struck at her with its sword, but Riley evaded
the sizzling blade. After feinting a jab to the fiend's throat, she
pivoted and drove her sword deep into the thing's side. As she

pulled the blade free, the Archfiend reared back, catching her with a wing. They landed in a heap in the dusty parking lot. As the fiend's claws searched for her throat, Riley frantically pushed the creature off her.

"Die!" the demon screamed, its talons digging at her. "Die!"

Riley slammed the blade's pommel against the fiend's head, breaking her hold. Once free, Riley backed away, foot by foot, sword in hand. The spell had vanished when she'd lost her concentration. Behind her, the fiend dug her claws into the dirt to propel herself forward. From all the blood pumping out of the demon's chest, Riley knew she had hit something vital.

The church steps were within reach. As Riley forced herself up onto the first one, she felt a wave of nausea strike her, the Archfiend's venom beginning to overwhelm her body's defenses. With what little remaining strength she possessed, she pulled herself up three more steps. *No more.*

With tortured gasps, the fiend halted just shy of holy ground. She stared up at Riley with clouding eyes, her lips moving, whispering. Some of the words were in Hellspeak, as if she was praying. Others were in English.

"Dying . . . " the fiend said. "Be with him . . . again."

Him? Did she mean Lucifer? No, Hellspawn hated him too much to worry about that. Perhaps it was another demon. "Was he an Archfiend?"

The she-demon nodded weakly. "You killed him . . . on the burning ground . . . "

The only place Riley had killed an Archfiend on holy ground was at the Old Calton graveyard in Edinburgh.

"Mine. You took him . . . from me," the fiend whispered, her wounds bleeding profusely now. Two of her eyes slowly closed.

"You were . . . " Riley wasn't sure exactly how to ask the question. "You and he were together? A couple?"

"Forever, but not . . . forever. Now we . . . no revenge."

Revenge?

That was why the demon had tracked her down; Riley had killed her mate. She hadn't even considered that there could be such a thing as love—or whatever was Hell's equivalent— between fiends.

"You did what I would have if one of you had killed Beck," she said.

The demon nodded. "Lost without . . . him."

"I am sorry, but he was slaughtering people."

"Doing . . . what we must."

Doing what Lucifer ordered them to do, just as the angels did what Heaven ordered them to do. Like in any war, there were always casualties on both sides.

"Will you see him again?" Riley asked.

In the tiniest of moments, she saw unfamiliar hope in the Archfiend's eyes.

"May . . . be."

"Then go find him. Stay with him forever. Be free of Hell's chains, if that's possible."

"May . . . be."

Then the demon took one last shuddering breath and died, the remaining eyes closing forever.

Tears gathered. If anyone had told her she'd cry over the death of an Archfiend, she'd have told them they were mad. Yet the tears fell for a creature that had known love and had lost all that mattered in her life.

Riley's father's voice came into her mind. *Now you understand. It's not as simple as it appears. It's never simple when pride is involved.*

This war would continue because Lucifer and the Archangel Michael were too damned obstinate to step back. Lucifer would never admit he was wrong, and he'd continue to play his endless games against Heaven. For whatever reason, God would allow that. Countless generations of humans and Hellspawn would sacrifice their lives and those they loved, all in the name of stubborn angelic pride.

"Rest in peace, demon," she whispered. "Find the Light. Because if it's not there for you, it's not there for the rest of us."

Chapter Thirty-Two

One of Riley's apprentices had done exactly what he'd been taught: He had sent out a text letting the trappers know there was an Archfiend at the church. Beck knew who it was after.

He ran stop signs, speeding his way to the church, fearing tonight would be when he lost the woman he loved. When he lost everything. How could he face each morning if she was gone?

Now, as he slammed the brakes on his truck, throwing it into park in the church lot, he uttered a single prayer.

Please God, let her be alive.

He flung himself out of the vehicle and sprinted as fast as he could, backpack on his shoulder and sword in his hand.

He was too late. The battle was over. But instead of finding Riley dead, he found her sitting on the stairs that led to the church's double doors, her bloody sword on the step next to her. Lying just off holy ground was the body of an Archfiend. One clad in armor.

Sweet Jesus.

Beck called out her name, but she didn't look up. As he drew nearer, he saw tears on her cheeks.

"Riley?" he said, skidding to a halt and going down on his knees.

Her jacket was shredded on the left side, bright-red blood seeping into the fabric. The blood on her hand and on her chest was black. Demon blood. It was too much like that night in the Scottish graveyard.

"Hey, ya with me?"

She looked up at him through the tears, then nodded. "I killed the one she loved. In Edinburgh. So she came to take her revenge."

She? He looked over at the corpse and confirmed it was female.

"The thing told ya that?"

Riley nodded. "I didn't know they could fall in love. I thought they weren't capable of that. Not like us."

It was one of the things he'd learned as a grand master, and it had surprised him as much as it had her.

Beck sat on the step next to his fiancée.

"Demons can grow close to each other. Sometimes it's what we'd call love, but mostly the relationship helps them gain more ground in Hell's power structure. Either way, ya kill one of them, the other suffers."

"When demons die, are they free of Hell?"

He shrugged. "Don't know. I hope so."

Riley looked over at him now, revealing a line of her own blood along the side of her face. "I hope so, too."

"How bad are ya hurt?"

"It's the usual for tangling with an Archfiend."

That didn't sound good.

"Let's get some Holy Water on those wounds, then we'll take the demon to Fireman Jack."

Riley wiped away the tears, smearing blood on her face. "Yes on the Holy Water, no on moving the demon. I'm staying here for the meeting."

He studied her face and saw the determination in her eyes.

"I know that look." He smiled, feeling his pride grow for this remarkable young woman.

"Seen it before, have you?"

"Oh yeah. So whose ass are we gonna kick tonight, Princess?"

She smiled back at him.

"I'll give you one guess. It's time to light a fire under National's butt, and this demon is going to be the gasoline."

~~*

After Beck had sent out a text to let the other trappers know the Archfiend was history—carefully avoiding any mention of who'd killed it—he poured Holy Water on her wounds. They pounded like someone kept thumping her shoulder with a sledgehammer. The wet jacket and shirt should have made her shiver in the cold night, but the heat of the poison in her wounds easily counteracted that. It was like being frozen and broiled at the same time. Riley really wanted to vomit, but taking small sips of water seemed to help. Another intense shiver overtook her and she groaned.

"You sure yer up for this?" Beck asked, sitting on the step next to her. "Because you look like crap, darlin'."

She sent an irritated look his way. "You know, sometimes your honesty is not a good thing. I'm staying, no matter what."

"Stubborn, just like yer momma," he said, shaking his head. "So what's the plan?"

"Just watch my back."

"Always and forever."

She took the bloodied sword and laid it across her lap as the first car screeched into the parking lot. Newly minted Master Remmers trotted toward them. When he reached Riley, he checked her out, then Beck, and finally the demon.

"Somehow I do not think tonight's meeting is going to be boring," he said, grinning.

"Nope," she said.

"You do know you're bleeding."

"Yup."

"Okay. Then I'm going to stand over here, out of the way."

"Congratulations on becoming a master," she said, meaning it.

"Thank you. Even if you can't use the spheres, if you want to trap with me, you're always welcome."

His support meant everything to her, especially now. "You rock, you know that, Remmers?"

"Only following in your footsteps, young lady."

Next to arrive were her apprentices, who had wisely waited until they'd received Beck's "all clear" text. Each of their faces reflected guilt for not staying to fight.

"You did right," Riley said, knowing what they were feeling. "No way you could have taken this thing down. We could all be dead if you hadn't followed my orders." She took a breath. "Don't worry—one day, you, too, can have all this fun."

Kurt winced. "Yeah, looks like a blast."

Jaye peered down at the demon. "It's a female?"

"Yeah. Equality in Hell. Go figure."

As more cars arrived, Beck rose and took a position to her right. His pack was at his feet, his sword resting on top of it, his expression all badass.

I love you.

Groups of trappers began to form about twenty feet out from her and the demon. She didn't know if they kept their distance because of the way she looked or because of Beck's vigilant "you mess with her and I'll rip off yer head" expression.

Simon walked right up to her.

He conducted the same assessment as Remmers. "Your third Archfiend, right?" he said quietly.

"Yup."

"Going to get in Master Northrup's face about this?"

"Yup."

"Good." After a nod at Beck, he walked up the stairs and took a position to her left. A grand master and one of the Vatican's exorcists as backup. Couldn't get any better than that.

When it was nearly eight, Harper and Stewart arrived. As they approached, both studied the scene.

"Blackthorne," Harper said, his eyes on her, not on the demon. "You okay?"

"Been better, but things are looking up," she said. More wishful thinking than a lie.

"Good job. By now you'd think the Archfiends would know not to mess with you."

"One can only hope, sir."

Stewart didn't say a word, just folded his arms over his chest, pensive.

Northrup arrived right at eight. The knots of trappers became more vocal as the National Guild's enforcer walked through them. He halted about fifteen feet away from Riley, frowning.

"What's going on? What are you doing here with that thing?"

Her stomach flipped again, and she feared she was about to throw up on the corpse in front of her. That would be memorable.

"Good evening, Master Northrup," she said, trying not to let derision coat each word. "In case you've lost count, that's *three* Archfiends I've killed. And no, I'm not moving off these steps until we get some things straightened out."

Northrup shook his head. "Grandstanding again. You know, the last couple of days all I've gotten is irate phone calls about how I'm treating you unfairly. I'm tired of your special-little-snowflake bullshit."

Her sword in hand, Riley stood slowly, revealing the rent clothes and the caked blood.

"Oh, lass," Stewart said, seeing the damage to her arm and shoulder.

"Jesus," Jackson murmured. Other trappers winced. They knew what that felt like.

Riley carefully wiped her sword on her jeans, taking her time, thinking through her reply. When the blade was clean, she looked down at the man who was standing between her and becoming a master. Between her and her future.

"For the record, this special little snowflake has been too busy not getting killed by Hellspawn to ask anyone to call you." She shuddered as her fever rose. "Is my application for master status going to be approved?"

"No."

"Then tell me: Just how many Archfiends do I need to kill to make that happen?"

"You're being ridiculous. You know why you're not master material."

"Color me confused on that," she said. She took the scabbard Simon offered and sheathed the blade, though tempted to leave it out.

"First, you said I was turned down because I *might* have cheated on the exam, except we had another master from out of state proxy the test to ensure everything was on the level. Then, you said it was because I was learning magic, but I applied for master status *four* months ago, long before I started working with a necro. So what's the real excuse?"

"We owe you no explanation."

"Oh yeah, you do." Riley sucked in air. "These guys," she said, angling her head toward the other trappers, "they follow the rules, and they're golden. But not me."

"You know why you'll never be a master. Your father sold his soul."

"He did and he got it back. He's in Heaven with my mom now because he saved the lives of everyone in the cemetery that day."

There were mumbles of assent from the trappers.

She took a step down. "So, how many demon corpses do you need to prove I'm worthy? Five, ten, fifty? Give me a number, and I'll keep piling these things at your feet."

"You're delaying the meeting and—"

"How many?" she shouted. "If I'm so freakin' special, give me a number!"

Northrup snarled. "There's no number, you stupid girl. You'll never kill enough demons to make master. We'll never allow it. Master Adams told me all about your father and how you're just like him. Lucifer is sending these demons to make you look good. We all know that."

"What?" Beck growled. "The hell he is."

"Even if he were, she's still killing them," Simon pointed out, his bright-blue eyes narrowed.

Stewart intervened. "What ya might not know, Riley, is that yer father filed two ethics grievances against the board. The last one was a week before he died. They're still languishing, sidetracked by this useless lot of bureaucrats."

Riley hadn't known that, but her dad hadn't shared much of the Guild's business. "So this really has nothing to do with me at all."

"Master Northrup?" a honey-smooth voice called out.

Somehow Riley had missed Justine's arrival, but there she was, impeccably dressed, this time in a green silk suit and a black leather coat and boots. This was Ms. Armando in full Reporter Mode, about to rip a hole in Northrup's life. Next to her was a cameraman, recording the moment for posterity.

For one brief instant, Riley actually felt sorry for National's fool.

Chapter Thirty-Three

The Guild's rep glared over at Justine. "I told you I don't talk to the press."

"We're here for the meeting. It's open to the public, right?" Justine said.

"Not tonight."

"The local Guild's policies-and-procedures manual states that the public are welcome to attend any meeting they choose," she responded politely. The light on the camera glowed, meaning this was all going on film.

"That's right. The meetings are always open," Jackson piped up. "It's just that most folks don't give a damn."

"I would think you would be concerned that such a move might send a negative message to the public, as if the Guild had something to hide," Justine said.

"Fine," Northrup warned, wagging a finger at the reporter. "But you be careful what you write, or there will be a lawsuit."

"You're not the first person to issue that warning," Justine said, moving closer, like a shark selecting a particular fish from a school of victims. "My research indicates Master Blackthorne did file grievances against the National board on more than one occasion. What do you have to say to that?"

"What else would you expect one of Lucifer's tools to do?"

Riley ground her teeth. She shot a look at Beck; his expression was venomous.

"I see." Justine continued on. "How is it that the National Guild can deny master status at whim, contrary to your bylaws, especially when the applicant has met your standards? In Ms.

Blackthorne's case, three times over. Are you not concerned about a discrimination lawsuit?"

"Blackthorne does not qualify. That's the bottom line," Northrup replied.

"Setting aside the matter of Ms. Blackthorne's application for the moment, is it true that there are *nine* other applicants being denied master designation, though all of them have fulfilled the Guild's requirements? That one of them, from Colorado, has been waiting over *eight months* and you are ignoring his master's requests for status updates?" Justine pressed. The cameraman moved in to get a close-up of Northrup's face.

"Nine?" someone called out. "I thought it was just Black-thorne."

The grumbling among the trappers increased.

"No comment." Northrup pointedly turned his back on the reporter. "As of tonight, the Atlanta Guild is on probation, and a new administrator will be arriving right after the first of the year. Until then, no more demons will be trapped. Clearly your masters are not doing their jobs, so you have no one to blame but them."

"What?" someone shouted. "Are you insane?"

Riley shook her head in dismay. Did this guy want to go back to DC in a coffin?

"If the demons find out we're not doing our jobs, they'll tear through this town," Jackson warned.

"No trapping for a week? Over the holidays? How do we pay our bills?" McGuire called out.

"That's your problem," Northrup replied uneasily.

Something felt off here. Was Northrup the bad guy, or just the messenger?

"That takes a lot of balls, comin' from you guys," Beck said. "It's been y'all who haven't been doin' yer jobs. We called for help last spring, when we were bein' slaughtered, and you were nowhere to be found. If the Demon Hunters hadn't stepped in, we'd all be dead."

"He's right," Harper said. "You were told what was going

down, but you didn't bother to send us any help. You said it was *our* problem. You even dragged your feet paying out the death benefits. We had to cover some of those ourselves so folks wouldn't lose their homes."

"I was told the paperwork wasn't right," Northrup replied, but he was sweating now, despite the chilly night air.

"The hell it wasn't," Beck spat. "You folks slow-rolled those payments because you've never liked this Guild. And I'm guessing it's because we call you on all yer bullshit."

As if on cue, Justine moved in for the kill. "Does this new administrator have anything to do with the National Guild planning to ban the use of all spheres that contain magic?"

"What?" Northrup said, seeming shocked.

She pressed on. "Is it realistic to expect this country's trappers to face deadly Hellspawn with Holy Water as their sole weapon?"

"What the hell is this?" someone called out.

"That the truth?" Beck asked, though, like Riley, he already knew the answer. "You sendin' us against the demons without the magic we need to stay alive?"

"That's an unfounded rumor," Northrup replied, but his sudden nervousness told another story. "It's been discussed, but not decided yet."

Riley heard the lie, and so did the others.

"That's not true, now is it?" Justine cut in. "I have in my possession a document that substantiates the claim, and it was provided by someone who used to work in the National Guild's office. This ban has already been put to a vote and passed, though by a very narrow margin. I also know that it was roundly condemned by two members of your board, who have been sworn to silence so that they could not publicly protest this decision before it was implemented."

Northrup's face had gone pasty white. "Ah . . . I might have been mistaken about the voting."

"You liar!" one of the trappers shouted.

"Yes or no. Has this been voted in?" Justine demanded.

The man gulped air now. "Yes."

"Yes? Then can you explain why this magical interdiction is set to roll out over a two-year period, but Atlanta will be first on the list to comply? In fact, it's six months before another city is required to follow the new rules."

"No, that's not right," Northrup said, looking confused. "Adams told me that it would be countrywide from day one. Everywhere, all at once."

"Why us first? That's not fair. We get the shaft while other trappers keep making a living?" McGuire demanded.

Even as Riley's body kept sending her messages that she wasn't going to remain upright for much longer, her mind went into overdrive. Why would Atlanta be first on the list, long before any of the others? Who benefited?

Lucifer. He wanted to make an example out of the city because they'd stuck it to him more than once.

"Now I get it," Jackson said, shaking his head in disgust. "This is why you've been all over Riley. You're looking to use her as a scapegoat, blame her for this ban. All it took was one complaint"—he glowered over at McGuire—"and you had exactly what you needed to keep your hands clean."

Northrup's face turned red, but he didn't deny the allegation.

"I complained because what she's doing isn't right," McGuire said.

"But you played right into their hands," Beck said. "The Holy Water is all fine and good, but the magic makes it kick ass. No magic and we're out of a job. Or dead. Is that what you want?"

The trapper shook his head.

"Is this really true?" one of the others called out from the back of the group. "Are they going to stop us from using the magic?"

"Aye. It's true," Stewart said. "I've verified it myself. The new rulin' was to be posted next week, once this ass made it back home safe."

"Why do you dislike magic so much?" Riley asked.

Northrup looked over at her now. "Because it's wrong. Always has been. We never should have been using it in the first place." He glowered at Harper now. "Either you'll abide by the ruling or we'll shut this Guild down. Permanently. You people have always been in our faces."

"Maybe we wouldn't have to be if you weren't such douchebags," Jackson said.

Northrup narrowed his eyes. "Bottom line, no magic and you get a new master to lead you. Master Adams will clean up this Guild. He said I should tell you all to take a look at the guy next to you. That trapper won't be here after the first of the year."

Harper walked up the steps until he could be seen by all of them. "You've heard what National has in mind. We can try to fight this, demand a recall election to boot these bastards out and fix what they've broken. Or . . . we can split off from the National Guild and go our own way."

There were gasps of surprise. Followed by a "Hell yes!" from somewhere in the back of the group.

"No way," Northrup said. "You can't demand a recall unless at least twenty percent of the guilds agree to it. You people are the only troublemakers. If you break away, we'll make sure that you won't be able to legally sell your demons. We will destroy you."

"Yer right about the twenty percent," Stewart said. "But if the folks I talked ta this afternoon follow through, we've got closer ta a quarter of the guilds eager for a recall. And that threat ta starve us out?" Stewart glowered at the man. "The International Guild is willin' ta underwrite this city's trappers. The traffickers will continue ta buy the fiends at the same rates. Only, National's cut would be goin' inta the local Guild's bank account from now on."

"You can't do that," Northrup sputtered.

"The hell we can't," Harper said.

"Why do we need these scum?" someone called out.

"That's a very good question," Riley murmured.

"So what's it going to be, folks?" Harper asked. "Recall or

break away? Think about it. We'll vote once we get inside."

The murmuring grew louder.

"You'd throw this all away because of one damned girl?" Northrup demanded.

"No, but we would for a fellow trapper," Stewart said. "Yer playin' with fire, lad, and ya don't have a clue how not ta get burned."

"Adams told me the International Guild has no role in the U.S.," Northrup insisted.

"Well, he's lyin' to ya. The U.S. guilds were originally underwritten by the grand masters. It's in yer charter, which clearly ya've not read. We have final say on what goes on over here. We've always given ya free rein, but that is about ta end."

"But he said—"

Justine's cameraman moved in closer now, distracting him.

"Master Northrup," she began. "Could you comment on accusations that one or more of your board members have been co-opted, that in fact some of you may be working for the Prince of Hell, and that's why you've failed to certify the new masters?"

Ohmigod. She went there. That hadn't been a strategy they'd discussed.

"It's not me you should be asking about," he replied, glaring at Riley now. "It's her family that's the problem, not us. You test her, and you'll see."

"Ms. Blackthorne?" Justine asked. "Are you willing to undertake such a test on camera?"

"Yes," Riley replied without hesitation. "Anyone have some really fresh Holy Water?"

"Like I'd believe it wouldn't be fake. I'm not stupid," Northrup said.

"As a lay exorcist for the Vatican, I have *papal* Holy Water. Will that do instead?" Simon asked. The steel in his voice said that denying his offer would have serious consequences.

Northrup was caught now. He couldn't dare deny the legitimacy of Rome's sacred liquid, and he knew it. Instead, he nodded knowingly. "When we're done showing Lucifer's brand on you, you're gone, Blackthorne. No license, you got that?"

If she wore the Prince's brand, it wouldn't just be no job. Her life would be forfeit as well.

"Come on up here so everyone can see this," Simon said, beckoning to her.

Riley handed Beck her sheathed sword, then took a step up to join Simon, her stomach still churning. The fever owned her now, and a fat bead of sweat rolled down her face.

"Make it quick. I'm not going to be upright for much longer."

As the cameraman moved closer, zeroing in on the scene, Simon held up an ornate metal bottle, turning it so the engraved crosses could be seen.

"This was blessed by His Eminence right before I left Rome."

He gestured and Riley held out her right hand. A single drop fell onto her palm. Unlike the time Father Rosetti had tested her all those months ago, this time there was only a pleasant hum through her skin.

She held up the palm so all could see that Lucifer's mark wasn't in residence. In particular, she watched for Northrup's reaction. His eyes widened in shock.

He really believes Hell owns my soul.

"You want them to know?" Simon whispered, gesturing toward her other hand.

Did she? So far only a very small number of folks were aware of her connection to Heaven. She looked over at Beck, and he gave her a reassuring nod. Then she tipped her head toward Justine.

He understood immediately. Beck walked down the stairs, whispered something into the reporter's ear, and Justine had the cameraman cease recording.

Once the camera's light went out, Riley turned over her left hand, and another drop of Holy Water fell onto the palm. She inhaled sharply at the sensation, then held up her palm so the others could see the crown, pulsing with white light.

"What is that thing?" McGuire demanded.

"That is Heaven's mark," Simon explained. "Riley made a

deal with one of its angels to keep me from dying after I was injured at the Tabernacle. In return, she owed them a favor. They kept their part of the bargain, and so did she."

"But she's . . . " Northrup began. "Master Adams told me she was working for Hell. He said he had proof. He swore to me she was dark."

"At one time Riley did have Hell's mark on her right palm. I saw it myself," Stewart said. "It's gone now because they have no claim on her soul. I filed a report with ya people that explained all this."

Northrup shifted uncomfortably. "I never saw it."

"Now you do the same," Beck said. "Let's see who you work for."

The Guild's man took a step back, then another.

"Come on, put it on the line. Riley did. Show us what you've got," Jackson said.

Northrup looked as if he wanted to bolt, but then he seemed to realize the camera was rolling again. "Okay, let's get this done, then."

The test proved he was his own man, which was actually good news.

"Then we're both on the level," Riley said. "But your Master Adams has been feeding you lies."

He nodded grimly.

"Have the required Holy Water tests been done on a monthly basis to vet the board members?" Stewart asked.

"Yes."

"Who conducts those?"

"One of our assistants."

"Where does that assistant get the Holy Water?"

"Ah . . . I don't know."

"I bet if you try some of the real thing, the results won't be the same," Beck replied.

Riley watched as the Guild's man processed that bit of information.

Yeah, you've been had. Riley sighed. If Master Adams had

sided with Lucifer, he wouldn't live to see the new year.

Abruptly, she swayed on her feet.

"Time to go," Beck said quietly. "You've done what you needed to do."

Not allowing Riley any time to protest, he handed over her sword, then scooped up both their backpacks like they weighed nothing.

"See you at the next meeting, Blackthorne," Harper called out.

She grinned through the pain. "You can count on it, Master Harper."

"I'll text in my vote when the time comes. Just let me know when that is," Beck called out.

"We'll let you know."

As Beck escorted her past the rest of the trappers, a couple said, "Good job." She only had the strength to nod in return.

Exhausted and sick, she finally reached Beck's truck. It took a tremendous effort to slide onto the seat. Then she remembered what she'd left behind.

"Beck? The Archfiend. Can you have someone take care of it? I don't want it to freak out the church folks."

Simon stepped up to the door. "I'll call Fireman Jack. He said he'd be happy to do a pickup anytime I asked."

Riley looked over at him. "Thanks. Have him send the trapping fee to the Atlanta Guild's benevolent fund." Because there was no way she'd make money off this fiend's death, not after learning why the she-demon had come after her.

"If that's what you want. When you're feeling better, give me a call. I'd still like you as my partner on the exorcisms."

That made her feel just a bit better. "I'll be there."

Her ex-boyfriend shut the door and headed back toward the church, cell phone in hand to contact the demon trafficker.

As Beck started the truck, her father's voice filled her head.

Well done, Pumpkin. You are truly a Blackthorne.

Chapter Thirty-Four

It was two days before the demon's poison finished its rampage through Riley's body, giving her a fever, a bitchy attitude, and no appetite. She probably would have healed faster if Simon had parted with more of the papal Holy Water, but she didn't want to ask. He'd need it for the exorcisms.

She slowly woke to find Beck on the other side of the bed, leaning against the headboard, reading. It was the Percy Jackson book she'd given him for his birthday, and he appeared to be about halfway through the story.

"What time is it?" she asked, groggy.

"About seven in the evenin'." He closed the book. "How you doin'?"

"I might even live. You don't have to sit by me all the time. I'm okay."

"You did this a couple times for me, so no sweat. Besides, if I'm not in here, your little demon watches over you."

She carefully turned her head toward him, not wanting to move her healing shoulder any more than necessary. "What do you mean?"

"A couple times I found him sittin' on the nightstand, watchin' you like a dog would when its owner's sick. He squeaked at me, but I didn't understand what he said."

She frowned. "It is wacked that one part of Hell wants me dead, and another part worries about me."

"'Wacked' is only one of the words I'd use."

She let out a long sigh. "What got decided at the meeting?"

"They're going for a recall vote. Northrup wised up and

headed back to D.C. It was either that or get lynched."

"What about Adams?"

"A grand master came down from Canada, tested him. He was one of Lucifer's," Beck said solemnly.

"Oh no. I was hoping he was just being stupid, not that."

"He was given a chance to explain things to his family, and then offered a choice between killin' himself or having the grand master do it for him. Adams chose suicide."

"My God. Right before Christmas. His family has to be devastated."

"He was divorced, no kids, so that helped a bit, but still . . . "

Silence reigned for the next few minutes. It was hard to feel angry at someone when you knew how easy it was to fall into Hell's arms.

Riley's stomach rumbled. "I think I need food."

"Soup and crackers?" She nodded. "I'll be right back."

As Beck left the room, she realized this was going to be their life from now on. One of them would get hurt, and the other would take care of them.

Which was a far better fate than Adams had received.

~~*

By Christmas Eve morning, Riley felt human again. As she loaded up on the omelet, bacon, pancakes, and sliced fruit Beck had made for her, he nodded his approval.

"Yup, yer gonna live."

She didn't reply, too busy eating.

"You gonna be up to goin' to Stewart's tonight?"

She washed a mouthful of pancake down with a gulp of milk. "Definitely. Will not miss that for anything."

"He invited me last year, but it didn't feel right, me bein' there."

"Why not?"

Beck shrugged. "Just didn't."

"So what did you do?"

"Went down to a bar, had a couple of beers, picked up this girl, and we . . . " He trailed off, perhaps realizing it wasn't wise to say much more.

"Ha! Busted. Well, at least you got the girl thing all sorted out this time."

"Honest, I don't even remember what she looked like."

"You are a total horndog."

"Former horndog." He pointed at the refrigerator, no doubt trying to change the subject. "That grocery list you had up there? I went out yesterday and got all that stuff. Figured you'd need it for tomorrow."

Riley hadn't realized he'd left the house, but then, she'd been pretty much out of it.

"No way we're missin' our first Christmas dinner together," he said. "I'll get yer momma's roaster pan out of the garage. You remember, the one you had me store when you moved out of the apartment?"

He'd thought of everything.

"Dinner it is. So when do we get to open our presents?" she asked.

"Well, we could open one now I guess."

Riley walked over to the tree, still feeling the tightness in her left shoulder. Once it stopped aching, she might have to start using some of Beck's weights to get back in shape.

Now that's a depressing thought.

She studied the various gifts under the tree. "Which one do you suggest?"

"The one in the gold paper," he said. "Just pick out somethin' for me."

She returned with both presents, and they tore eagerly into them. Beck had his unwrapped first and smiled as he held up a bright-blue shirt.

"Nice. That'll go really good with my suit."

"Or your jeans," she said.

When Riley lifted the lid off the top of her present, she gasped; a beautiful red dress sat inside, one made of the softest wool. She held it up in wonder.

"Wow, Den. It's gorgeous."

"I bought it in Edinburgh. I could just see you in it."

"How'd you know my size?"

"I might have checked the tag in the green dress you wore in Scotland. It fit real fine, so I figured it'd be close with this one."

She stood, holding it up against her body. "It's perfect. I'll wear it tonight at Stewart's party."

"I'll do the same with my shirt," he said, beaming. He looked down the hallway toward the bedroom. "You feelin' tired?"

She eyed him, then grinned, knowing what he had in mind. "I could be . . . "

Beck scooped her up in his arms before she said another word.

~~*

He'd made love to her as gently as possible, reaffirming that once again, they'd defied death. As they lay there after the loving, he could see the newly healed scars and knew how close the demon had come to killing her.

"Riley, about our weddin' . . . "

She turned her head toward him. "Yeah?"

"You not settin' a date is drivin' me crazy."

"Why? We're going to get married."

How could he explain this? "Remember when I told you how things weren't good when I was a kid?" She nodded. "Well, they were worse than I said. And no matter how far I've grown away from that, I'm still . . . " He took another deep breath. "I'm still that little boy, hungry, alone, and sleepin' on a pile of dirty laundry because I didn't have a bed, wondering why nobody loved me." He began to shake from the memories.

"Oh God, Den," she said, then carefully scooted over to place her head on his shoulder and her warm hand on his chest. He knew that position had to hurt, but she did it anyway. "I wasn't stalling because I don't love you."

"I know. It's not a rational thing when I'm like this."

Riley gently kissed his cheek.

"First, there was this guy named Paul who wouldn't back off, wouldn't let me be the loser everyone thought I was. Then there was his daughter, a little girl named Riley with the prettiest eyes I'd ever seen. Then suddenly she wasn't a kid anymore," he said, looking over at her. "She's a beautiful young woman, and now she's mine. No matter all that, I'll always be that little kid, fearin' all the good stuff is gonna end."

There was silence from her, and it scared him.

"What did I say wrong?" he asked.

"Nothing. Do you have any idea how much I admire that little boy, who has turned into such a good man? How I'd marry him tomorrow if only . . . "

He rolled toward her now, touching his forehead to hers. "If only?"

Riley blinked back tears. "I want to marry you. I swear I do. But I want . . . "

"A fancy weddin'? You just need time to save money for it?"

"No, not fancy."

He wiped away one of her tears. "Tell me what you want, and I'll make it happen."

"So much of my life I've had no control over. Losing my parents, the condo; I almost lost you *and* my soul. I want our wedding to be a beautiful memory we both can hold in our hearts for the rest of our lives. Because I'm only getting married once, and I want it to be perfect. I want that memory to carry us through the bad times."

"So what's perfect for you?"

"Sunshine, flowers, the people we love watching us become man and wife."

"Sometime in the spring, then," he said, sighing.

She nodded.

"What keeps us from getting a license?" he pushed.

"They expire, don't they?"

"No. Not at all. In Georgia, they're good forever."

She lifted her head to look into his eyes, smiling now. "Then let's get a license. Let's let that little boy inside of you know that everything is just fine."

He'd take what he could get. "Okay, the license will keep me from freakin' out for a bit longer, but you *have* to set the date and tell me what it is sometime before the first day of the year. I want to know when yer goin' to be my wife."

He expected to see panic on her face; instead he saw relief.

"You got a deal. But you have to do something for me."

"Which is?" he asked, wary.

"Bring your kilt home when you're done with the grand master training. You're wearing it at the wedding."

"I am?"

"You are."

Before he could protest further, his woman kissed him so passionately that all his arguments were absolutely forgotten.

Chapter Thirty-Five

Stewart's house, just like the year before, was tastefully decorated for the holidays. Though there were no outdoor Christmas lights, greenery cascaded from the porch railings and a massive evergreen wreath with a big red bow hung from the door, welcoming all.

Stewart met them at the front door. Riley received a careful hug in deference to her healing injuries. Beck, of course, received the obligatory bone-jarring slap on the back.

"Look at the pair of ya. All decked out right and proper. Merry Christmas!" he boomed.

"Merry Christmas," Riley replied. As soon as they were inside and their coats off, she handed him their present, a festive green box containing a bottle of whisky.

"I hope you don't have this one," Beck said. "It's Penderyn, from Wales. It's got that peat in it you like."

"Wales?" Stewart said. "Peated, ya say? Never had it before. We'll have ta break it open later this evenin' and give it a try. How did ya come by it?"

Beck grinned. "I had some help from MacTavish."

"That old reprobate," Stewart said, laughing. "Come on, there's family ta meet, lots of fine drink and food. We have much ta celebrate this year."

He hadn't been lying about that family. Some had flown all the way from Scotland or beyond. His children, their spouses, and offspring filled the house with their rich brogues and laughter. Little kids scampered around, issuing squeals of joy.

As the raucous conversation flowed around them, Riley

leaned over to Beck.

"It's like we're part of the family," she whispered.

"We are. Have no doubt on that."

"Last year it was just Dad and me. I'm so happy they all came this year."

Beck looked over at their host—who was regaling one of his daughters-in-law with a tale—and nodded. "So is he."

Later, after they'd settled at the long dining room table, Stewart rose, holding up his full glass of whisky. Once conversation died down, he called out, "Merry Christmas to ya all!"

Shouts of "Merry Christmas!" and "Happy Christmas!" came his way.

Then Stewart sobered, his eyes on Riley. "Sadly, some of those who should be here with us have been called home before their time. Too many, it seems. It's been a rough year. So on this night, I send our prayers and love ta those folks, most especially Paul Blackthorne. He was a good man, a good friend, and one helluva demon trapper."

He took a deep breath. "This evenin' we share our table with his bonnie lass, Riley, and her young man, Denver. They are Paul's legacy, and as much family as the rest of ya. Rest in peace, my friend, for ya'll always be missed. *Slàinte mhath.*"

"*Slàinte mhath,*" many called back.

Her eyes misting, Riley took a sip of her wine, thinking of her father and mother. *I miss you. I love you. Merry Christmas.*

~~*

Once supper was done—Riley found she could barely move— their host beckoned her and Beck away from the boisterous group, who had gathered near the tree in anticipation of opening the presents.

"I've got somethin' ta show ya."

They ended up in Stewart's library, where he handed over a newspaper. He tapped a finger on a particular article, one with Justine's byline.

RECALL ELECTION SLATED FOR
NATIONAL DEMON TRAPPERS GUILD
CLASS ACTION DISCRIMINATION LAWSUIT THREATENED
ATLANTA GUILD DEMANDS ACCOUNTABILITY

"Oh boy. Justine's a tigress, isn't she?" Riley said.

"A married one. The best kind," Stewart said, winking.

"Hey, I got good taste in women," Beck said.

Riley shot an elbow into his ribs and received a satisfying "*oof*" in return.

"Can we really kick these guys off the board?" she asked.

"We'll find out," Stewart said, clearly energized about the news. "The votin' starts on Thursday. If the recall doesn't pass, Harper has five other guilds lookin' ta go independent. There's a lot of shady dealin's goin' on; the problems we're havin' with this bunch are only the tip of the iceberg. It's a shame. They were good until about five years or so ago. Then it changed."

"So there's still a chance I might make master?" Riley asked.

"Possible. We'll see soon enough."

Riley nodded, setting the paper on the table.

"Ah." She looked over at Beck for support, and he nodded back. "When we get married, I wondered if you'd be willing to, well, walk me down the aisle?"

The Scotsman blinked repeatedly as his eyes grew moist.

"I'd be honored ta escort ya ta marry this fine young lad," he said. "I've grown verra fond of ya this last year, Riley. Yer just like a daughter ta me."

Her own eyes began to brim. "Thank you. You mean so much to me, too."

"Ya thinkin' of havin' the weddin' here? I know ya love my back flower garden so much, and we have plenty of space upstairs in the ballroom for a reception."

Riley couldn't believe her ears. "Here? In the flower garden?"

"Certainly. Mrs. Ayers can help with the cookin'. She'd love it."

"Oh my God, that's perfect. Thank you, Angus."

She hugged him hard and he returned it, his eyes nearly as wet as hers now.

"Ah, well, now we best get back ta the rest of the family. The bairns are eager ta open their presents." He turned to Beck. "Later, we gotta have a taste of that whisky ya brought. Let's see if those Welsh folks are as good at distillin' as they claim."

As they walked out of the room, Beck dropped a kiss on her forehead.

"Did you have something to do with him letting us get married here?" she asked.

Beck shook his head. "His doin'." Then he grinned. "So yer really gonna marry me, huh?"

"Looks like it."

"Then that's another miracle in a life full of 'em."

~~*

They shuffled into their house close to midnight, tired, happy, and still full of food. Riley collapsed on the couch, then promptly nestled into Beck's arms.

"That was awesome. I love his house. Yours is neat, but man, that library. I could spend my whole life in there."

Beck chuckled. "Spoken just like a teacher's kid."

"Once you're home for good, Stewart will be going back to Scotland, right?" He nodded. "I'm glad for him, but I'll really miss him. He's just so cool."

"It'll be a year or so before he leaves, once he's sure I'm ready to take it all on by myself. Then you and me have to make a decision."

His serious tone caught her notice, so she wiggled around until she could see his face. "About what?"

"That house you love? Stewart doesn't own it. The International Guild does. So once I take over his work, we can move there. That is, if you would be okay with that?"

Her jaw dropped open as her brain seized up. Beck reached over with a finger and gently pushed her mouth closed.

"Yeah, blew me away when he told me, too. It's a big decision. Now, I love this place, but Stewart's house? Damn, it's right fine."

"That. Is. Amazing."

"Thought you'd like that bit of news."

"But there's gotta be a catch."

"There is. Unlike Stewart, I'll be travelin' more, almost all of it on the East Coast. He didn't do much of that because of his leg. Accordin' to the folks in Scotland, they want me 'oot and aboot,' as MacTavish put it."

She laughed. "Travel, huh?"

"Yeah. You can come with me, or stay put; it all depends on what you want to do."

She snuggled in next to him. "I'll see. You know, that's one big house."

"Yup. Lots of room for books. And kids."

She closed her eyes, trying to imagine what it would be like to live there. Mornings in the kitchen, nights in the big room with the fireplace. Someday, children running up and down the stairs, playing hide-and-seek.

"Riley?"

"Yeah?"

"We've got a visitor."

She opened her eyes to find the Magpie perched on the coffee table in front of them. He looked around, nervous.

"Hi, guy. Merry Christmas." Then she realized that might not be what a demon wanted to hear.

He grinned in response, showing all those nasty sharp teeth, and set his bag of loot down. He rooted around in it, then pulled out something silver and laid it in front of her, followed by a pleased squeak.

Riley leaned over to study it and smiled. "It's the earring I found in Centennial Park all those years ago. He likes to keep it safe for me," she explained, though it was more like he kept stealing it. She'd find it somewhere, then he'd steal it all over again.

The fiend rummaged around in the bag again and came up with another earring, laying it alongside the first one. It was its mate.

"You are the bomb, demon! Thank you! How did you find it?"

The Magpie smiled back again.

"Hold on, I have something for you."

Riley pulled herself off the couch and went to the Christmas tree, picking up a small cylinder wrapped in green paper. When she returned to the couch, she found Beck watching the demon in wonder.

"He always like this?"

"Yup. He's great. Just very possessive."

She opened the little present, popped the top on the plastic tube, and ran a line of glitter on the tabletop in front of the Magpie. It wasn't just the usual kind of glitter, but included tiny gold stars and brightly colored crystal diamonds.

The demon gasped, fell to his knees, and touched the offering with deep reverence.

"I was going to get him some with little prisms in it because they were really neat, but that would have just messed with his head."

"How?" Beck asked, leaning forward.

"Because he's very OCD. See?"

Beck watched as the small demon carefully sorted the glitter out into distinct piles according to color, then according to shape.

"I'll be damned. Look at that."

The Magpie held up one of the little red diamonds, then hugged it to his chest. Then he squeaked at her.

"Thank you. I'm glad you like it," she replied. He squeaked again.

"What did he say?" Beck asked, curious.

"That I'm the nicest mortal he's ever met."

Her fiancé laughed. "He's got that right."

A second later the demon and all his loot were gone, the tiny pitter-patter of feet indicating he was headed somewhere at high speed.

"Now I've seen everything," Beck said. He nuzzled her ear. "Merry Christmas. How's about we go to bed now?"

Riley heard the huskiness in his voice and knew what it meant, but decided to mess with his head.

"What about the presents? I got you some really cool ones."

"We can open 'em in the mornin'. We need our rest."

"Merry Christmas, Den," she said, kissing his cheek.

"Merry Christmas, Riley," he said. Then he shot a look at the gifts under the tree. "Well, maybe just one . . . "

"Gotcha!"

Chapter Thirty-Six

Beck's last few days in the States had been busy. In addition to dealing with Guild business, he and Riley had gotten their marriage license, then headed to South Georgia, where they'd spent time with his buddy Tom Donovan and Tom's daughter down in Sadlersville. They'd also visited his ex-girlfriend Louisa, her husband, and their baby. When he'd held the little girl, he'd seen a wistful look in Riley's eyes.

Someday. Just not yet. There was too much to be settled before they started a family, and they were both young. When they did have their first baby, he knew he'd be ready.

The bittersweet part of the trip had been visiting his mother's grave, especially after she'd saved him from Hell. He'd never understood Sadie, but when he'd needed her the most, she'd been there for him. In her own way, she'd paid off her debt. If God was merciful, she'd be set free soon.

As Beck knelt in front of the grave, he spent some time telling her how things were going, as if she could hear him. Perhaps she could. Then he wept, and it was Riley who held him as he finally vented his grief. The lost little boy wasn't alone anymore.

~~*

Once back home, they'd made the rounds, spending time with Peter, who'd returned from his family vacation, with Riley's other friend Simi, then visiting Mrs. Litinsky and Mort.

Beck had gone out for a night with the trappers that involved too much beer and a designated driver. Riley had helped Simon with another exorcism.

Beck made sure that he and his lady spent their last day together as lovers should. It was a day he would remember forever. Even when they said goodbye at the airport with a scorching kiss, it wasn't enough.

Never will be. Like his beloved granddaddy, Beck had found the one woman who would stand by him, and he had no intention of ever letting her go.

Now, as he sat on the plane, his phone pinged. He smiled, knowing who it was.

MISSING YOU ALREADY. IS IT MARCH YET?

I'LL BE HOME SOON. I PROMISE.

STAY SAFE. I LOVE YOU.

"I love you," he whispered.

Because if it weren't for Riley Blackthorne, he wouldn't have known what it was like to have a future.

Epilogue

Beck arrived in Edinburgh the afternoon of the thirty-first and checked into the hotel MacTavish had booked for them. All his superior had said was, "Get some rest. It'll be a late night."

Beck did as ordered, taking a combat nap for a couple hours. When he awoke, groggy, he dragged himself into the shower. As the hot water sluiced down his body, he shook his head to clear it. As always, his thoughts were on the woman he'd left behind and how he wished she was with him now.

As promised, MacTavish arrived at six.

He said, "Good evenin', lad," and had the bellhop hand over a garment bag, which held Beck's kilt and all the trimmings. Beck wisely kept his groan to himself. At first, he hadn't been good with all this fanciness, but now he was beginning to like it. Not that he'd ever admit that to Riley.

By the time he'd finished dressing—and he swore it took longer than Riley when she wore all her makeup—MacTavish was decked out as well, wearing one of his clan's modern tartans, mostly red, blue, and black.

"What's goin' on that we need to get all duded up for?" Beck asked.

"Supper at The Witchery with two influential members of the Scottish parliament," MacTavish replied, adjusting one of the flashes tucked into his socks.

Beck knew of the restaurant, had even saved up money to take Riley there, though it was pricey. Given the way things had fallen out during her visit, they hadn't had the chance. *Maybe someday.*

So, on the last day of the year, he hung with Scottish politicians. He made sure to be polite as he was introduced around as Grand Master Beck from America, handed a glass of expensive single malt whisky that was older than he was, then served excellent Loch Duart salmon. It was surreal.

The conversation remained genial and had nothing to do with demons or Hell or Lucifer. He appreciated that. They were "buildin' bridges," as MacTavish called it. Beck held his own as the token Yank and even generated a few laughs.

His situation and this setting were as far removed from South Georgia and a life of poverty as he could imagine. And yet, Beck knew this was where he was meant to be.

Silently, he offered a toast to the Fallen angel whose soul now resided on top of the Blackthorne mausoleum. Without Ori's help, he'd have died at Sartael's hands, and he'd never forget that. Then he took another sip of whisky in honor of Paul and Sadie.

Once dinner was over, a quick cab ride delivered Beck and his superior to a private club on Princes Street, where there was more whisky, along with hand-rolled cigars. It was like living in a dream.

"No doubt yer wonderin' why we're here," MacTavish said.

"More bridge buildin'?"

"Aye, it never hurts ta glad-hand the power brokers, and there's a few of them in this room. Someday ya might need one of these folks ta help ya, and if they remember ya as a good soul, that makes it much easier."

MacTavish took a deep sip of his whisky. "And this particular club has one of the best views of the castle, which will become verra important right soon."

Because of the fireworks.

With that thought came a genuine flare of guilt. Beck had really wanted to stay in Atlanta with Riley and celebrate their first New Year's together as a couple, but Edinburgh knew how to throw a party. Stewart had insisted that Hogmanay—as the Scots called New Year's Eve—was not something to be missed, so Beck had made the difficult choice. He might not have the chance again.

"Heard from Riley?" his superior asked, eyeing him.

"Nope. She's not set the weddin' date yet. It's drivin' me crazy."

MacTavish chuckled. "Women are like that, lad. She'll tell ya in her own good time."

"I made her promise to tell me by New Year's. Doesn't look like that's gonna happen."

MacTavish just smiled when Beck's phone pinged and he checked the text. It was from Riley, as if she'd known he was talking about her.

LOOK WHAT WAS IN THE PAPER TODAY

The text included an image of an engagement announcement. He caught the headline and grinned.

"She did it!" He handed the phone to his companion.

"So now yer really on the hook," MacTavish said, scanning the text. Then he smiled. "Did ya read all of this?"

"No, not yet."

"Allow me. See if ya catch the other important bit." MacTavish cleared his throat. "'Ms. Riley A. Blackthorne and Mr. Denver Beck are pleased ta announce their engagement. Ms. Blackthorne is a *master* demon trapper in the National Demon Trappers Guild, the daughter of—'"

Beck snatched the phone away from him.

Blackthorne & Beck

Ms. Riley A. Blackthorne and Mr. Denver Beck are pleased to announce their engagement. Ms. Blackthorne is a master demon trapper in the National Demon Trappers Guild, the daughter of the late Master Paul Blackthorne and Miriam (Henley) Blackthorne. Denver Beck is a grand master initiate in the International Demon Trappers Guild, the son of the late Sadie Beck. An April 6th wedding is planned.

"My God, she finally made master!" Beck exclaimed. He knew he was drawing attention from others in the room, but he didn't give a damn. This was too important. Riley had achieved one of her dreams.

MacTavish beamed impishly.

"You knew about this, didn't you?"

"I did. I promised Angus I'd let her tell ya in her own way."

"You old fox. Both you and Stewart."

Then Beck looked back at the announcement. "She even set the wedding date," he said, smiling. And she'd told him right under his New Year's deadline.

Beck dialed Riley's number and she answered, laughing.

"Hey you!" she said. "Think you can stand being married to a master trapper?"

"Hell, yes. You deserve this, Princess. Paul and yer momma would be *so* proud of you. Oh, and I see we're getting married in April, huh?"

"Yup. Me in my dress and *you in your kilt* and all the extra things that go with it. Stewart will be in his, that's for sure."

"Yer really gonna hold me to that?"

"I am, Den. I love you, but I love you *even more* in a kilt."

He laughed. "Understood. Happy New Year, pretty lady. I love you. I'll see you soon!"

"Happy New Year!"

He ended the call and found MacTavish's eyes dancing with delight. The grand master pointed out the window. Above the centuries-old fortress, a curtain of fireworks exploded in the night sky, the brilliant colors raining down like angel fire.

"Happy New Year, lad. May this one be filled with love, with peace, and with fewer demons."

"Amen." Then Beck blurted, "She's like those fireworks," gesturing toward the night sky. "Riley. She brings light into my life. I wouldn't be here if it wasn't for her." *For her fierce love.*

"And ya bring an equal amount of light into her life, which is why yer gonna be just fine. Hell doesn't stand a chance with the pair of ya. In fact, I feel sorry for Lucifer." MacTavish grinned.

"Well, just a wee bit."

He raised his whisky glass. "*Slàinte mhath*, Denver."

Beck raised his glass as well. "*Slàinte mhath*, Trevor."

~~*

The Gastro-Fiend was secured in the wire-mesh bag, howling like a badly tuned bagpipe. Kurt high-fived Richard, and there were smiles all around. Now that Kurt had reconciled with his girlfriend, the only demons they trapped were the real ones.

Behind them, cheers erupted as the Peach Drop signaled the start of 2019, only a few hours after Beck had celebrated his own new year. Riley had timed her announcement just perfectly and was still smiling that she'd pulled it off.

"Good job, guys," she said, pleased. These two were going to be kickass trappers. All they needed was polishing. Once Jaye rejoined them, it'd be even better.

"Thank you, Master Blackthorne," Kurt said, grinning.

She took a bow. "Happy New Year. How's about we ditch this noisy thing with Fireman Jack and go find ourselves some pizza. It's on me."

The two of them hooted and headed for the car, Richard dragging the furious demon behind him.

Riley looked up at the stars, imagining them in the night sky over Scotland. Over the man she would be marrying in the spring.

"Happy New Year, Den. I love you."

Then she headed after her apprentices, because there was a smelly demon to sell, yummy pizza to eat, and a life full of love to celebrate.

The End

About the Author

A resident of Atlanta, Georgia, Jana Oliver admits to a fascination with all things mysterious, creepy and laced with a touch of the supernatural. An eclectic soul who has traveled the world, she loves to research urban legends and spooky tales. Then write about them.

When she's not hunched over a keyboard, she enjoys Irish music and fine Scottish whisky.

Thank You!

Thanks for reading *Mind Games*. I sincerely hope you enjoyed it.

Please tell other Demon Trappers fans about the novel, post reviews on Goodreads and the various online booksellers' sites, etc. I would really appreciate it.

If you've never read the other books in the Demon Trappers series, please check out the following websites for details:

www.DemonTrappers.com

www.DemonTrappers.co.uk

If you'd like to stay in touch with me about new books, guest appearances and just about everything else:

Join my newsletter at my website! I share book news and snippets with all my subscribers.

Or follow me on social media:

Facebook: www.Facebook.com/janaoliver
Twitter: @crazyauthorgirl
Instagram: CrazyAuthorGirl19
Or at my website: www.JanaOliver.com

Thank you for sharing in another Riley and Beck adventure!

The Demon Trappers Series

Be sure to check out the rest of the books in this great series by Jana Oliver

U.S. (U.K.) Editions

The Demon Trapper's Daughter (Forsaken)

Soul Thief (Forbidden)

Forgiven (same title)

Foretold (same title)

Grave Matters (same title)

Mind Games (same title)

CPSIA information can be obtained
at www.ICGtesting.com
Printed in the USA
LVOW13s2304230617
539174LV00013B/241/P